the
crash

BOOKS BY CATHERINE MILLER

99 Days With You
The Day that Changed Everything
The Missing Piece
The Girl Who Couldn't Leave

All That is Left of Us
Waiting for You

Christmas at the Gin Shack
The Gin Shack on the Beach

the
crash

CATHERINE MILLER

bookouture

Published by Bookouture in 2022

An imprint of Storyfire Ltd.
Carmelite House
50 Victoria Embankment
London EC4Y 0DZ

www.bookouture.com

ISBN: 978-1-80314-144-2
eBook ISBN: 978-1-80314-143-5

In Memory of my Aunt Lain and Uncle John
Together Forever

PROLOGUE
MAY 1982

There was nothing about their meeting that wasn't clichéd. It was the same story for plenty of people that had gone before them, and there would be many others that would also meet in a similar fashion. The thing is though, it wasn't ordinary. Because nothing ever is. All these complex dynamics where we meet or we don't. Where we become friends or never cross each other's paths. For this couple, in *this* moment, it was extraordinary. It was that infamous spark that's so often referred to. The ones that don't always get jotted down in history like they should. Sometimes life is full of moments that only the individuals involved ever get to notice. This was Mike and Susan's moment. This was their spark.

For anyone who knew them, it was hard to comprehend that they'd never met until the end of their school years – at the disco, of all places. Despite being in the same year group for the entirety of their secondary school days, Mike and Susan had never officially met. They'd been on school trips together but not on the same coach, and as they weren't timetabled into the same classes they didn't hang out with the same friends. Their paths had never crossed. Until *now*. In the school dining hall, which was still entirely recognisable as such despite the PTA having attempted to deck it out with paper streamers everywhere, banners with good luck messages painted on, and a disco ball doing its best turn.

'I'll Fall In Love Again' by Sammy Hagar crooned from the DJ's stereo system. Susan had not long ago requested it, the only one brave enough amongst her friends to ask for a particular song. She was also the only one wearing a dress, one her mum had made from silver sequinned material. The others had said they were going to and then turned up in their usual jeans and motif T-shirts. When the song started to play, her friends, Julie and Lisa, abandoned her and giggled at their achievement.

It made Susan's world shift slightly. They were doing it to belittle her and, rather than embrace the friendship they'd held for the past five-plus years by dancing with her, they were going to laugh on the sidelines instead.

Fine, Susan thought. If that's how they wanted to play it. Rather than bow away with shyness as they were expecting, Susan decided to dance like no one was watching. If she was dressed like a disco ball in a room with one especially installed then she might as well dance like one.

Closing her eyes helped. It was easier that way to ignore that the friendships she'd thought of as lifelong were starting to disintegrate. If they were still laughing at her, it was impossible to hear with the music tumbling from the speakers and her self-made optimism bouncing around the school hall. She was sweet sixteen. The world was her oyster. She wanted to believe that, even if Julie and Lisa didn't. She'd finished... school was over. The fate of their exams was decided and, right now, there was nothing to do other than celebrate.

That was when Susan bumped into a solid object and opened her eyes in a reflex action.

'Thought I'd join you,' the solid object said.

'Wow. Yeah. Okay.' Susan smiled. 'I only have two left feet when my eyes are closed.'

'It's an interesting way to dance.'

'Figured I would try and embrace the disco mood. Really I was trying to ignore the fact my friends have abandoned me.' It was too early to add 'so-called', but even as she danced she knew the shift had arrived.

'Miserable lot,' the solid object said. 'I can't understand why anyone here wouldn't be dancing like mad. We're only going to get this moment once.'

It was true. They were only going to get this moment once. Susan liked him instantly.

'I'm Susan,' she blurted out, realising that having only ever glanced at him, she'd never got round to introducing herself.

'Mike. With any luck my requested track will come on soon, but neither of us are going to stop dancing until it has.'

'What did you ask him to play?'

'You'll see.'

'I'll hear really, though, won't I?'

Mike's somewhat ill-fitting suit might have been worn by his dad in the fifties but he laughed as they danced, somehow coordinating both their questionable dress sense and a way round each other. Not touching, but connecting all the same.

A new track started and Mike did an elated bout of air drumming.

'A Flock of Seagulls?' Susan stated as soon as she recognised the song.

'"I Ran".'

'"So Far Away",' she finished.

While they continued what they considered to be groovy moves, most of the other dancers left the floor. Susan's friends were no longer giggling now they'd realised she was enjoying herself and had moved on to the next thing to collectively laugh over. The food buffet was now open for business and everyone in the hall was swooping in its direction. But Mike and Susan weren't going to be swayed by a prawn vol-au-vent. They were here to see this tune through to the end. They were here to dance like they might never get the chance again.

Susan found herself wanting to be the woman in the song. Wanting the spotlight to be on her – and it was, even if it was a disco ball, so technically it was a series of small spots. And she didn't want him to run away. Her friends were doing that all too readily. The notion of the song being just for her was silly: they hadn't known each other when he'd put the request in. He wouldn't have been able to guess that her friends would abandon her to dance alone. But whatever had come before, *this* was the moment when it happened. It was the time they looked into each other's eyes and knew. Neither of them were going to run away, not when this was the beginning.

Years later, she would find out that the song *had* been for her. That Mike had been looking at her from afar for a long time, and when he'd been queuing up to put in a request he'd witnessed her friends leave her and decided to go for it. Because we only ever get this moment once. He'd decided *that* moment was his. And the song choice was down to the opportunities he'd had before, but run away from.

When the song ended and a slow one came on (the DJ had needed to do something to compete with the buffet), they'd gravitated towards each other. They'd held on tight. Because somehow, in those moments, they'd connected. One moment of connection that they knew would last beyond that evening.

And they were still each other's slow dance partners thirty-nine years later. Thirty-nine years in which they'd married, purchased a family home, had three children (a girl, Isabelle, and two boys, Stuart and Phil), and two granddaughters (one from Isabelle and one from Phil) with another on the way, and navigated life's highs and lows together. It was hard to comprehend that now, with their fortieth anniversary of being together just around the corner, they were in the depths of becoming strangers. Of life having cast them further apart rather than together.

Because in the end, the song was right. Running away was still an option. It was as if it was written in the stars, because that was the clichéd inevitability of life. She'd fallen in love with her high school sweetheart and, as some people liked to point out, that kind of love wasn't meant to last.

But did it have to be like this? Did they have to lose the magic of the last forty years? Susan could hear in her head that she'd already half admitted defeat. It wasn't a war after all, where she should prepare herself for battle. It was her life, where she needed to make sure *she* was happy. Looking back, it was hard to pinpoint when they'd lost their way. Where the magic had slipped away to. The answer was to try and work it out together. She couldn't fix this alone.

Pulling herself away from the school disco photos she'd been poring over and before she changed her mind, she grabbed her laptop. She should consult Mike but, as he was hiding in his shed as he so often did, it was time to make a decision for herself. Who knew? Perhaps running away together to rekindle what they'd once had was the answer. And if attending a school disco wasn't possible, perhaps they could do something similar. They needed to give themselves one last chance. Perhaps, rather than being lost, their spark was buried. Maybe they just needed a disco ball to light the way. She went ahead and booked the eighties weekend for them without daring to knock on his shed door. She really had to hope he'd be on board with this as much as she was. After all, she was going by his motto from that first time they'd met: *we're only going to get this moment once.*

She just had to hope their lifetime of moments wasn't over.

CHAPTER ONE

ZACK

When the chainsaw entered Zack's chest, there was a very real sense of this being the end. It wasn't supposed to be on, so this shouldn't be possible. And yet there were spurting shots of what looked like tomato ketchup, but was definitely arterial blood. The chainsaw *was* on and that fluid was Zack's blood.

Of course, this hadn't been part of today's plan. Today's plan had been to continue the project they'd been working on for six years. Zack and his company co-owner and best mate, Larry, had been giving up their Saturdays to landscape local care home gardens. At some point, they'd started recording what they were up to and were now local celebrities in their own right, after being dubbed Oxfordshire's answer to *DIY SOS*. Larry currently had the camera rolling, while Zack was supposed to be giving a safety demonstration of chainsaw use ahead of woodcarving a dead tree trunk, a hobby of his that he'd perfected over time. Moments ago, he'd been talking to the camera about the features and safety checks required before turning the chainsaw on. Only it *was* on when Zack hadn't plugged it in yet. He was unexpectedly giving a demonstration of what might go wrong without having intended to.

As he watched his own demise, it was surprisingly like an animation. As if he were watching it on telly rather than taking part in the main event. Perhaps it was because, as yet, he hadn't felt any pain. There was no instinct to move from the impact because there was too much disbelief in his mind over what was happening. Shock didn't arrive as an after-event because he was going into it instantly. In just split seconds his world was being torn apart in the most literal fashion possible, and his limbs weren't responding quickly enough to stop it.

The blood spurted out as if someone was having fun with a water pistol filled with strawberry-coloured syrup. It was as if a paintballing event had been kitted out with only red balls. And in that moment Zack's vision only saw red. He didn't see Larry abandoning his filming to run and help. Nor the staff members calling the emergency services. Or the cleaner apologising profusely for having plugged the chainsaw in at the same time she'd plugged in the vacuum cleaner. It was all lost at the same rate he was losing blood.

It was ironic really for this to be happening to him aged thirty-three, when he was living his life as wholesomely as he could. As a youngster, he'd spent his life being told not to over-step the mark. Zack's response as a teenager had been to nod in the right places, even though he'd been thinking he could decide for himself. This mentality meant that more often than not he went ahead and did it anyway. That sense of caution was always such an adult point of view. His parents had been so risk-averse he thought they wouldn't have known a good time if it hit them square between the eyes.

In rebellion, he'd spent his teenage years doing everything he shouldn't. He'd been living his own UK-based version of *Jackass*, never more than one step away from his next risky manoeuvre or gaffe with his mates. His mum had said one too many times that he'd send her to an early grave for him not to feel guilty when it actually happened. When he was fifteen, his mum had gone out shopping, never to come back. A heart attack in the supermarket car park as she'd been loading bags into the car. She'd gone before he got to say goodbye or ever murmur the word 'sorry'.

At first, he'd continued with his recklessness as a way to release his anger at the unfairness of it all, but then his dad had become unwell with signs of early dementia. That was the point he turned his life around, caring for his dad, training at college, and setting up a business with Larry. The care home that had housed his father for the remaining years of his life had been their first volunteering project. Zack had been twenty-seven when his father had passed away after gradually deteriorating for years. He still visited that garden now on the pretence of maintenance work, but really he was there to remember his dad.

So with his misspent youth behind him, this was not how he'd expected things to end. However much he missed his parents, it was far too soon to join them. And what was it they said about your life flashing before you? Was this it? The final curtain. A sudden rush of pain brought his vision back and told him not quite yet.

At the realisation that the chainsaw had chewed down deeper than just his skin, he took in Larry's expression. Larry: his long-term prank-loving best buddy and co-worker. His mouth was in a perfect O that appeared to be screaming, but Zack couldn't hear the noise what with the heavy vibrations from the chainsaw and the loud whooshing going through him. Larry's phone camera was no longer poised to record like usual, the device limp in his hand. His green eyes flitted in every direction as the water gun spurts kept hitting him in the face, as if he were Zack's direct target.

'I don't think we should put that video out,' Zack said, as he finally managed to stop the chainsaw running. As he did, the pain pushed through in an instant. It stopped him from breathing it was so severe. It was like nothing he'd ever experienced before and his knees crumpled beneath him. As he fell, he glanced down and one thing was clear... he shouldn't be able to see the inside of his chest filling with gushing blood to the beat of his heart.

'I don't think you should be worrying about videos right now,' was the last thing he heard Larry say before he passed out.

It wasn't exactly the profound statement that he wanted to hear as the last words ever to meet his ears. But there it was. He'd turned his life around. He'd done good deeds in a way that had meant something to him. None of that was enough to stop him from accidentally ending his own life. As he closed his eyes for the final time, he gurgled an absurd laugh. This wasn't how a life should end. Not when it felt like he'd only been at the beginning. Not when he hadn't finished what he'd set out to do.

But just like that, his light was out. His time was over. And once it stopped, his heart would never beat again.

CHAPTER TWO

CHLOE

Not for the first time, Chloe wondered if her sisters realised they always sat on the same side of her hospital bed when they visited. Alice was always on the left-hand side with Leona on the right. She didn't like to point it out in case they became conscious of the fact and changed it up. It was one of those things that was strangely reassuring, akin to putting on some lucky socks. Somehow this formation of her sisters spelled good luck. And she was sure she was due some of that. Congenital heart disease gave her the frequently used pass card to the John Radcliffe Hospital. It was her local heart centre, which had been taking great care of her for all her twenty-eight years on the planet. The only problem being that for every admission, it was becoming increasingly harder to gain a get out of jail free card. She'd spent far too many weeks and months in this kind of hospital environment with her sisters visiting every day. A side room of a ward was pretty much her second home, vying for the position of primary residence.

Opening her eyes for the first time after surgery, the consistent formation that greeted her meant she knew where to look to find them. She peered to the left and saw Alice first.

'Don't try and speak yet. You need to rest. The doctor said everything went well.'

Chloe realised she couldn't speak even if she wanted to. There was a tube in her throat which was going to prevent that for now.

Instead, she felt for a hand from both of her sisters and they responded readily. She closed her eyes and concentrated on their strength. She would never have made it here without their constant support. She was the youngest of the three, born five years later than her older siblings. She'd been described by her mum as an unexpected, but very much loved, surprise. Her parents had taken her illness in their stride, but when they'd both fallen ill with lung cancer (a shared heavy smoking history had been blamed), they'd been stopped in their tracks. When Chloe was fourteen, they had passed away within a month of each other and it was Alice and Leona (both adults by then) who'd taken on the responsibility of her care. Losing their parents had left a gaping hole in their lives, but they'd muddled through together and were as close as could be as a result. Half of Chloe's lifespan had now been spent without her parents and she wouldn't be alive without her sisters. There had been more than one occasion when she'd wanted to give up. When both mentally and physically she'd decided it was the end. But their care had made her hold on that bit longer. Whenever she'd been unwell they'd been at her side, and the fact that she was here feeling their hands in a different room to the one she'd been in before the operation meant the transplant she'd been waiting for had happened.

She was lying here with a new heart. *A fresh start.*

After her eyes tired from concentrating on Alice and Leona, she tried to focus on the changes. The heart that was beating. The lungs that were expanding. Admittedly, that wasn't happening without assistance currently. It was a surprise to find she couldn't feel her organs in the way she had before. Everything felt numb. As if whatever pain relief they had her on was cutting off any connection. Perhaps that was deliberate. Even though the procedure had been explained to her in depth, she couldn't remember what they'd said about nerve endings and how much time it would be before the adjustments took place.

But did that matter? She was alive. It was one hurdle crossed which, if she was honest, she hadn't thought she would achieve. Death had been a close companion for too long not to expect it to be her next destination. It was both miraculous and startling to discover she was going to get to experience another lifetime.

She hoped to spend a smaller percentage of this one in a hospital bed surrounded by her sisters, filled with concern. She drifted back to sleep, dreaming of all the different places she might be able to go with Alice on the left and Leona on the right of her, keeping her steady as they always had. Because while it was a second chance, certain things should never change. Some things exist to remind us of our good fortune. Chloe's sisters had undoubtedly brought her plenty of that. She hoped that would continue for a long time. It made a delightful change to wake up with some hope in the room beside them.

CHAPTER THREE

ZACK

There were many things that were unsettling about waking in unknown surroundings, especially when the last thing Zack could remember was the moment he had felt his heart stop beating.

The sight of heavy packing and tubes coming from his chest told a different story to the one he'd expected. Even though he'd been royally unlucky, it would seem he was still in the same earthly realm. Not the heavenly one he'd thought he would be visiting, with his mother and father waiting. Every inch of him ached and pulsed while also being numb and otherworldly. It didn't seem real. He was clearly in intensive care and it was God knows how many days since he'd last been conscious. He flicked his eyes around, the only part of him that he was able to move, half expecting to see Larry there, still gawping.

That thought made him remember what they'd been up to at the time of the accident. For the past six years, in his parents' memory, Zack had been making over care home gardens free of charge. Initially he'd only intended to do one, but that home had been part of a group of care facilities and when the key workers had expressed a hope that they could all be up to that standard,

Zack had decided he would use his Saturdays to volunteer to landscape them as well. Larry had helped from the off, and gradually they were working their way around each facility, throwing themselves into the process. Generally they learned what hobbies the residents had and created a design to suit. Some gardens had ended up with allotment spaces, others had an area for mini golf. It hadn't taken long for the media to become aware and they'd soon had other local companies offering items and services, making the whole process much easier: it was only costing Zack and Larry time. The other benefit had been that their weekday work for their landscaping business now had a waiting list. Locals were keen to support their enterprise, especially those with relatives in care. They'd also built up a huge TikTok following by creating updates on their volunteer projects and other practical DIY videos. Their mini golf makeover had netted millions of views, the one with the residents having a go being the most popular. Ironically, the one they'd been recording at the time of Zack's incident was supposed to be a safety video. A prelude before carving the tree stump into the requested seahorse. Only he'd never got that far. Instead, he was here.

In an effort to find out what was going on, Zack tried to push himself up, but the pain was unbearable and he screeched with agony. He couldn't even scream normally: the sound was muted by how scratchy and dry his throat was feeling.

'Stay there, my love. We can't have you trying to get up like that yet,' a voice said to him. He glanced to the side to see a woman in scrubs bustling around, and soon the movement was making him sleepy all over again. It was as though the little energy he had was being zapped directly from him.

'What happened?' he managed.

'Can you remember anything, sweet?'

'Chainsaw. Heart. I should be dead,' Zack managed to croak.

'You certainly should be, but you're one lucky young man. The odds were truly in your favour that day.'

'Why?' He didn't feel particularly lucky. The pain was too severe to liken this to luck.

'After your accident, a heart became available that was an exact match. If it wasn't for that, you wouldn't be here now. It would seem all the good karma you've created meant fortune was shining on you.'

'A heart?' The numb, otherworldly sense came into focus. As if he was here, but also wasn't.

'Yes. Your own was, for want of a better word, mangled. The accident caused some irreparable damage. But as you were given immediate first aid and brought to a specialist unit, they managed to get you onto ECMO. It's a type of artificial external heart that can only be used for a short period. The fact you got a transplant in that timeframe is nothing short of a miracle.'

'A miracle?' Zack repeated, not entirely taking in or understanding anything this guardian angel was saying.

'The doctors will come by soon. I've paged them. They're going to be delighted to hear you've started to respond now. They've already started talking about submitting your case to the *British Medical Journal*. One of the most complex surgeries they've performed, they reckon, because of the nature of your injuries.'

Zack made his best attempt at a nod. He was already too fatigued to chat any more. It all sounded quite impossible. Having never wanted any media attention, it would seem not only was he famed as the local answer to Nick Knowles, now he was going to be in a medical journal as well.

Before the doctors even arrived, he'd returned to a deep snooze where his dreams took him to other places.

He was with his daughter, walking her to school. It wasn't something he usually did, but he was doing it knowing it would be one of the last times before she was due to go to secondary school. After that, having her dad with her would be a definite no. It was only a ten-minute walk, but every second was precious and he was going to hold on to them.

That jolted Zack awake. There was no daughter in his life to dream about, but there had been such clarity to the thought, it was as if it was real. It left a lingering sense that he was supposed to be somewhere else. Even though his medical state dictated that he couldn't be anywhere else but here. He searched for where that place was in the folds of his brain. As if the answer would be nestled nicely in some part of his grey matter. Only it wasn't there. Of course it wasn't. Because with a frightening clarity, he knew the answer was in his heart.

The heart that wasn't his. The heart that was telling him it wanted to be somewhere else.

CHAPTER FOUR

SUSAN

Often, Susan watched Mike's shed from her vantage point at the kitchen sink and wondered what was so exciting about it. There was no radio or TV inside and he wasn't one for spending lengthy periods on his mobile phone. So it often raised the question of what exactly he did in there for *hours* on end now that he'd taken early retirement. Ever since that had happened earlier in the year, he'd been more withdrawn. Further away, even though he was closer.

In truth, Susan knew the essence of what he was doing. He *tinkered*. He claimed he was fixing things or trying to, but mostly he was taking things apart, never to be reassembled again. She couldn't recall the last time he'd fixed something for the house.

As far as she was concerned, he was tinkering his life away and didn't have much to show for it. Whenever she questioned him on the matter, she was met with blank looks. As far as *he* was concerned, it was a good use of time. Maybe Susan would have been more inclined to agree if he'd actually managed to fix her Dyson like he'd assured her he would. Instead the parts were all over the shed, and she'd long since given up and purchased a replacement.

Rather than spending more time together, Mike was in the shed for even more hours of the day. She had hoped they'd find some new hobbies to enjoy as a couple, but as yet that hadn't happened.

At ten thirty, as always, he came to join her in the kitchen for a cup of tea and a biscuit. Susan found it hard to believe they'd become so dull that this counted as a date.

'I've booked us a holiday.' She'd been holding on to that news for too long and it was a delight to finally spill the beans. She figured if she only told him relatively last-minute there'd be less wiggle room to get out of it.

His face contorted as if she'd spilled a real tin of cold baked beans into his lap. 'What'd you do that for?'

'Because even if things have been strained, I didn't think we should let forty years pass by without celebrating.' Susan placed the usual plate of digestive biscuits and mugs of tea before them. The choice of biscuits seemed as stale as their marriage. Even they were always the same.

'Should have just got me a card. Don't need to be wasting our money on holidays.'

'It's not a holiday. It's an intervention.'

'Inter-what?'

'An intervention. I figured it's time we decide what we're going to do, once and for all.' She hadn't meant to be quite so direct, but now she had been she was rather pleased with herself.

Mike sighed heavily, as if the thought of going on holiday with her was taxing. 'Where are we going then?'

'I'm keeping that as a surprise. I just wanted you to know that you need to pack for a long weekend. We won't be back here until Tuesday next week.'

'When do we leave?'

'Tomorrow morning.'

'Right.' Mike turned his attention to his tea and digestive biscuit.

Susan wasn't sure what she'd hoped for. But some excitement or thanks would have been nice. Instead, Mike sounded like he'd been treated to a prison sentence and was trying to come to terms with the fact.

'It'll make a change from your shed at least.'

'I suppose,' Mike said, despite having a half-eaten biscuit in his mouth. 'Should have known the bloody shed would have to come into it.'

'Well, it's true, isn't it?' Susan really had to hope he'd rather come on holiday with her than spend more time in that place. It didn't even have a nice smell anymore. More mouldy than musty.

'What's true?'

'That a holiday will make a nice change.'

'How much did it cost?'

'What does that matter? It's an anniversary gift to ourselves.'

'From our joint savings?'

'We *need* a holiday.' Susan was desperate for one. She couldn't understand his aversion to going away.

'It's not a need. It's a want.'

'If you're so worried about the cost, let me assure you, it's remarkably cheaper than a divorce would be. I haven't forgotten that's what you mentioned the other week. So, like I said, it's an intervention. I've decided a holiday is the way forward.'

There was still the option of going by herself. It might be more enjoyable, if this was the treatment she was going to get from him all weekend. She'd not realised how worn down she was feeling about his attitude and knew her outburst was entirely justified.

'I don't know what you want me to say.'

It was Susan's turn to sigh. She was so familiar with this default response. As if he hadn't been around for the past forty years and had no idea how to interact with her when she was upset. *I want you to say you love me. I want you to say that our family and I are the most important things in the world to you. I want you to find the passion you once had for us, which you seem to have buried in your shed.* Those are the things she wanted to shout loudly into his face. But they were words she'd already spoken. Words that even then had evoked the same response. It was as if, even when what he needed to do was being spelled out to him, he still didn't understand.

'I'd like you to pack a bag and not complain about it.'

'Any clues as to where we're going?' Mike put his hands up in surrender. 'And before you say anything, it's not a complaint. It's a genuine enquiry... do I need my swim shorts or not?'

Half a smile found its way onto Susan's face. She didn't dare produce a whole one in case the change in attitude didn't last. 'You do need your swim shorts. In fact, I'd say pack for every eventuality.'

'No limits on the weight of my luggage then?' Mike asked, his gaze settling on her, watching for tells.

'No fishing for more clues.'

'Are we going fishing?'

'It's a surprise.'

'I thought it was an intervention?'

'It's going to be a surprising intervention. If we get that far.'

'I have to hope my swim shorts still fit, in that case.'

Susan's smile switched to a full one. Perhaps it was the years of practice, but sometimes they had the ability to wind each other up and defuse the situation in a matter of minutes. She often came close to wanting to throttle him but soon after would be laughing, forgetting that the idea even went through her head a short time before.

'You'd best go and check,' Susan said, when she saw the

time. Their habitual tea break date was over, and once again they had been close to the wire with another argument. She really was holding on to a lot of hope that the holiday would do something to resolve matters.

'I'll do that later. Best get back to it.' Mike nodded in the direction of his shed.

Man cave it was not. It was far too lacking in luxury to be described as such. Hovel was more like it. And yet its appeal had no bounds.

'Go and pack now. If you need to get anything new, you only have this afternoon to sort it out.'

'Well, whose fault is that?'

Complaint number one. He couldn't help himself.

'I've told you early enough that you have time to get sorted. Don't ruin it by returning to your hole, for no actual important reason. Try and make *us* a priority for once.'

Susan placed the dirty things into the washing-up bowl. She wasn't going to state her case anymore. This was going to be a make-or-break weekend. Already the dial was leaning towards break. If getting him to pack was going to be this much of a problem, maybe that was all she needed to know. But if so, she was still going to go and enjoy what she could of the weekend regardless and call a solicitor on their return.

It wasn't much of a surprise to see him wander back to the shed ahead of doing what she'd suggested. It didn't mean it didn't hurt though. It didn't mean it hadn't been hurting for months now.

As she packed a red sequinned dress that she'd been waiting for another suitable occasion to wear, she was reminded of the expression one of her friends had used. She'd described what was happening as a thousand papercuts. Micro wounds that smarted and stung and by themselves weren't enough to stop anyone in their tracks, but when a person was covered in them it was no longer possible to carry on. She'd reached a point where she felt as if she was covered, nicked with stinging cuts from head to toe, and she really hoped that what she had planned was an opportunity to heal. But at the moment, with only one of them packing their bag, maybe it was already a hopeless mission.

CHAPTER FIVE

ZACK

Considering how close to the brink of death Zack had been, he was doing much better than most of the medical staff had expected. The novelty of unknown medical professionals rocking up at the end of his bed, discussing his case and declaring him a miracle, hadn't worn off yet. He was sure it would with time.

'Shit, man!' Larry declared when he came to visit. 'I've never been more scared in my life. Can't believe you're sitting here drinking tea like nothing happened.'

Larry plonked himself down and lightly whacked Zack with a rolled-up newspaper in the process.

'Would you be careful? I'm not completely out of the woods yet!'

'I'd stay here as long as you can, mate. Some of these nurses are fittt-ta-ta,' he said, in a way that made him sound like he was riffing a guitar.

'I'm not doing so well that I'm here chasing skirt. And have some respect, the people you're referring to have been saving my life. I'm very grateful for that... the odds were totally stacked against me.' Over the years, he and Larry had chased far too many nurses at the rest homes they'd been working at. Or rather, they'd frequently been chased. A shiver ran through Zack momentarily as he considered the last encounter with Elodie, which had made him solemnly swear to remain a bachelor for the rest of his days. She'd made a good attempt at ruining his life and had put him off relationships forever.

'Yeah. I was pretty sure you weren't going to make it. The staff at St Francis's care home were amazing. If it had just been us, I would have freaked out, but they carried out first aid as if dealing with injuries like that was an everyday thing.'

'I can't remember any of that.'

'You were passed out. It's probably a good job you have no recollection.'

An awkward silence followed as the terror of what had happened travelled through them like a ghost passing through the room. Zack was able to recall the event up until he passed out with surprising clarity. He remembered the look of fear in Larry's eyes.

Moving back to an easy-going conversation didn't seem possible after that. They weren't used to really talking about the big subjects. Normally it was always small talk, and that usually involved discussing what they were working on next.

'Was it bad?'

'It was like a frigging *Saw* movie. All fun and games until you realise it's not a joke. I genuinely thought for a moment or two that you were pulling a prank on me. That at any second you'd get up and reveal you'd used a prosthetic or something. I mean, you didn't wail or anything! I was the one screaming. I couldn't understand how it had happened. We're always so careful with stuff like that. It was just one of those really unfortunate accidents.'

'Yeah,' Zack said, not sure what else to say. He'd been the one foolish enough to leave the plug by the socket, not thinking someone would kindly put it in and flick the switch on.

Even though the medics were declaring he was doing brilliantly, there were still wires attached, his wound was still vacuum packed, and it was going to take a while to heal. He wasn't going to be able to help with any garden makeovers anytime soon, if ever again. Fortunately Larry had roped in his nephew, so their paid scheduled work was still going ahead.

'But you're okay. That's the main thing,' Larry said, tapping Zack's knee with the newspaper again.

'I'm not dead, so that's a start.'

'Technically, I think you were for a bit.'

'I'm trying not to dwell on that fact.' Nor the fact that his heart was no longer his own but seemed to have a memory, if his strange dreams were anything to go by. 'What have you got there? Please don't tell me you released the footage?'

TikTok had been earning them a bit of money through associated adverts, but the video of his injury wouldn't be in keeping with what they usually shared. He hoped that Larry wouldn't have added what he imagined to be the most gruesome outtake ever. He didn't want that out in the world. If anything, they were better off deleting it completely, so neither of them could go over the trauma. The thought of seeing it again made Zack's stomach turn.

'Nah. Can't even watch it, Zee. I think that clip is best buried to save anyone ever knowing how unlucky you were. I've not posted any kind of update. I figured you wouldn't want any fuss. Figured we could just go quiet for a bit on the social media front and hope no one notices.'

'What's going to happen with the garden project?'

'My nephew Billy and I will finish this one. We reckon we've only got three or four days' work so it'll be finished soon enough. Then the next one can go on pause until we know how you're doing and when you'll be back to work.'

'I don't think it'll be anytime soon. Three months' minimum recovery time, the doctors are saying.'

'That's not surprising. It's going to be more than just healing going on. Your new heart needs to knit itself in and get itself cosy. Which reminds me... I've been doing a little research.'

Zack's brow almost went into cramp at the thought. 'Research? Do you even know what that is?'

'Pah. Maybe I don't mean research. To be honest, I just stumbled on it and thought maybe it wasn't coincidental.'

'What are you on about?'

Larry threw the newspaper into his lap, narrowly missing his chest.

'Bloody hell! Watch out, would you? I've not long had open heart surgery and you're trying to finish me off like an absent-minded paperboy.'

'Sorry, Zee. You've survived worse and have the scar to prove it. It's the fifth page you want.'

'Please don't tell me my run-in with a chainsaw made the local paper.'

'No, thankfully. Everyone kept quiet about it like I asked them to.'

Opening the paper to the correct page, Zack only needed to catch a glimpse to know what Larry was on about. *Family pay tribute* were the only words he needed to read.

He was on the sidelines, attempting to watch two matches at the same time. His elder son on the nearest pitch, his younger son on the next. His eyes were beginning to strain from trying to follow both in order to cheer in the right places. But he was thankful they'd moved up one of the matches, with the weather set to change later. 'Go on, sons,' he shouted, tucking his gloved hands deeper into his pockets.

Zack jerked with the sudden flashback and pushed the paper away. 'I'm not supposed to know about any of this.'

'I know. I doubt it's even connected, but the date made me think. Anyway, forget I ever said anything.'

Zack made sure the paper was closed, trying not to take in

any of the details because as soon as he'd seen the article, he knew his friend's instincts were spot on. Of course, there were various other places his transplant might have come from, but already his heart was telling him that this was *it*. As if it had grabbed hold of the piece of information it had been after. 'I'll keep it. I'm just not sure I want to read it yet. I'm not sure I ever will.'

'I understand.'

Zack wasn't sure if anyone would understand how he was currently feeling, especially when he wasn't certain what these solid flashbacks meant. 'It's a lot to take in. Being alive was surprise enough, but finding out it was only because someone else... you know.'

'You don't need to say anything, mate. I just thought you'd want to know if you could.'

Zack coughed and had to hold on to his chest so it didn't hurt. 'Thanks. It's been odd waking up knowing it shouldn't have been possible.'

'Well, I'm very glad you have. And if this has put you off woodcarving, you're always welcome to join me fishing.'

That made Zack smile. Ever since they'd been schoolboys together, Larry had been going fishing with his dad and constantly encouraging Zack to join in. He had once, but the whole affair had been cold, with smelly bait, and he'd not caught anything. It hadn't enamoured him enough to try again. But Larry had never given up encouraging him to join in. Perhaps this time he would.

'Maybe I will. Once I'm out of here and signed off on being active.'

'Do you know how long it'll be until you're out?'

Zack and Larry had spent their lives in each other's pockets since their school days. They were more like brothers than friends. Having grown up together, Larry and his family had provided amazing support when Zack's mum had suddenly passed away and subsequently when his father had been ill. He couldn't imagine a world without them all in it and now they were his family. This hospital admission was already the longest time he'd spent apart from Larry.

'Once I don't have any of these accessories, we'll be good. The doctors are hoping within the next few weeks. My wound needs to be fully healed and they want me mobile first. Don't expect me to be racing around like usual straight away.'

'I'll pop in again tomorrow. Let me know if there's anything you need. Can't have you hanging round here in stinky boxers. My mum will sort out any washing for you. She sends her love, by the way.'

Zack appreciated the sentiment from his surrogate family. 'Kathy can come visit if you give her fair warning about how things are.'

'Now you've given me the word, you know she'll be in as soon as possible. She's been clucking like a hen with worry about you.'

Zack smiled at the image. Ever since his mum had passed, Kathy had stepped seamlessly into the wings, supportive when needed, but never overstepping. No doubt she'd been inconsolable since his accident.

'I'll be glad to see her,' Zack agreed, before Larry said his goodbyes.

Once Larry was gone and with only the newspaper for company, Zack had to decide whether it would be fair to take a glance into the world he shouldn't know about. The life that had been lost in order to save his own. He'd been told a limited amount of information about it since he'd been awake. He knew donations were always anonymous. That later on he could send a letter of thanks to the relatives if he'd like to.

So the article Larry had shared was pretty much sticking a pin into a board of names of people who had died that day. Who was to say this was the one?

But then there was that knowledge again. The dreams that weren't quite dreams, telling him he had two sons and a daughter. The thoughts he didn't seem to have any control over: when he had them, or what they told him. They were shifting inside him separate to his own thoughts, and each one made him want to acknowledge this heart's desires more and more. But how could that happen if he never knew its history? This newspaper had the information he needed to know. It was about the heart inside him. It was a fact, not a guess; he was sure because its rhythm was pulling him towards it.

For a moment, he had to have a word with himself. It was like he was willing it to be true, in the way he might want a football team to win or a bet to come in. He was looking for an answer so he was convincing himself this was it.

But his certainty didn't feel unfounded, not deep down. It was coming from somewhere else. It was coming from within. An inexplicable undercurrent. It was the pounding of his heart shouting: *This. Is. My. Story.*

Before any further hesitation, Zack flicked open the paper and read the headline properly this time, allowing the words to sink in.

TREE CRASH RESULTS IN TRAGIC DOUBLE FATALITY

His cardiac monitor temporarily gave out an extra-loud bleep as if to acknowledge the event. And with it came an overwhelming sadness that in order for this heart to be beating now, it meant a man had lost his life. Browsing the words for more context, there weren't the details that Zack was hoping for. He wanted to know his name and instead all it had were the facts of the accident.

It wasn't an easy thing to digest, but in reading it he understood a bit more. Zack's heart transplant was only half the story.

There had been another death and, Zack reasoned, if one of them had signed up to be on the transplant list, it was likely they both had. In fact, he knew it. It was clear to him that it wasn't one person who gave a life that day, it was two. And that meant somewhere there was another heart beating. That was the place his heart wanted to be. Only it wasn't a place; it wanted him to find a person.

And as he was alive because of the decision this man had made to donate his heart, he was going to do whatever this new heart desired. If it wanted him to find the other heart, then so be it.

The only question was... how was he going to do that when it wasn't simply a case of asking? However nice a concept reuniting the hearts was, already it seemed like an impossibility. Zack was a man of his word, though. So he whispered a gentle promise that he'd do everything possible. And as he said the words, he already knew his heart was thankful.

CHAPTER SIX

CHLOE

Chloe had waited for her surgery for so long it was inevitable she was loaded with expectations. In fact, she had a veritable suitcase full of them.

She'd expected to wake up feeling brand new.

She'd expected to feel on top of the world.

She'd expected to be out of hospital as soon as possible.

She'd expected to be able to do some of the activities that had made her breathless before.

What she hadn't expected was to come out of this feeling heartbroken. As if what they'd nestled in her chest wasn't a working organ but a stone.

'They'll be here at two,' Alice said, when she returned to the side room. 'That's something to look forward to, isn't it?'

There was a brassy hope in Alice's voice that Chloe didn't want to crush. Because she really wasn't looking forward to another physiotherapy session where she felt she was getting nowhere. Where her suitcase-sized load of expectations weren't being met.

'Do you want me to read to you for a while?'

'That would be nice.' Chloe adjusted her position slightly in the cocoon she'd created in her hospital bed. It was a nest for her new stone heart. The one she felt she needed to protect no matter what.

Her own heart hadn't developed properly in the womb. When she hadn't even been a flicker in her parents' eyes, in the first six weeks of foetal development when they hadn't known they were expecting, the tube that should have become her heart didn't follow the blueprint it should have. Because of that she'd ended up with multiple defects that needed to be fixed. Her first heart surgery had taken place when she was so young she had no recollection of the event. And it had been followed by five more as after each one, new problems would occur. The last one prior to the transplant was meant to be relatively simple, a valve bypass, but she'd ended up with an infection which had caused her heart to enlarge and put her on the transplant list. That had been eighteen months ago, and what a long haul the wait had felt like, when she'd spent more time in hospital than not.

She'd been unable to protect the heart she was born with, but this new one was special. It was faultless and all she had to do was recover, only she didn't have the required energy levels she needed to be enthusiastic about that right now. It's why she was so thankful for her sisters. They always took it in turns to distract her.

On the days she visited, Alice had been reading from a series of crime novels. The chapters and tense pace were just right for Chloe's depleted energy levels. Alice would always read to her, and Leona would play music while they tackled a puzzle together. She knew it was intentional to occupy her and it was a nice way to pass the hours when she wasn't able to pursue her favourite hobby: art. Holding even a pencil for any length of time caused her sternum to ache, so she'd not even tried. Instead, she had pictures she'd created dotted about the room. They were a good source of encouragement for the things she wanted to get back to, even if it would be another six weeks until she'd be able to consider starting her first sketch. They were all different symbols of love and hope from different places around the world. It might be a tad indulgent, but they were preferable to the boring landscape prints that had been in place.

As sisters went, they were very different. Alice was the sharp one. She was a hairdresser and always worked the weekend so she'd have Monday and another weekday off to be with Chloe. A pair of scissors would be the emoji of choice to represent her. Exact and to the point, she always said what she was thinking and got things done. Leona was more laidback and worked as a freelance photographer. Her work was varied and that suited her to the ground. Her emoji would rather obviously be a camera. That or a sun lounger. If Chloe had to choose what symbol represented her, it would be an easel. Something that never looked the same because with a sweep of a brush the colours on the canvas would change. Unlike her sisters with their permanent vocations, Chloe did seasonal work for a local art gallery in the summers when she was well enough. The owner, Rowan, had become a good friend over the years and displayed her work, which sold in dribs and drabs. Today, Chloe was a steel blue mixed with forest green. She'd spent her whole life feeling different, and even she wasn't able to guess the pattern of her life. But she liked to think, like an easel, it had an arty messiness to it and there was a beauty to her imperfect edges.

As Alice reached another cliff-hanger ending of a chapter, she stopped reading, knowing the physios would arrive at any moment. And they did, right on schedule.

Great! Chloe thought, keeping the downcast sarcasm to herself. She often found her sisters didn't appreciate anything other than outward enthusiasm – Alice more so than Leona – so the zip remained firmly over Chloe's lips.

'Are we ready to sit you in the chair for a bit longer today?

Shall we go for an hour?' Leah the physio said, with an enthusiasm only someone young and the right side of thirty would be able to conjure. She was joined by a male counterpart and it was a sad fact to know they'd be doing most of the muscle work. Chloe's strength seemed to be away on a cruise that the rest of her hadn't been invited along to. Simple tasks were causing major fatigue and something like putting her own clothes on, which she was managing before the transplant, were a major obstacle that required assistance.

'Okay, we'll do the same as we did yesterday.' The machine they'd used to help her to get from sitting to standing was already being wheeled into the room. It had been evident from day one that Leah wasn't here to muck around. She meant business and that business was getting Chloe on the move. 'Do you mind giving us a bit of space?' she asked Alice, knowing there wouldn't be enough room for an extra person present with the equipment they were using. It was also a step to protect Chloe's dignity, and Alice gave Chloe's hand a quick squeeze before leaving the room.

Every move she took, getting from lying to sitting to raising her arms to the right place on the machine, required assistance. None of it was under her own steam. If it weren't for Leah and her assistant, she'd still be like a limp leaf on the bed.

'How are you feeling today?' Leah asked, as they sat side by side on the bed. In truth, Leah was there to stop Chloe flopping over. Her muscles weren't even opting to support her against gravity.

Chloe let out the biggest sigh of her life, which at least meant her lungs were doing the job that they should be. She just wished she wasn't so numb, so she could feel her chest expanding. 'I thought I'd be feeling better by now.' There was a sweet odour coming off her that reminded her of the days of long and complicated infections following her valve replacement surgery. She really had to hope she wasn't getting another. They were supposed to be in the past.

'So how are you feeling if you're not feeling better? I know what you're not, just not what you are.'

It was a shame standard responses weren't going to wash here. 'Fed up.' At least she could be honest with Leah. She was a concerned professional, and they were a whole lot easier to handle than concerned sisters. 'I never thought recovery would be this hard. I thought I'd flourish, and instead I feel like my heart is a bird and my ribs are a cage, and if I move it's all going to collapse and break.'

'I can assure you what we're doing now is only doing your body, and your heart, the world of good. We won't be breaking anything. Is that why you've been wanting to stay in bed most of the time?'

Chloe knew what she wanted. She wanted to stand up unaided and walk out of here without even having cause to pause. That's what she'd been imagining in her head when she'd gone into theatre. She really was having a hard time with the fact it was proving to be so entirely different to what she'd hoped. 'I want to get up. I want to be well. But I'm scared that the only way to keep this heart safe is to tuck it into a nest and keep it there. I don't seem to have the energy for much else.'

'Fortunately your blood results are looking good, so hopefully this is just a hiatus. Sometimes our minds and our bodies don't cooperate in the way we want them to. Sometimes we have to wait until they're both on the same page.'

Was that it? Might it be as simple as waiting for a couple more days for her body to catch up to the idea? Surely it had had more than enough rest time already?

'I feel so exhausted. Even before the surgery I had more energy than I do now.'

'Give it time. I promise you, if we carry on doing this daily, it'll be much easier this time next week. Gravity has a marvellous effect on your muscles. Are you ready?'

The next part of this process was to haul herself up to standing, ready to get into the chair. She wouldn't mind, but that wasn't the hardest part. That would be the period of time where she had to remain in the chair without falling asleep and slumping over.

'Ready as I'll ever be,' Chloe said, holding on to the hope that really it was just a case of her body and mind needing to align themselves. If only there was a dial in her chest that she could turn on and carry out some kind of manual overdrive. She wanted to be in control and sensed she wasn't.

'On three?' Leah said, her assistant murmuring agreement.

'On three.' Chloe nodded her own consent.

She found it was best to get this part over and done with – the moment of hoping her weak limbs would at least pull her to standing, with the physios and their equipment helping. She always felt like it was someone else they were moving. This couldn't be her life, her body, her existence. She wasn't able to shake the numb feeling and at times it almost took her outside herself. As if she was floating above this scene of a woman struggling to move, rather than being the person moving.

When she was comfortably propped up in her chair, they promised it would only be for an hour if she was okay.

'It's so nice seeing you upright,' Alice said, when she was allowed back into the room on everyone else's departure.

'I wonder what they do if people refuse to move?'

'What are you wondering about that for?' There was a look of horror on Alice's face, as though she could tell Chloe was ready to give up.

'I'm not sure. I've been in here long enough to think about these things.'

Because her heart condition had caused multiple admissions and required multiple surgeries, it had created a lifetime of being careful and following medical advice. There had been a lot riding on this heart transplant. It hurt to know it wasn't the perfect remedy she'd imagined, and giving up, staying in bed, was a hugely tempting option.

'I know it's tough, Chlo, but you're doing so well. Please don't give up on us yet. Do you want me to read a few more chapters? Make the time go a bit quicker?'

Chloe nodded. Her sisters were always such a comfort. Alice knew that not only was sitting up physically draining, it was also painful. Being narrated to always made it more manageable somehow.

It also meant Chloe didn't have to admit she wanted to start refusing the physio sessions. She wanted to protect this heart, and as it was behaving like it was broken, curling up around it seemed like the best way to shield it from harm. Right now, staying still seemed like the safest option.

CHAPTER SEVEN

ZACK

The day of Zack's discharge came about much quicker than many of the medical staff had imagined it would. He was even given a guard of honour by the nursing staff, who all clapped him when he was wheeled from ICU to a general ward.

He was rather embarrassed as he'd really done nothing to warrant such attention. He'd been unfortunate. Unfortunate souls didn't generally deserve applause. That should be for the medical professionals who'd managed to perform an actual miracle by piecing him back together again.

It was a relief to be leaving the hospital itself without as much pomp and ceremony. He didn't want a fuss. He was never one for being the centre of attention. Even with his localised fame, he only did that because of the additional help it ended up bringing.

Larry landed on the ward with his usual tardiness. He'd never been one for early mornings and it was a running joke between the pair of them.

'Take your time, why don't you?' Zack smiled at his friend.

'Don't go getting your knickers in a twist. The parking's awful here. Took me ages to get a spot.'

'Any excuse, eh?' Larry never functioned fully until he had a cup of coffee in his hand.

Larry raised his arms. 'No excuses. Not on this occasion,' he said, with a cheeky grin at the ready. 'Do you need me to carry those for you?'

'You better had. I'll get shouted at if I try to myself. Nothing heavier than a kettle for the next nine weeks apparently.'

'No wielding chainsaws in that case?'

Zack shivered at the recollection of the reason he'd ended up here.

'Too soon, right?'

'Yeah, I think so. That gave me a hellish flashback.'

'Sorry, mate. Bit insensitive of me. By the way, Mum's insisting you come over to ours to start with, and she's going to cook us dinner. I hope that's okay, Zee? You know what she's like. There was no saying no.'

'It's fine by me. I could do with one of Kathy's meals after being in here. Preferably a roast, if she's taking requests?'

'She'll do whatever you ask for. Have you got everything?'

Zack nodded and went to give his thanks to the nursing staff before they made their way to the car park. He had his own flat, which he'd bought with the inheritance his parents had left him. After his mother had passed away and during the following years, Kathy and Don's house had become his second home. He'd never been gladder of his substitute family and going to theirs today, rather than an empty flat, was comforting in lots of ways.

'Could you have parked any further away?' Zack laughed.

'The physios told me to. Said they don't want you slacking as soon as you leave.'

'Yeah, right. This is the furthest I've been since I got here. I'm worn out already.'

'Clearly we need to build your stamina back up!' Larry glanced at Zack. 'All jokes aside, mate, you don't know how nice it is to be heckling you to walk further. I really thought... well, you know.'

Zack did know. He also knew all too well how different he felt now. This wasn't the same Zack leaving hospital as the version that went in. His muscles were deconditioned and there was a scar on his chest that came with a constant ache. Getting back to full fitness and continuing the gardening project that he'd started in memory of his parents should be the first thing on his mind, but instead it was something entirely different. A wish that wasn't his. 'I'm going to make a strange request.'

'O-kay. Like what?'

'That paper you gave me.'

'Yeah?'

'Is there any chance you could do a detour and take me past the crash site? I'd like to pay my respects.'

'Fine by me,' Larry agreed with a nod of his head.

Ever since he'd read the article, Zack had become more and more convinced of the connection and he wanted to do something about it. But what could he do in the circumstances? His new heart was tugging him in that direction. Every day, a snippet of a memory that wasn't his had appeared. He wanted to say thank you and goodbye in the only way he knew to be possible. And Zack wanted to see if he could find out any more about this couple. Who were they and what was it his heart was hoping for?

Larry drove more carefully than he usually did. He wasn't normally one for slowing down as much as he should for round-abouts or corners, but Zack was obviously precious cargo these days.

'Do you think it is linked?' Larry asked, as he steered them towards the edge of the forest where the accident had taken place.

'When I read that article, I felt strangely certain. I mean, it could be from various other places, but in my heart of hearts, which feels like such an odd expression to use, it feels like it must be true. A gut instinct, if you like.' Zack didn't like to mention the memories he'd been experiencing that weren't his own.

'I can understand that. I had the same thing in a way when I was reading it. Seemed like too much of a coincidence, so I figured I should show you. Shall we get some flowers to pay our respects? I'd like to, if that's okay. Whatever happened to them meant I still have my best friend.'

'Yeah, that seems fitting.' Zack nodded and stared out of the window when a tear started to pierce the corner of his eye. It was overwhelming to think that the previous owner of his heart might have been on a car journey such as this one with no idea of how it was going to end.

The closer they got to the spot, the more Zack's emotions churned up inside him. He'd waited in the car when Larry went to get flowers, saving his energy for this short venture, knowing he was already fatigued.

'I'd best take the price off,' Larry said, when he got back to the car. 'Do you want to leave any kind of note?'

'No. It should be anonymous. I don't want to upset any of the family if they were to visit – I'm not supposed to make contact. Besides, I'm not sure I could write down what I'd want to say without giving away who I am.'

After setting off again, it wasn't long before Larry pulled into a layby. The area they were in was the edge of a forest, under a canvas of trees dense enough to create shade despite the sunshine. It made Zack think about what had happened. It wasn't often that a car careered into a tree trunk without cause. Perhaps the change in light had been a factor. Possibly a deer in the road as it roamed the woodland and strayed onto the tarmac. Maybe fatigue after a long drive? Or was there even a chance it was intentional? He wished the memory fragments he kept seeing would tell him something more concrete. It was hard to even pinpoint the chronology of the memories at times. He'd seen a daughter at three different ages of her life, but how old was she now? What was her name? And were they real windows into someone else's life?

'You ready?' Larry asked.

It was a good question, seeing as neither of them were taking the lead. Zack's mind felt like it was in a different realm at times and this was one of those occasions.

'Look, don't be surprised if this ends up being the first time you see me cry.' There had been tears shed for his mother and father, but he'd managed to never break down in front of his best friend. But this felt different. More acute. Not something he'd be able to regulate.

'Ditto, mate.'

They climbed out of the car before waiting until the road was clear of traffic. It was a countryside lane and if they hadn't been exactly sure what tree to look out for, then the flowers already in situ were a helpful indicator.

It was a solid oak, set a little way back from the side of the road. They would have had a few metres of travel before plunging into the trunk. As it had been a whole month since it happened, some elements of the crash weren't as evident as they might have been. Nature had continued its course, and any remaining tyre marks were worn away and covered with new growth. But the marks on the tree were still evident; it seemed to have buckled somewhat from the impact. To get to the floral tribute, they had to step down into an embankment that was filled with foliage before clambering up to the other side. With every step Zack took, he begged his heart not to offer another flashback. He was having a hard enough time dealing with the memory of his accident, let alone processing the details of this one as well.

'These flowers are pretty fresh,' Zack said, more as an observation than anything. 'Someone must have been here more than once.'

'They may have been to the same shop by the looks of things.'

The bouquet Larry was holding was almost identical to one of the three that were laid by the tree. He popped his one next to them all. 'I don't really know what to say, other than to say thanks for saving my mate. I don't tell him often enough, but I'd be lost without him. And I really thought I had lost him until you came along and saved him. We will never meet, but I just wanted to say how grateful I am.'

Larry stopped his speech with a croak in his voice and quickly wiped his face with the sleeve of his top. 'I'm going to wait over here. Give you a bit of time to yourself.'

With Larry already something of a mess, it meant Zack didn't mind that his eyes were now wet too.

It was a lot to process. He'd not imagined he'd feel so emotional being at the spot it had happened. He'd been present when his father had passed at the rest home. It had been a gentle affair and the staff had done everything they could to make Zack's dad comfortable, knowing the chest infection he'd caught was going to be the one to overwhelm him. When he'd passed, it had been expected. But these two recent deaths had happened in entirely different circumstances and it filled him with another kind of grief. There were plenty of spots over the world that could be marked as somewhere that a life had stopped or started. But this spot was where something else had happened... a baton had been passed. One life had stopped and another had started. It was hard to comprehend that the heart now beating in his chest had stopped here, only to start again, giving him a new life.

Zack didn't know what to say. Some types of thanks were so huge, words alone didn't feel like they were enough. So instead he read the cards on the flowers already there.

Dear Susan and Mike,

The best neighbours we ever could have wished for. We'll miss you more than you'll ever know.

Much love,

Penny and Stan x

His throat contracted. *Mike.* The name he'd been after. The person who'd given him life and was trying to tell him his tale. It took a moment before he was able to push on to reading the next.

Dear Mum and Dad,

We'll always be grateful for everything you've done for us. Look after each other in death as you did in life.

Love Isabelle, Stuart and Phil xxx

Mike's three children. If Zack had wanted to dismiss the memories he'd been having, that one fact told him they were real. One girl and two boys. Reading that was enough to make Zack's usually dry eyes flood. Zack's, or rather Mike's, heart contracted. The article he'd read hadn't contained names. It had only mentioned they were a couple in their late fifties. But here they were with names and children. It was a lot to process. There was so much said and unsaid within the words on the cards. No wonder he'd had a sense of heartbreak lingering around him since he'd woken up. He was hoping being here might be enough to put that to bed, but it was peeling it further open. Making it all the more real.

There wasn't a note on the last bunch of flowers, which was

a relief. Zack wasn't sure he could handle finding out anything more. He wasn't sure what he'd expected to gain from being here. In a way, it was in the hope of finding some closure. To be able to say thanks in the place where a life had ended in order for his to start again. He'd not expected it to open small doors into the lives he was now somehow intertwined with.

As he cried more tears, not concerned about what Larry thought, he realised there was no closure to be found here. He wanted to say thank you to Mike, but how was that possible when he wasn't here? He wanted to know more about him. Where he'd lived, what he'd liked to do. Perhaps if he knew more about him, he'd be able to pay tribute to Mike as he had for his dad. Maybe he'd feel better about what had happened here if he was able to do more than lay flowers.

Instead, there were only questions. He had so many of them with nowhere to place them. And the biggest one of all was, if he had Mike's heart, where was Susan's?

Susan was wearing a red sequinned dress she'd had for years, but she still looked fantastic in it. Having watched their eldest nephew marry, they'd sneaked outside into the cool night air. Their teenage children were lighting up the dance floor and as they gazed at the stars, they both wondered how long it would be before they would watch one of their own children wed.

There she was again. The wife that wasn't his. The one his heart longed for him to find, but he didn't know how to. The only concrete certainty he'd discovered here was what was missing, and he had no clear course forwards. All he knew without doubt was that Susan's heart was still beating somewhere, and that he had to find out where.

CHAPTER EIGHT

MIKE

Mike's favourite thing to do these days was take his granddaughter, Lily, to the park after school. They did it once a fortnight when his daughter, Isabelle, had to work later on a Thursday. It was the one activity where he felt totally immersed. He had to concentrate entirely on the five-year-old and her constant chatter made it an easy task.

At any other time, the thoughts seeped in all too readily. Because it had been over six months now and he'd still not managed to talk to Susan about the one thing he needed to.

He'd planned to. There was a very solid plan, in which he took Susan away on holiday, but as with so many things, he'd failed to bring that to fruition. And now instead, she was taking him and he was trying his best to be happy about it, even if it wasn't what he'd hoped would happen. Right now he would give anything to be at the park with Lily and at least feel in control of his thoughts again.

Susan plugged the postcode into the satnav, ready for him to drive them to their destination. Not that she was letting him know where that was.

'I hope it's not too far away.'

'I told you... Mr Grumpy Pants has to remain at home. It's a clean-slate weekend, remember?'

'A man's allowed to hope without being perceived as grumpy, thank you very much.' He knew he'd been grumpy for months now, but having it pointed out wasn't helping.

'I'm still not giving you any clues, although as you're driving, you'll soon be able to work it out.' She finished adding in the information and turned the small screen to face him in the driver's seat.

'Hmm. Southampton postcode. Off to the airport then?'

They'd flown from there before on family holidays and skiing trips so it was an obvious guess, but Susan didn't give him any further indicators.

'Although, that's further north in the city if my memory serves me right?'

'I'm not going to be giving any more clues.'

'More? I don't think I've had any.' Mike attempted to keep some lightness in his voice.

'I'd drive if I were you. It's going to be the quickest way to find out.'

So he did. And when they arrived at a hotel, part of a chain, Mike almost kicked himself for not trying to push harder to get his plan into action. 'Is this it?'

'Looks that way, huh?'

'Uh-huh.' It was all he could muster as a response. It might not be what he would have chosen, but he needed to embrace this time with his wife and at long last get round to telling her the thing he should have told her when he'd retired.

CHAPTER NINE

ZACK

In the days following his discharge, once he returned home from his stay with Larry and his family, Zack didn't feel at all well. He wasn't sure if it was a general malaise that had overcome him, needing to recover from visiting the crash site, or something more like a stomach flu.

The first thing that had caused it was seeing his reflection in a mirror, his chest changed irreversibly. He didn't have one of those scars that he'd seen in movies: a neat line down the sternum. His was a mashed-up mess, as if someone had taken a chainsaw to his chest. Which of course he unintentionally had.

That had made him want to do nothing else other than curl up and cover himself with a blanket, and never move from his flat again. Accepting the change in his body didn't come in an instant. It was going to take time to adjust, and recognising he needed to rest was part of that.

The second thing was that Larry had been kindly keeping his promise of coming to visit and escorting him on walks. They'd both figured he'd need to build up his stamina. They'd gone on a walk and not got very far before Zack found he needed to throw up, and he had to make use of a drain along the side of the road, but the drain stunk, which made him heave all over again.

That walk had been cut short and he'd not felt up to going out again since.

Today would be his first venture out after that, but could it be classed as that when he was going to be heading straight back to the hospital? One week following discharge the cardiac team wanted him in again for a check-up.

It was a routine appointment, something they did for every patient who'd had this surgery, but he knew he needed to be at the hospital because he felt far more broken than he had when he was discharged a mere week ago. He'd hoped that going to the crash site would be a cure of sorts. A way to feel better about everything he knew, but shouldn't really know. Instead it was as if he'd been unplugged. The emotions from visiting the crash site had exhausted him to the point he no longer knew how he felt. Because were the feelings his or Mike's? And now the problem was he had no idea where the socket was to get his own charge back.

Larry chose more convenient parking spaces today, collecting him right outside his flat and being lucky enough to spot one close to the hospital entrance this time round.

'Do you want me to get a chair, mate?' Larry had a look of concern on his face, not dissimilar to the one he'd had when Zack was dicing up his chest with a chainsaw.

'How far is it? I'm not that bad, surely?'

'I don't want to frighten you, Zee, but your lips are beginning to turn blue.'

'That doesn't sound good.'

'Doesn't look too great, if I'm honest. Look, I'll get one to wheel you sharpish to the cardiac department and they can fix you up. I hope you've been taking your meds like they told you to?'

'Scout's honour.'

Zack slumped into the porter's chair once Larry had managed to locate one. He felt like a bean bag with all the stuffing knocked out of him.

'It's not far. I'll get you there as soon as I can.'

Zack didn't like the fact there was fear in his best friend's voice again so soon after the accident. Hopefully this wasn't on the same scale as before, but as he looked at his hands even they had a blue tinge to them. It was as if his whole system was about to shut down.

The cardiac department wasn't on the ground floor. They needed to go up one level, so Larry found the lifts in the behemoth hospital and they both silently willed the doors to open as quickly as possible. When the steel doors of the large lift opened, there was enough space to fit a circus but, despite its size, Zack still felt the walls pressing in on him.

It was hard to breathe. This really wasn't how he wanted to go. He didn't want to survive a chainsaw incident only to go and be swallowed up by the lack of air in a lift. But by the looks of everyone else, it was only Zack that was struggling. He wished he knew what his heart was doing, but the disconnecting numbness was still there.

Susan was in labour, the baby's heartbeat dipping dangerously low, and he was pleading with her to push, wishing he could do it for her, knowing she was exhausted. Moments later, their baby daughter gave out the wail of her life and he'd never known tears of relief like it.

'We're nearly there. Don't go passing out on me now.'

'Everything okay?' a woman in scrubs asked.

'I'm not sure. He's here for a check-up, but he's been looking worse the past couple of days and even worse on the car journey over here.'

The woman in scrubs pressed at Zack's neck, asking Larry more questions at the same time.

They were lost on Zack. He picked out words only. Things

like 'transplant' and 'sick'. The lift was beginning to feel like an oven. He was pretty sure no one should be able to talk in this heat. He flopped his head to the side in the hope he'd be cooler that way. He wasn't sure he had the strength to keep it up.

'I'm coming with you. I'll be able to get help if we need it on the way,' the woman said as the lift doors opened, allowing a rush of cool air in at the same time.

As soon as they were rushing along the corridor, Zack's hearing returned. He was able to sit up again and was no longer overwhelmed by the fear he might die because he couldn't breathe.

'Slow down a bit,' he said to Larry.

'Slow down? This lady was ready to call the resus team! We're getting you to somewhere with some staff about.'

'I feel fine!' Zack said, not fully aware of the antics in the lift.

'You certainly didn't look fine. Here we are.' Scrubs woman opened the door for them. 'I'm going to hand over to my colleagues while you check in. Any other problems, you pull that red cord there.'

The instruction was for Larry, and she pointed to a cord hanging from the ceiling that wasn't unlike a light pull.

'Fuck, man. Please don't do that again.'

'It wasn't deliberate. Honest.'

'I know it wasn't, but for a minute there you looked like death warmed up.'

'I felt like it too. At least my hands are pink again.' Zack admired how his hands once again appeared to belong to a body that was pumping blood around in the way one would hope.

'I've let them know what happened,' the woman in scrubs said as she reappeared. 'They're going to keep an eye on you and will be running some extra checks. I'll get back to where I should be heading, if you're all okay?'

'What caused it?' Larry asked.

'We won't know for certain without checking, but it might have been something as simple as a panic attack or an episode of syncope.'

'Syncope? That sounds bad.'

'It's just another word for fainting. Anyway, your actual doctors will carry out all the relevant checks. Take care, okay?' The woman in scrubs rested a hand briefly on Zack's forearm before heading off to save someone else.

Zack knew then that all superhero capes were actually made from scrubs. Or at least they should be.

'I do feel fine now,' Zack said to Larry, who was staring into the empty space where the doctor had been.

'I'm not sure *my* heart will handle it if you do that again.'

'Strangely, I feel better than I have all week. I don't think I even need this chair.' Nimble as anything, Zack hopped out of the chair and did a little jig to prove how much better he was feeling compared to only minutes beforehand. And something told him there had to be a reason.

They were waiting in a queue for the cinema, ready to watch Romeo and Juliet. *There was a swell to Susan's stomach, their lives about to change soon with their firstborn now in the third trimester. They were squeezing as many dates in whilst they still could.*

'Sit down, Zee. You are genuinely going to give me a heart attack with turnarounds like that. I don't think anyone should go from fainting to dancing that quickly.'

Zack stopped his mini jig of euphoria. Of course this wasn't natural. No one should go from feeling at death's door to joyful dancing without a shot of adrenaline or some kind of medical intervention. He'd not had one of those so there was only one other explanation, and he knew if he voiced it too loudly they might be getting Larry to wheel him off to an entirely different department. But the memories had been increasing the closer they'd got to this place. They were trying to tell him something.

The realisation was enough to make him sit down again.

She's here.

Susan, or at least her heart, was *here.*

Mike's heart wanted something, Zack was certain of that. And the longer it pressed on him, the more it was becoming a need of his own. To do what his heart desired would be fulfilling a wish, even if he wasn't entirely sure what that was.

Sensing that the change in him must be because the other heart was here meant that he just had to work out who had been its recipient. Maybe then the sense of heartbreak that kept taking over him would go away. Maybe then he could work on being Zack once more.

CHAPTER TEN

CHLOE

With every book, puzzle and crossword that Chloe was supported through, she found herself tugged further away from leaving hospital. Her sisters were gladly supplying their endless optimism, but even they had to admit she wasn't doing as well as they'd hoped. Of course, they hadn't said this to her face, but when there had been raised voices in the corridor it had been hard to miss a word: her sisters felt the doctors weren't giving them clear answers. There was no sign of infection. All her vitals were as they'd expect them to be, better in fact. Everything indicated the heart had taken well. They couldn't explain her weakness and fatigue through any of the tests they'd carried out and were 'perplexed' (their choice of words), stating system shock might be a factor.

Hearing the word 'perplexed' in reference to her medical status had been no comfort at all. For two days, much to Alice and Leona's collective horror, she'd refused to get out of bed for her physio sessions. She was done with it all. If the doctors were hazarding a guess at her being in shock, then she was going to behave as such. If she were at home and unwell, spending the day in bed would be an option. She'd decided to indulge in the same, even though she was in hospital and everyone else seemed to be opposed to the idea.

'You'll end up with a blood clot if you stay in there too long,' one of the nurses told her.

'I'm going to take my chances,' she said defiantly. Even though she knew she shouldn't be taking any risks with this new heart, right now, resting seemed like the right thing to be doing.

That comment made her stay in bed another day. Her sisters hadn't dared say anything to agree with the nurse, knowing Chloe might dig her heels in more than she already had.

Today they'd both come in, ready to do battle once more with the medical team. She was so lucky to have such great advocates in her sisters, in the absence of their parents. She just wished she could find the same kind of strength and enthusiasm at this stage.

'We wondered if you'd like Logan to pop by? See if that would cheer you up?' Leona suggested.

'What?' That did get Chloe's attention. She even pushed herself up at the suggestion.

'It's only an idea. We've just been racking our brains over what to do.'

'I do not want to see Logan. Not ever. Least of all while my body's doing a good impression of a limp eel.' Logan had been a fellow patient she'd met during one of her admissions and they'd started dating. It had been on and off for about two years when Chloe had been in her mid-twenties. There was a definite pattern of it being on when he'd been an inpatient and not when he was out and she remained in hospital. The final straw had been when he'd got jealous about her qualifying to be on the transplant list. His heart condition wasn't as serious as hers, and he'd responded as if she were receiving a get out of jail free card at no cost. She'd realised that was a rather toxic attitude to take, and she didn't need that in her already fragile existence.

'We just thought a friend might be able to encourage you.'

'Logan is *not* a friend.'

'We weren't sure how you left things. Forget I suggested anything.' Leona peered at the floor as if she had known, but they were desperate.

'Have either of you booked a holiday yet?' Chloe wanted to change the subject. Booking a holiday was all they'd talked about pre-surgery.

'We wanted to wait until you were better. We're not going off without you!' Alice said.

'You could, though. I wouldn't be upset. You all spend far too long here waiting for me to pull it together and at some point we have to accept that it might never happen.' Chloe hadn't meant to sound quite so melodramatic, but sooner or later they all had to face up to the fact that it might be true. She'd been dying for at least half her life. With the solution not being the rosy picture they'd all imagined, there had to be a moment when they faced up to reality.

'We don't want you talking like that,' Leona said.

'We don't want you thinking like that either,' Alice added. 'We know you spend a lot of hours without us here. We need you to knock that out of your noggin. Once you're feeling better, which you will, then we'll book a holiday for all three of us.'

'No plus ones yet then?' Chloe knew her sisters were perpetually single, because who wanted a relationship with someone who was tied to a hospital sick bed? Any romances they'd had always seemed to be short-lived, unless they were keeping such things quiet for fear of upsetting her. She doubted that, though, as they'd always been as honest as possible with each other. That's why she was trying to get across how she was feeling, even when it got rebuffed. It was always well intended. Maybe she'd try again tomorrow to express how this wasn't the recovery she'd hoped for. That the second chance she should be experiencing had hopped away by itself on the night bus and was nowhere to be seen.

'We don't have time for plus ones. We'd much rather be with you,' Alice said.

'Dear Lord, please will one of you get me a sick bowl?'

Leona actually went to grab one before realising Chloe was joking.

'Genuinely, girls. I don't want you missing out on your lives because you're so busy focusing on mine. It's not right. You've been doing it for too many years.'

With Chloe being the youngest, her two older siblings had taken responsibility for her when their parents had passed away. That was fourteen years ago now. Fourteen years of putting their lives on hold for her. They'd formed a tight circle around Chloe, continuing the care their parents had previously provided. But some days Chloe worried that they were risking their chances of a fulfilling life for the sake of hers.

Alice placed a hand on Chloe's. 'Until you're better and out of here, we're going to focus on you as much as we like. Then we'll book a holiday. We're not about to go off without you. Nor is visiting you preventing us from finding our plus ones. We're still in our thirties, so there're plenty of years ahead for that kind of nonsense.'

There was a knock at the door, followed by a head ducking around as it opened. 'Ready for today's physio session? We thought we'd try before lunch today.'

There was a steady silence in the room as Alice and Leona exchanged a discreet glance. They knew not to push, but they also wanted her to try.

Chloe took a breath and, in a way that was hard to fathom, it felt different. As if the alveoli in her lungs were like butterfly wings unfurling for the first time.

'Yes, I'm ready,' she said, excited to find out what this feeling meant.

'We'll give you some space,' Leona said, gesturing the physios in before leaving the room.

When the physios rolled in their machine, Chloe found herself getting up into a sitting position on the side of the bed without help.

'My goodness. Someone's obviously had their Weetabix today.'

Chloe found herself smiling, the first genuine one in days. 'It was cornflakes actually, and I feel – dare I say it? – better!'

'Well, that's tremendous news. Perhaps you were right to have your time in bed. Maybe your body did need some respite.'

'The doctors kept mentioning shock, and I figured whenever I've had a stressful event I've taken myself to bed. I do feel revived somehow.' It was hard to explain the kind of static-electric sensation that was pulsing through her. She'd felt awful for weeks, but when the physio had opened the door it had washed away in an instant. She wished every physio session felt like that, but this was a start.

'As you've managed to sit up yourself, I want you to try and pull yourself up to standing. We're going to be here for support. If it goes well, we can try it without the equipment tomorrow.'

Even though she'd been weak and wasn't close to her pre-surgery fitness level, she still managed, with effort, to get herself upright. Having her back straight was such a novel experience that she remained like that for a while, just appreciating the fact that some kind of switch had been flicked, allowing her to start recuperating as she'd hoped. It was the first step of many, but even this early sign that things were going to be okay was like seeing a firework in the night sky for the first time. It was unexpected and brilliant all at once.

'Amazing!' Leah exclaimed. 'Do you feel up to taking a couple of steps? We just need to take the brakes off and this can move forward. We can bring the chair for you to sit in when you need to rest.'

There was a beat of hesitation in Chloe's head because of the fear this might put her body into shock again, but the desire to walk was far stronger. Now that her limbs were cooperating she was going to cash in on the feeling as much as possible.

For the first couple of steps, while pushing the frame forward, the floor was like a foreign object, hard and unyielding. They'd put some hospital-issued slippers on her feet to ensure she didn't slip on her surgical stockings, but they were thin and didn't stop that strange sensation of having contact with something that wasn't a bedsheet.

The third and fourth steps brought about a greater sense of familiarity. The patterns of movement were something that she'd never really had to give much thought to, but here she was having to remind her body what it needed to do at each stage. It filled her with a sense of gratitude, from previously being at a point where she'd begun to believe it might never be possible again. And here she was, very slowly putting one foot in front of the other.

Admittedly it was with help, the physios supporting her and guiding the frame, positioning her feet if they went wayward, but it wasn't long before a few steps became ten and they were starting to head for the door.

'Are you okay to keep going?' Leah asked from by her side.

'I want to get out of the door.' It wasn't the main door of the hospital, but even seeing the outside of her room was going to be a major achievement.

'If you need to stop at any point, you let us know.'

Chloe gave a firm nod in agreement.

The next ten steps were far harder. She didn't have a stride. It felt like she was treading water and getting nowhere. It was frustrating to put so much effort in and appear to be not much further forward now that she'd given herself a target.

She decided to stop counting steps and just concentrate on how she was feeling. There was more strength in her limbs right now than there had been for weeks. She tried her best to harness that sense of power to pull herself up straighter, to make her legs step forward as much as possible.

The gap was gradually closing and, using everything she had, it was time for Leah to open the door.

The gasps of her sisters, and possibly some of the nursing staff as well, were audible. Even though it was in surprise, it was one of the nicest noises Chloe had heard for a long time.

'Bloody hell, Chloe. Looks like you want that holiday more than we realised,' Leona said.

It was quickly followed by a round of applause from everyone there, and perhaps a tear or two being wiped away if she wasn't mistaken.

'I think I'll have that chair now, Leah, if you don't mind?'

She plonked into it without ceremony. She might have found some strength, but it would be a while until all her muscles were toned enough for full cooperation. She was out of breath as well and it was a welcome sensation. The fact that she'd done something physically exerting, and it had shifted that awful numb feeling, was bracing.

Her sisters crowded round on their usual sides. 'That was amazing.'

'More of that, please!'

'Fingers crossed! But for now, I think I might be in need of an extended nap in the chair.'

Once she'd been returned to the usual position in her room with the help of the physiotherapy staff, her sisters bade her an early goodbye, satisfied that she was starting the journey to recovery. It made a nice change to have an afternoon to herself. She loved her sisters dearly, but sometimes the intensity of them being there felt as if she was under a microscope.

At least they all had a bit more hope to hold on to today. Except, by the time the dinners came round, that sense of euphoria had left Chloe. It was as if whatever switch had been flicked on had been flicked off again.

There were all sorts of reasons for it. Exhaustion being the most likely. But she couldn't escape the sense that it was gone. She cried in the night as if she were mourning its loss, but come the next day, by breakfast time she perked up again.

In the days that followed, the cycle continued every day and night. During most of the daylight hours, the switch was on. She had energy. She engaged with her physio sessions and grew stronger by the day. But at night, it was as if all her vitality left her. She was a limp piece of lettuce in her bed again.

It didn't make sense, but if her body was going to choose to only be in shock mode at night time, it was a much better deal than before. This way her sisters saw how much she was improving and didn't have to know about the contrast in the evenings. She wasn't even certain the medical staff had noticed that during the hours of darkness she felt like an entirely different person. Why would they when for much of that time she was sleeping?

It didn't matter, she kept telling herself. Mentions of returning home were already beginning to happen and that was what she wanted most in all the world. As they'd not managed to pinpoint why she hadn't progressed as expected in the first place, she wasn't about to tell them it might all be an illusion. That in the wings, the locked-down version of herself was waiting to come and take over. She was frightened that if she admitted to it, it might actually come true.

She was just tired, she reminded herself. Rebuilding yourself from the ground up was not going to come without fatigue. That was all it was. Nothing else made sense.

CHAPTER ELEVEN

SUSAN

'Checking out?' Mike's expression was a mix of relief and confusion.

'Yes, dear. However lovely a weekend in Southampton might have been, that was never the actual plan.' Susan folded the last of her clothes back into her suitcase and gave the hotel room a sweep to check everything was packed away.

'And the actual plan is?'

Susan was surprised Mike hadn't worked it out. They'd talked about it often enough over the years and never got any further than looking through a brochure.

'I'll tell you when we get to the car.'

It was easier that way. As they made their way to the car park in silence, Susan waved towards the docked ship they were going to be heading for.

'What? On there?'

The ship was like a small city, far bigger in fact than the hotel they'd just been staying in and more or less eclipsing the view. It looked rather majestic sitting there, and had managed to swoop into dock at some point since they'd arrived. If it had already been in situ, she had to hope that Mike would have worked it out, but even now he seemed to be slow on catching up.

'Yes, Mike, we're going on a cruise. We've always talked about one, and never got round to it. So I've taken matters into my own hands.'

'I hope neither of us get seasick.'

'And of course that's the first thing to say about it.' It was always concern or worry with Mike these days, never a glad word to say about anything.

'Well, it's true.'

'That's why I only booked for the weekend. A taster. If we're both fine, we can go for a longer one next time.'

'So what do we do... walk there?'

'They have a secure car park and we'll be escorted from there. It isn't far.'

Without further grumblings, Mike loaded their cases into the car and drove them the short distance to where the car would remain while they were away.

'Are we stopping anywhere on this cruise then? Or is it all at sea?'

'We get to stop at Amsterdam.'

Mike raised an eyebrow. 'Interesting.'

'Oh, and as we're celebrating forty years of being together, it's also an eighties theme. I thought we could do with some reminiscing.'

'Wow. Okay, so when you told me to pack for every occasion, I didn't manage to include a different era.'

'That won't matter. What really matters is that we enjoy ourselves. Learn to enjoy each other's company again.'

'I've always enjoyed your company.'

'You know what I mean.'

Susan didn't want to have to spell it out. They'd been together for a very long time, but without doubt at some point they'd drifted apart. They might still share a bed, but that was all at times.

'I'm looking forward to it already.'

The short sentence gave Susan a warm fuzzy feeling in her belly. For someone who'd forgotten how to be positive, it was quite the statement. She just had to hope they'd make it through the weekend without arguing again. Life was for living and enjoying, and neither of them had been managing to do that in the hiatus they'd found themselves in. It was time for a change and it needed to be a lasting one.

CHAPTER TWELVE

ZACK

After realising what Zack needed to find was in the hospital, his next moves were relatively limited. The thing was, now he'd worked that out, he knew he had to find her, but how to go about finding a heart inside a stranger's chest?

He'd decided to do the only thing he was able to and that was wait. Day in and day out of waiting. He'd found a bench in the central part of the second floor near to where he'd had his outpatient appointment and he was spending many hours sitting there, occasionally going for strolls to the nearby quarters of the hospital without intruding onto the wards. The benefit of this strange new routine was the fact he always felt much better at the hospital than he did when he was away.

He would read the paper for most of the morning, dwelling on far more details in the news than he normally would. He'd make notes of the flashbacks he was having in case they somehow held a clue. At lunch he'd grab something from the shop or the canteen, then he'd return to his stakeout post, not really sure exactly who or what he was waiting for. As far as he knew, the heart he was looking for may have passed him by many times over. How would he know when there were so many people filtering in and out of the hospital?

But even though it was impossible, he also felt certain that he knew. That what he needed was somewhere here, but he just hadn't come across it yet. And when he did he'd know.

He'd become so relaxed in this new ritual, on occasions he'd lain on the bench and attempted to have a snooze. It was in one of these snoozing stupors that his phone rang and gave him a moment of disorientation before remembering where he was and why.

'Helllooo.'

'Zee, mate. Where are you?'

'Out for a walk. Thought I'd better build myself up a bit.'

'Really?' There was a note to Larry's voice that told him he'd at long last worked out that he was off his trolley.

'Mostly.'

'Mum said she saw you sleeping on a bench in the hospital. Doing her voluntary bit in the League of Friends as usual and reckons she's seen you a few times.'

'Ah.' Why hadn't he figured out his second mum would see him? The fact she volunteered here had escaped his thoughts until this reminder. He peered about to check if Kathy was still around.

'What's going on? Honest answers only.'

'You're going to think I've lost the plot.'

'I've been thinking that for some considerable time. Long before the accident, though.'

Zack brushed the tiredness away from his face. The problem was he hadn't managed to convince himself that he wasn't losing the plot. 'Do you want to come here and I'll tell you?' He'd rather Larry was here so he could see his expression for himself and gauge how mad it seemed.

'Sounds like you need to get out of there and get some fresh air. How about we go to that pub down the road and get some lunch?'

'No, I can't.' Zack hadn't tested the opposite of his theory, other than going home to the flat to sleep at night.

'Can't? How come, mate?'

'I'll explain when you get here. Bring snacks.'

After giving detailed instructions on where Larry would find him, it was a little over half an hour before his friend joined him on his bench with a sharing bag of Doritos.

'I'm pretty certain there are more upmarket places you can people watch. What's made you want to hang out here so much?'

'It's to do with when we were here before.'

'Thought so.'

'How did you know?' It was going to be a relief if Larry had already worked it out.

'Well, it's obvious, isn't it? You're worried you're going to need medical attention again. What better place to be than a hospital? If you pass out, someone knowledgeable like that woman the other day will be on hand. It's going to be far better for you to pass out here than at home alone.'

'Strong theory, but that's not it.'

'Ah, I get it. You need to offer your thanks to the stranger in scrubs who got us to the cardiac department without you dying on me. Neither of us managed to get any details so you're waiting here until you spot her. Your *guardian angel*.'

Zack didn't have much recollection of the woman. She'd been a saviour, but since he'd been spending his time here he'd seen about twenty people a day that met the minimal description he had in his head. 'It's not that either.'

'You've got me then. Unless it's a hare-brained scheme for a TikTok video to raise money.'

'No schemes or fundraising. You'll laugh when I tell you.'

He wasn't even sure how to word it without it sounding questionable.

'No laughing. My mum has made me give that up.'

'It's going to sound crazy, but I feel *better* when I'm here. And it's not because I'm around medical staff like you suggested. It's because I think the other heart is here. Ever since we went to the roadside tribute, I've had this sense of something unfinished. That the other heart and this one need to be reconnected, if only for a while.'

'You're right. That does sound crazy. Do you think perhaps you're reading too much into it? Like your electrolytes have gone out of sync or something?'

Zack wished it was easy to explain away. For it all to be made clear by numbers on a blood test. 'Nah, it's not like that. I know it sounds ridiculous, like my mind might be going into overdrive, but it's an actual physical thing. When I leave here I feel ten times worse. I'm pretty sure the quality of hospital air can't explain it away, unless they're accidently pumping additional oxygen into this corridor. If you walk home with me, you'll see what I mean.'

'Do you want to head back now then? Mum won't forgive me if she sees you here twice in a day.'

'Can we stay a bit longer? An hour or two. I've been trying to work out where she is.'

'She? Do you know any of this for certain?'

'That's the thing. I keep having these flashbacks to memories that aren't mine. They're Mike's and I'm sure it's him nudging me towards finding Susan. Or her heart, at the very least. So I mean *she* as in Susan. It's the heart I need to meet. Whatever form it's in now.'

'Flashbacks? Are you sure that's not a side effect from one of your meds or something?'

'I know that would make it easier to explain, but I'm being genuine. I keep having recollections of time spent with my two sons and my daughter. The card I read at the roadside from Isabelle, Phil and Stuart has confirmed that's not made up. It's not in my head, like a doctor might phrase it – this is in my heart and I swear it's filtering thoughts through to me.'

'And you think waiting out here is really the answer?'

It was a relief that Larry didn't seem to be dismissing what Zack was saying entirely. 'I've been testing out other parts of the hospital, near different wards, and this is the place I feel at my strongest.'

'Aren't there other ways you could find out, though? Some official channels? It doesn't seem right that you're sitting on an uncomfortable bench when you should be convalescing at home.'

'Honestly. I feel so much worse by the time I've made it home. I'll prove it to you after we've waited a while longer.'

They didn't say much more to each other as the next hour stretched out before them, each of them intermittently raiding the bag of crisps. What was there to add? Zack didn't know what more he could say to convince his best friend or himself that he wasn't losing it entirely.

Words weren't always needed, though, when actions were far greater. He didn't need to tell Larry when showing him was the far easier option.

Because with every step they took further away from the hospital, Zack became a different man. Weaker, more feeble, barely able to manage his own weight as Larry helped to get him up the stairs to his flat.

'See what I mean,' Zack gasped.

Larry aided him to the sofa before replying. 'It doesn't make sense. Are you sure you're not having some kind of cardiac event and I should be calling an ambulance?'

'It's because I'm away from her. You saw that I was fine at the hospital.'

Larry rubbed his hands in his hair and then drew them

down his face. 'This ain't right. I don't know what's going on, but I can't leave you like this. I need to take you back to the hospital.'

'And they won't find anything wrong with me, because I'll be fine again once I get there.' Zack had already got his breath back enough to form sentences.

'Look, we're mates, right? And I don't want anything to ruin that, but I've gotta say it... To me, it seems more like you're having a panic attack. You've been through what must be a crazy high level on the trauma scale. You've had the biggest shock of your life in discovering you've survived, only with someone else's heart in your chest. It's bound to have messed with your mind and your normal harmony. Even if you don't want to go to see a doctor at the hospital, it might be worth seeing your GP or something? See if there's someone you can talk to about everything that's happened.'

Zack clicked his teeth at the thought Larry didn't believe him. 'I promise you. This isn't in my noggin. This is for real. You'll believe me when I find her.'

'And if and when you do, what then?'

'Then I start to heal.'

At least, he had to hope that was what would happen. Because the truth was, as much as he was unable to explain the sense of being incomplete that had overtaken him, he didn't know the answer to Larry's question. 'What then?' seemed like the most terrifying question in the world when he didn't have a clue what the answer was.

CHAPTER THIRTEEN

CHLOE

Walking around the block and climbing the stairs independently were the final hurdles. Chloe knew this from weeks of observing the comings and goings of patients and listening to snippets of conversations through the view her side room door allowed her. She'd also been there herself previously. They wanted to make sure she'd be able to wander around the house she shared with her sisters independently. Not that she needed to. They tended to wait on her hand and foot whenever she returned from a long stay in hospital.

She knew she could play these small nuggets of knowledge to her favour. If she didn't complete those hurdles, they weren't going to send her home. Not yet.

It was contradictory to how she should be feeling and what she should be aiming for. Home was the ultimate goal, wasn't it?

It should be, but there was still the rotten feeling she was experiencing every night that was making her want to stay. Like somehow she was safe here, but wouldn't be at home. The thought that any kind of medical emergency could occur at the house filled her with dread. Her sisters had been through so much already. She didn't want them to have to go through that too.

Leah's knock was so familiar now, she didn't have to wait until she'd entered the room to know it was her. 'Ready to give it another try?'

Chloe was so much better, Leah no longer had to attend with a colleague. She was able to take herself to the ensuite toilet, walk around her room freely, and get in and out of bed herself. She'd even managed a set of stairs supervised by Leah without too much trouble, but when it came to walking any distance, she was complaining of a tight feeling in her chest.

It was a fib.

A little white lie because in truth, the pain didn't come when she was walking along the corridor. It came in the middle of the night, clamping itself to her as if the two sides of her sternum weren't healing as they should be. It was such a star-tling contrast to how comfortable she felt in the day that it took her breath away, and she'd be alone in the dark knowing some-thing was dreadfully wrong. The pain pinched her so hard she wasn't able to call out and let anyone know. Then, in the morn-ing, it was as if it hadn't existed. As if it had been a nightmare that had terrorised her and no one would be able to make sense of it.

She hadn't managed to tell anyone about what was happening at night, so it made sense to speak the truth of it now, especially if it prevented the thing she was dreading... being discharged from hospital.

'I can't go any further,' Chloe said, as they reached the ward doors. She held her ribs and imagined the pain that was haunting her at night as if it was happening to her now.

'How about we stop a while? See if that pain eases and we can carry on in a bit?'

Normally at this point, Leah would concede to the pain Chloe was telling her about. Was this the start of her physio beginning to realise she was putting it on? Other than her sisters, Leah probably knew her better than anyone else, given the frequency they'd seen each other all the times she'd been an inpatient at this hospital.

'I'm not sure. This pain, it makes me feel a bit faint.' That might be a step too far. Faking pain was one thing. Faking fainting was going to another level. Perhaps she should just be honest with Leah and tell her she was scared? But it was difficult to explain when she didn't really know what was going on.

'I can get you a chair, but why don't we wait it out? See if it passes.'

That's what Chloe kept hoping. That this would pass, as it had when she'd gone from not being able to sit herself up to being able to manage it independently. Something had shifted then and she was busy waiting for the second shift. She was desperate for her journey to be a smooth one, but she was quickly learning that wasn't how post-transplant life worked. The problem was, she didn't understand why at certain times of day she felt wretched. When she explained it to the doctors they dismissed it as fatigue.

'I don't think I can.' Chloe let her knees buckle slightly before saving herself. She had no plans to actually throw herself on the floor.

Leah whisked up a chair for Chloe to sit on like magic. She took it up thankfully, beginning to genuinely feel some of the fatigue she was feigning.

'Is there anything you want to tell me?' Leah asked, apparently sensing there was more to this than Chloe was letting on.

Chloe nodded. 'Back in the room,' she whispered.

When they got there, Chloe was exhausted. Maybe she didn't have to fabricate additional aches and pains as well.

'What is it you want to tell me?'

'I'm not making it up.'

'I didn't say you were. It just seems like there's something on your mind.'

Chloe took some gulps from her glass of water. She didn't mean to immediately go on the defensive. 'I'm scared. Something doesn't feel right. This was supposed to improve things, but I still feel broken.'

'I know it hasn't been easy, but we need to take things one step at a time. I'm sure I've said that to you a lot but it's true. I think maybe the idea of how far walking the block is has become a stumbling block in itself. The thought of it is overwhelming, which is why we never make it off the ward.'

'Maybe.' Everything was overwhelming for Chloe currently. It was as if she was experiencing life in an entirely different way with a different set of feelings. Sometimes those feelings didn't even feel like they belonged to her.

'How about the next few times we try this, I set up some pit stops along the way? Break it down into small stints and try to get further each time?'

Chloe nodded and offered a brief smile. 'It sounds like a good idea.'

Leah reciprocated the smile with much more meaning. 'Great. Your sisters are desperate to have you home. I bet you can't wait to get there.'

After Leah had departed, that sentiment settled in her stomach like curdled milk. She should be desperate to get home and here she was stalling. She wondered, if she really tried, whether she was capable of walking far enough for them to decide she was well enough for discharge. She'd be tempted to sneak out when it was dark to try herself, but she knew as soon as night time came, she'd be bedbound and unable to get out, let alone walk any distance. And that was why, for now, she was staying.

But that didn't stop everyone encouraging her in the opposite direction. Over the following days, her sisters were doing everything in their power to inspire her to walk that much further. To be honest, she was beginning to feel like a dog on agility training lessons, with clicks and treats being used for good behaviour. On the first pit stop efforts, both of her sisters waited at one of the resting places. From their position, they would cheer and say things like, 'You can do it, Chlo!' On that attempt, she made it to Alice, but not as far as Leona. Their collective disappointment was palpable, but their words didn't match their moods and were still full of positivity and encouragement. 'You'll manage it next time,' they both said, in variations of the same sentence.

'I just don't feel strong enough. Not yet.'

She'd not told any of them that by the end of the day she was so worn out she was immobile. That this peak performance was mirrored by a complete contrast.

When Alice turned up by herself the following day, Chloe was secretly glad. The constant joint cheerleading was well meaning, but it also made her feel so much worse for disappointing them both.

'Maybe today's the day?' Alice said.

'What? The day I get the gold? I don't think so.'

'You never know. You had that sudden leap in strength a couple of weeks ago. Maybe the same will happen again at some point.'

'Maybe.'

'As Leona's working today, I thought I'd bring someone else along as a cheerleader. I hope you don't mind.'

If she did mind, she didn't get the chance to voice it as the invited guest was in the room before she had time. It was Logan. Her idiot of an ex she'd expressly said she never wanted to see again.

'Heard you had a new heart. Your sister thought I should say hello.'

Chloe noticed how her sister wanted it and not him. And

her heart responded, but not how she expected. It was as if it jumped backwards, it was so repulsed by his presence. She didn't blame it, but didn't appreciate the fact it left her feeling dizzy.

'Are you okay?' Alice asked.

Chloe shook her head, unable to speak.

'Do you want me to get someone?'

'Go,' Chloe managed, pointing first at Logan, then at the door so he'd understand.

'I told you it was a bad idea, Alice. We tried at least.' He left, sounding like he'd been doing Chloe some kind of favour, which she'd been too ungrateful to accept.

As soon as he was gone, her heart seemed to right itself again, the dizzy sensation passing.

'What did you bring him here for?'

'I bumped into him. He was asking after you. I thought, as we haven't managed to encourage you, seeing other friends might help.'

'Logan is not a friend. I told you that. He didn't worry about upsetting my last heart so he certainly doesn't get any input on this one.' She had a feeling it wouldn't let him if he tried.

'I'm sorry. I figured anything was worth a try.'

'Are we really at last resorts? Because that was *the* last resort.'

'We just want you home. It's not the same without you there.'

'I want to be there too. I'm just scared.'

'We're all going to be there for you. I promise it'll be okay.'

Chloe always admired the fact her sisters swore to that promise. Anyone able to state 'it'll be okay' when armed with nothing other than blind faith was to be respected and admired.

'I hope so,' she said, unable to muster the same faith herself.

'Today, I'll let you tackle the walk with Leah. I'm not going to cheer you on like it's the school sports day one hundred metres. I'm going to be here waiting for you, like always.'

When Leah arrived and it was time for yet another attempt to get round the block, Chloe decided not to feign pain. Instead, she took the anger at seeing her ex-boyfriend and the fury it had caused her heart and turned it into fuel. It spurred her on to take one step and then the next.

Of all the things that were going to make this achievable, she'd not expected hatred to be it. But apparently her new heart disliked her ex as much as she did. And the knowledge that they were agreeing on something made her efforts all the more pleasing.

She passed the first chair and the second without feeling the need to sit and take a rest.

'This is amazing! Keep going,' Leah said.

When they were off the ward it started to feel impossible. All the anger in the world wasn't going to be enough to get her all the way along the corridor. She moved more sluggishly and the labour of breathing was becoming marked.

'There's a bench halfway along this corridor. Let's see if we can make it there. You can have a rest and then we'll head back.'

Chloe spotted the seat in the distance. It was occupied, but that wasn't going to stop her. She'd probably collapse when she got there, but she was determined to make it.

And as if a magnet was suddenly pulling her along, she carried on her journey, one step at a time.

CHAPTER FOURTEEN

SUSAN

The cruise ship had taken them to another dimension as far as Susan was concerned. Mike had complimented everything he'd seen so far. He liked the grandeur, the decor, and the many facilities. Even their cabin, although a tad cramped compared to the hotel room they'd stayed in the night before, was the nicest room he'd ever stayed in. Such praise was so rare it made her wonder if the real Mike had been body-snatched as they boarded the ship.

For their first evening meal on board, they were joined at their table by three other couples. Susan had forgotten all their names by the time their starters arrived, but that didn't seem to matter as they compared their memories from the eighties.

'We used to have a terrible nightclub that did nights for the schoolkids. Think it was called something awful like Club Zone, wasn't it, Tina?'

'God, yes. I remember that place. All mirrors and black-and-white decor like they were trying to create an Escher drawing.'

'It worked though, didn't it? Once you were in, it was quite the job to find your way out again.' The rotund gent laughed at the memory.

'We met at our school disco,' Mike said.

It was a pleasant surprise to hear her husband joining in, let alone referencing the start of their relationship.

'Gosh. Does that mean you've been together all that time?' Tina exclaimed like it was a miracle.

'Yes. Forty happy years together,' Mike confirmed.

He reached under the table for Susan's hand and gave it a squeeze.

That one small gesture was enough to make her want to cry and rejoice at the same time. Affection, especially relatively open displays of it, were a rare treat. It was probably months since she'd been in receipt of a handhold. What hope it possessed.

The rest of the meal involved an exchange of stories from their youth. The places they'd been, the things they'd done, the bands they'd seen.

Mike regaled them all with stories Susan had thought he'd long forgotten. Like the time they'd travelled all the way to a gig in the Winter Gardens in Margate, only to find it had been cancelled after the band had completely trashed their previous venue. Or when they hadn't been able to afford tickets for a concert so instead had found a patch of grass to lie on outside the arena, and listened to it with their eyes closed as if they were on the right side of the stadium wall. And the details of that first night. The day they met. The day they fell in love. She still felt surprise that he'd chosen that song for her before they'd even properly met. Before they'd known it would spell a lifetime together.

'I loved that song,' the wife of the rotund man said, before starting to hum the tune.

'I wonder if we can put requests in here. We should ask for it to be played before the weekend is over,' the rotund man suggested.

'Oh no. We don't need to be that sentimental,' Mike said.

Susan felt it like a slap across her cheek. Here they were recalling the good times, but they weren't the here and now: they were in the past. Her husband didn't want to hear a song that would remind him of happier days. He didn't want to drag his wife to the dance floor as though they were kids again.

'I'm sure your wife would love to. If she's anything like mine she loves reminiscing, especially the best bits.'

The rotund man was right. She really was going to have to remember his name.

After dinner, they filed into a huge theatre to watch a show by a band covering hits of the eighties. Some of the actual eighties stars would be performing the following evening. The band was good and she found herself humming along to some of the tunes, but her mind was elsewhere. She wanted to pinpoint exactly when things had changed between them and what had caused everything to feel different. Because surely there had to be a reason?

It was later, when they were back in the cabin, that she asked the question: 'Why don't you want to hear our song?'

'Do we have to go over this just before bed?'

'It's not a difficult question.'

'It is if you don't like the answer.'

'What does that mean?'

'It means you always do this. Bring up something deep and meaningful just before we're going to bed, and we're always tired so it ends up in an argument unless I say exactly what you want me to say.'

'What?' Mike was making her sound like a grade-A manipulator. All she wanted to know was why. Why were they no longer in love in the same way they'd once been? It always went unanswered. 'That's so untrue. I just want to know what's changed. What happened to the Mike that would whisk me to the dance floor whenever we heard that song, or any other song for that matter?'

'Maybe I left him in the eighties.'

'More like in your forties. I just don't understand why you wouldn't want to.'

'Getting old isn't a crime, you know.'

Susan flopped down to sit on the king-sized bed that dominated the room. 'I never said it was. I just want to know why you wouldn't want to hear our song. Why don't you want to dance with me?'

'I never said that I didn't want to dance with you. I just, I don't know...'

Susan huffed with impatience. It was hard not to. It always felt like there was so much left unsaid. And she never managed to get around to asking the question she wanted to ask... *Is there someone else?* For months she'd wondered if it was a possibility, but even voicing the question would feel like a betrayal of their marriage. It was a silly notion, but she always felt that saying it would mean the end, whether it was true or not.

'Shall we go to sleep?' Mike switched the main light off, leaving only a lamp lighting the room.

Shall we get round to fixing our marriage? she felt like countering, but this was where things were so often left – nothing fixed – but could that even happen when she'd never worked out what was broken? How could she get to the bottom of it when Mike was always so ready to brush matters under the carpet?

Maybe tomorrow was the day to finally ask the question she'd been putting off. It might spell the end, but as she laid her head on the goose-down pillow listening to the waves and the sound of her husband already snoring, she accepted that this weekend was going to go one of two ways. And however much hope the brief handhold had given her earlier that evening, it wasn't enough. It wasn't bridging the gap between them as they lay in bed now. It hadn't given her an answer to what had changed. It hadn't given her her husband back.

And if he wasn't able to navigate dancing together for a song, perhaps it was time to start accepting they weren't going to be able to navigate the rest of their days together either. She knew that however much asking the question frightened her, she needed to ask even if it meant the end.

CHAPTER FIFTEEN

ZACK

In the weeks Zack had been occupying the bench, he'd offered it up for others more in need on numerous occasions. He was a gentleman, after all.

When she arrived, however, he found he couldn't move like he usually did. It was as if someone had come along and applied superglue to his jeans. How was he supposed to move when his limbs were suddenly lead, unable to cooperate?

Zack's heart leapt, as if it were on a rollercoaster ride, giving him a sense of euphoria. In an instant he knew this young woman was who he needed to meet. But he was at a total loss as to what to say or do.

'Would you mind if we have a seat?' the woman with her said.

'Of course, sorry, bit slow today.' Zack willed his limbs to move again, peeling himself away from the bench to move aside as he had for every previous person in need of a perch.

Only this wasn't anyone. This was *her*. This was Susan, only not.

'Tough, isn't it? The surgery, I mean.' Zack cracked his T-shirt down slightly to show the top of his scar. He didn't want to lose her as quickly as he'd found her, so he was prepared to flash a bit of skin in her direction if it meant they found their common ground.

'How did you know I'd had a heart operation?'

'Lucky guess, with you coming off the cardiac ward. Am I right?' Was it possible she didn't sense they were connected in the same way that he did?

'The recovery's been hardcore,' she said with a smile. 'Take a seat. There's room for two. Leah doesn't need it.'

Leah looked like she'd been running around the hospital all day and could in fact do with a rest, but graciously she got up and allowed Zack a seat all the same.

'Are you okay for ten minutes, Chloe? I'll go and write up some notes now, and then we'll do the same in reverse.'

'Yeah, sure.'

'Great. Don't go anywhere and I'll be back in ten.' Leah jogged along her path back to the ward.

Chloe. Her name was Chloe.

'So... Hi, Chloe.' God, this felt awkward. He'd been waiting here for days upon days. Why hadn't he thought more about what he'd actually say when they finally met? It was hard to think with his heart practically vibrating. As side effects of a heart transplant went, he'd not read anywhere that he could develop spidey-senses, but at this moment in time, they'd definitely been set off.

'Hi. Do I get to know your name? Otherwise I'm at a disadvantage.'

'My name's Zack. Nice to meet you.' He offered a hand.

When she took it, a jolt akin to electricity leapt up his arm and confirmed everything he needed to know. She *was* the one. She had the other heart. And hopefully that one touch was all it was going to take. That was the connection his own heart had been after and now, perhaps, it would behave and he wouldn't have to hang around hospital corridors.

'What are you here for? Are you still waiting to be released?'

'Er.' Zack took a second to formulate his thoughts. She was younger and prettier than he'd thought she'd be. He'd been looking for a version of Susan, someone in their fifties perhaps, but Chloe must be in her twenties. Her bleached-blonde hair was dyed a pastel pink at the ends, making her look younger still. He couldn't say he was here waiting for her. It would seem insane. It *was* insane. 'I had a follow-up. Still pacing myself though, so figured I'd stop for a rest.'

'Cool.' Chloe glanced in his direction. Maybe she'd had the same sensation he'd had. Maybe he'd never have to explain the real reason for this moment because she already knew. 'Is it okay to ask what surgery you had? I'm not sure if it's the done thing, but I've not met many people my age with a matching scar.'

The question didn't help him work out what she knew, but if he only had ten minutes, he wanted to cash in on every single one of them.

'I had a gardening accident that damaged my heart. I would have died if it hadn't been for the fact I managed to get a transplant. The doctors say I'm a walking miracle.'

'It sounds like you are! That's quite the way to recover.'

'I was astonished to wake up and I'm doing my best to be thankful for every moment. What about you? Why did you need a new heart?'

'I haven't told you what type of heart surgery I had yet.'

'Oh, yeah. Sorry, I just guessed.' He hadn't guessed. He *knew*. But did she know that he knew? And what would she think if she did? This was as stalker-like as he'd ever been. It wasn't a natural instinct to hang around to meet a woman for days on end. But here he was. And now he'd so easily slipped up.

'It was a good guess.'

It was hard to tell from the way Chloe's brown eyes were taking him in whether she had any clue what he already knew. 'What caused you to need the transplant?'

'Congenital heart disease. My heart didn't develop properly in the womb and I've had various surgeries over the years. This place is like a second home. My own heart had finally had enough. They couldn't do any more to help it, so they placed me on the waiting list. We waited over a year for this one.'

'Wow. That's a lot of waiting.'

'It was. And I'm still waiting. I take it you've been discharged?'

'I was, a few weeks back. It's taken some getting used to. When are you hoping to get home?'

'Soon. I've been working on it for weeks, but my body didn't seem to want to cooperate at first.'

The thought of Chloe, or at least her heart, not being at the hospital filled Zack with a new kind of fear. If being near her had indeed been making him feel better, what was he going to do if he wasn't able to locate her?

'Do you think you'll want a friend on the outside? Not meaning to sound too forward or anything, but I've found I've needed to build myself up slowly. Walking has been the main thing that's helped. A little more each day. So if you want a fellow heart transplant patient who goes at the same pace as you, maybe I can give you my number. We could stay in touch? Check on each other's progress.'

Chloe's eyes took Zack in for a moment, no doubt weighing up whether or not he was a complete weirdo. He was behaving like one, sitting on a bench for days on end seeking out his partner-heart. This wasn't some kind of romance set-up, though. Not when primarily he felt like an electric car that was depending on a specific charging point. He'd not considered the fact that it was a mobile one and even if he felt fine tonight having met Chloe, he didn't want to risk leaving the hospital knowing that one day soon she wouldn't be there. Now they were in touch he had to keep it that way.

'Sure, you can give me your number, although my phone's back in my room so you'll have to write it down. It'll be nice to have someone to chat to. My sisters are rather protective though. I doubt they'd let me go out for walks alone anytime soon, so at least being with someone else might mean I can get out of the house.'

'Do you live with them?' Zack wanted to know more, but as Leah rounded the corner, he knew their time together was over. 'Scrap that. You'll have to answer by text. Our ten minutes is over.'

'Ah, yes. I see that window is over all too quickly.'

Thankfully he had a pen in his bag, and so he tore the first page from the book he was reading with only the title and author name on it, leaving enough space for his phone number.

'Here. Answer my question as soon as you get back to your room. That way we'll both have each other's numbers. You can let me know when you'll be discharged and we can meet up.'

Chloe's cheeks blushed. 'Sure. That'll be fun.'

'Are you good to go?' the physiotherapist said.

Getting up, Chloe used Zack's knee for leverage and that buzzing sensation ran through his body again. A jolt. A connection. A miracle?

As soon as she took her hand off, he wanted to grab it to experience it all over again. The question was, did she feel it as well? Was it one-sided, or did she realise their new hearts were connected? That being together was making their hearts happy.

'Don't forget! Answer the question when you get back to the ward.'

'Will do. See you,' Chloe said, before walking along with the expectant physiotherapist.

Before she got back to the ward, there'd been at least two glances over her shoulder in his direction.

Rather than look away like he usually would, Zack happily stared at his own miracle, very possibly with his jaw dropped open in a wide smile.

He'd *found* the other heart. Now he just had to hope that in doing so, he would no longer feel as if death was knocking at his door every night. Maybe now, he would get to feel well twenty-four hours a day.

When he heard his phone ping, he was confident it was her, which meant it was time to go home. Now the connection had been made, he needed to know if being away from her would come with the usual consequences.

CHAPTER SIXTEEN

CHLOE

Chloe had typed her first message to Zack as quickly as possible so as not to overthink it. Doing so meant she didn't think long on how much to reveal to a stranger. And wasn't it odd that he didn't feel like a stranger? Instead it felt like she'd known him a very long time.

Since then, they'd been regularly messaging each other. As soon as she'd returned home, he'd asked to meet up for their first walk and here she was, after her first night in her own bed, getting ready.

If being back in her space wasn't surreal enough, the nerves and excitement running through her entire body were new and terrifying.

'Did you sleep okay?' Leona asked from her position at the toaster, as Chloe joined her sisters, who were waiting in the kitchen.

'I think so. If I don't remember it, I'm pretty sure the answer is yes.' Being back in her own bed had been a slice of heaven. For the first time in what felt like years, she'd had a good rest without the overwhelming fatigue that had become her night-time companion. Maybe being home was the thing she'd been in need of.

The kitchen table had a spread fit for multiple guests at a bed and breakfast. There were cereals, a fruit bowl, yoghurts and two plates full of English breakfast items ready so that everyone could help themselves: poached eggs, bacon, sausages, fried mushrooms and hash browns. It was a welcome sight and she knew her sisters had gone to extra effort to celebrate her return.

'God, I've missed home.' Chloe hadn't realised quite how badly until being there.

'And we've missed you.'

They'd collectively inherited the house from their parents when they'd both passed away. All three girls had a share of their home now, but had vowed to keep it for as long as possible. Chloe knew this was, in part, due to them taking over the role of carers for her in the absence of their parents. She often wondered what her sisters would do if one of them ever found a lasting kind of love. What would happen if one of them wanted to leave, or would they all end up with their husbands still living here?

'Tuck in then.' Chloe started to fill her own plate and encouraged everyone else to do the same. 'I'm going to go for a walk this morning.' She tried to time this statement to match a moment when Alice and Leona had their mouths full. They were less likely to protest then, but of course, it didn't stop them completely.

'We'll come with you. Make sure you don't overdo it,' Alice was quick to offer.

Chloe's cheeks blanched and hiding behind a glass of milk wasn't going to disguise the fact. 'I'm actually meeting someone. They've had a transplant as well so they wanted to exercise with someone who'll be going at the same pace. As in, neither of us will be running, just in case you're worried I'm about to take that up.'

'Are you sure it's not overdoing it? We thought you'd be taking it steady,' Leona said.

'It's all part of the programme we've been given by physiotherapy. We'll be building ourselves up gradually, I promise. It'll be nice to go with someone who understands what it's like, and it means you don't have to worry about me being alone.'

This announcement brought about a sense of unease between her sisters. That somehow, by becoming friends with someone else and planning to walk with them, she'd betrayed the household. She wished it wasn't like that, but how was she supposed to tell them Zack was making her feel better in a way that none of them ever could? That he'd sent a pulse of electricity through her that marked an immediate attraction she'd only experienced a few times in her life? Hopefully once she'd scheduled in some walks with each of her sisters, they wouldn't be so put out.

They wouldn't let her help with clearing away the breakfast things, so she sloped off to have a shower and get ready in her room, where her nerves kicked in. She wasn't sure what was making her stomach churn more: the apparent unhappiness of her sisters being deprived of taking her on her first walk, or the knowledge that soon she would see Zack again and didn't know what to expect. Tall, dark-haired, muscular Zack, who she sensed she knew even though they'd barely met.

One thing she did know was that she wanted to look more human than she had at their first meeting. She'd been in hospital for so long at that point she must have smelled like stale wee or bleach, or any of the other odours that always seemed to permeate the hospital corridors.

Having her first shower back at the house had left her feeling like new.

Zack arrived early, but by that time Chloe was ready. She

had a sense that she'd been waiting for this moment ever since she'd left hospital, and it wasn't a struggle to walk away from the disappointment that continued to linger in the house. He was taller than her by more than a foot, so she had to peer up to get a glimpse of his long brown hair, which was pulled back into a ponytail.

'Do you think they're still watching?' Zack said when they were partway down the street.

'I did warn you that they can be a bit intense. It all comes from a good place.'

'I don't doubt it. It's nice to have people looking out for you. Most of my family are surrogate so you can always loan one out to me if two sisters is too many.'

Chloe laughed. There was a warmth filling her that was like sherbet tingling on her tongue, only the sensation was grasping every limb. 'You might regret that offer, and I don't mean to sound ungrateful. It can be all a bit "waiting for God" at times, and it shouldn't be like that when we're all so young. Besides, if I were to loan one of them it would mean picking my favourite, and I could never do that.'

It was Zack's turn to laugh. 'I'm sure you could if I really pushed you, but don't worry. I'm not going to make you choose which one to give away.'

'Have you had anyone to support you?'

Zack glanced at her in a way that sent tingles down her spine. His eyes were crystal blue with darker iris lines so clear it was hard not to stare.

'I've got my best friend, Larry. We've known each other since our school days and he's always been there for me. He's as close to a brother as it gets. His mum is always looking out for me as well. Treats me like her second son. They've been there for me since before my parents passed and even more so since.'

'That's good.' Chloe could feel her conversational ability

clamming up. His eyes were leaving her far too spellbound for what was an innocent walk.

'Where should we head? Where's your nearest green space?'

'The park isn't too far. Or if we go a bit further we can take a seat by the river.'

'Shall we get to the park and see how we're both feeling? We might need a seat by then.'

Chloe agreed and, as they chatted, the awkwardness that had overcome her gradually eased. They talked about the music they liked, what they'd wanted to be when they'd been growing up, and what their favourite foods were. They were fairly generic subjects, but it struck Chloe how refreshing it was not to be talking about hospitals or anything to do with being ill.

'Do you want to know something a bit strange?' Chloe wasn't sure why she was venturing onto this subject, but it had been bugging her since they'd first met.

'What's that?'

'I think I know you.'

'Do you?'

'Have you been on the telly or on the news or something?'

'Oh. Maybe.'

'So you have? Please tell me where from so I don't lose my mind.'

'I'm one of the guys who has been making over the care home gardens. We've had a fair bit of news coverage. Could that be it?'

'Oh my goodness. That's totally it! The Gardening Guardians they've been calling you, right?'

Zack glanced at the ground, a flush to his cheeks that hadn't been there before. 'That's it.'

'I knew that I knew you. I just couldn't work it out.' That explained the sense of familiarity she'd been experiencing.

At the park, they found a bench to rest and recover before considering going any further.

'Do you mind not saying anything to anyone? We've managed to keep my accident out of the press and I'd like to keep it that way.'

'Of course. I won't say a word. Anything we share on these walks stays between us.'

Knowing Zack was one half of the Gardening Guardians made the fizzing sensation she'd been experiencing increase. She'd already got the impression that he was a genuinely nice guy, and here was the proof if it had ever been needed.

When Zack asked if she wanted to do the same again tomorrow, she said yes in an instant.

CHAPTER SEVENTEEN

ZACK

Zack had no clear idea if Chloe had sensed the connection. He'd hoped she was going to come out with it when she'd wanted to ask him a question, and it was a disappointment when it was connected to the care home gardening project. Unlike Zack had hoped, the simple act of meeting Chloe had not improved his medical woes.

He'd imagined that reuniting the two hearts was going to be enough. That in doing so they'd have the reunion they were after and all would be well again. They'd both be able to move forward and get on with their lives. Instead, Zack had continued to feel rubbish whenever Chloe wasn't in the vicinity.

It had been a huge relief when not only had she agreed to meet up for a walk the day after being discharged from hospital, she'd also given him her address.

Having that ahead of time had meant he'd been able to arrive early to help him get closer to a sense of normal. He likened it to guzzling an energy drink after not sleeping all night. Being near her gave him a buzz of vitality that he couldn't fathom, but he also didn't want to question what was going on. He was giving in to it without fully understanding why.

What he hadn't been able to work out so far was whether she was having the same feelings he was. Did she sense that their hearts had once been a pair? Did she feel the same magnetic pull that he did, that was enabling him to function? Bringing the subject up wasn't proving to be as easy as he'd hoped. It was hardly a matter that would trip off the tongue, so he was waiting for the right moment. A clear indication that he wasn't barking up entirely the wrong tree.

Only it hadn't happened during their first walk. Or their second. And here he was arriving early for the third with the same eagerness to know, but with no clear idea of how to bring up the subject.

Chloe's other sister answered the door today and introduced herself as Leona. He was pretty certain she was taking her turn to look at the mysterious man their sister had met in a hospital corridor and was now going for regular walks with.

'Do you want to come in for a drink while you wait? Chloe's just getting ready.'

'I am just here, you know. It's not going to take me that long to get my shoes on,' Chloe said from behind her.

'Not today in that case.' Zack attempted a smile, but Leona seemed to be too busy assessing every aspect of him to respond in kind.

'I was only being polite. Another time, Zack, when Chloe isn't busy keeping you all to herself.'

'I'm sure that can be arranged.'

Chloe let out a sigh as they wandered along the garden path and headed in the same direction they had for the last two days. 'Sometimes there is far too much oestrogen in that household. It's like me being back has totally tipped the balance.'

'Would you ever consider moving out?'

'We've never discussed what would happen if one of us did that. I know it's naive to think that we'll always be living happily together, but it's as if none of us can move on until we know how things work out. Even now I'm out of hospital, it feels too early to bring it up. I still feel... fragile.'

'Is it worse at any particular time of day?'

Chloe glanced at him as though it was a strange question, which of course it was. He was struggling to swerve the conversation in the direction he was hoping it would go.

'I always feel rubbish overnight, as if the day has taken away every piece of energy I have. But then by morning I feel okay again. I'm hoping, given time, it'll improve. I can't see me heading out nightclubbing anytime soon, though. What about you?'

'The same. The nights are the worst.' Zack wanted to explain that he thought it was because they were apart overnight, but he didn't know how to without making it sound like a strong come-on. That wasn't his angle. He'd not got over the trauma of Elodie, the healthcare assistant who'd worked at the last care home they'd landscaped. She'd been so eager to go out with him it had been hard to say no, and when he had finally conceded, less than a week later she was trying to tell him she was pregnant with his baby. As far as he knew, it wasn't normally that quick, and he'd not been wrong in his assessment when a DNA test after the baby had been born confirmed he wasn't the father. In the months he'd waited to find out, the two due dates he'd been told (the medical opinion and Elodie's being different) had been enough to make him suspicious. He was certain it had been a deliberate honeytrap attempt, and the ordeal of not knowing plus all the drama that ensued had put Zack firmly off relationships. Not that it had been one, but it was enough of a headfuck to make a pledge to bachelorhood that he intended to keep. Besides, Chloe reminded him of a fragile pixie with her petite features and pink dip-dyed hair. Some days she looked like she might break if he spoke too loudly. He wanted to protect her, nothing more. With the flash-backs he kept seeing, his head was all over the place, so anything romantic was the last thing he needed. He wanted to steer a careful path. He wanted to let her know his theory and for them to solve how to wean themselves off what was likely to become a dependence on each other.

'Tell me more about yourself. Where do you live, for a start? Have you always lived near here?' Chloe asked.

'I've got a flat in Abingdon. It's not far from where I grew up. I was a bit of a tearaway as a youngster. That started at a young age and I think it put my parents off having any more children, so I'm an only child. My mum passed away when I was still at school and my dad become unwell after that, and eventually needed to move into a home. I set up a landscaping company with my friend, Larry, when we were in our early twenties, and we've been doing that ever since, including the voluntary project to make over all the care home gardens in the county of a weekend.' If she'd been after an info dump about his life, he was more than happy to give one.

'I didn't realise the care home project was only continuing at weekends.'

'It started with one garden in the home where my dad had stayed, but it soon became a bigger task and extended to all the care homes in the Oxfordshire catchment. I don't like having to do the news coverage, but it does help with donations and promotion for our own business.'

'It's nice that you're doing it in your parents' memory. I lost both my mum and dad when I was fourteen, so I know what it's like to have a chunk of your life missing.'

'I'm sorry to hear that.'

'I'm lucky that I have my sisters. They've done everything they possibly could for me ever since.'

'I'll have to take you to the garden dedicated to my dad sometime. It's in walking distance, once we've built ourselves up a bit more.'

It didn't seem like long, but soon they'd been chatting about the various aspects of the project for a solid half-hour. It wasn't getting Zack closer to telling her, because for every question he answered she came up with another. They talked so much they ended up heading to the river rather than stopping at the park.

'I haven't been here for ages. Well, I haven't been able to make it this far. Maybe I am improving after all,' she said.

'If we stick at this daily, we should get better and better. We'll be stars at the cardio rehab classes when we start.'

'I understand if you're ever too busy to come over. My sisters will be more than happy to fill your shoes.'

'I like coming over. I enjoy your company, but if I'm treading on toes you let me know.'

'No, it's not that. They want to take me out for a few afternoon trips to make up for it. I just don't want you to do it because you feel obliged now we've started this.'

'I'm not here because it's an obligation.' There was another half to this sentence, but it escaped him before he was able to put it into words.

'Well, that's good. I'm glad.'

Chloe's phone interrupted their conversation.

'Home,' she said.

'I'll give you a moment,' Zack said, making his way towards the murky river.

Gazing into the depths wasn't helping. He didn't want to deceive Chloe – he wanted to be frank with her – but even in his head it had an air of lunacy. The idea that her sisters were going to start taking her out of an afternoon was giving him the jitters. What if he didn't know where she was? How would they both fare if they weren't in close proximity?

Perhaps he should let it happen, just to see how they both ended up feeling. Ever since he'd discovered her, apart from during the night, he'd made sure that he was near to her house. Even when they weren't out walking, he was spending the extra hours waiting in his car around the corner so they wouldn't be too far away from each other. Maybe what they were both experiencing at night time was genuinely just fatigue. He needed to let it happen and see how it would work out.

'Sorry about that,' Chloe said, joining him at the riverside.

'Everything okay?'

'They were worried that we weren't back yet. I explained we'd just gone a bit further today and they didn't need to be concerned about us being out half an hour longer than yesterday. I think my parents would be less worried if they were still alive.'

'I guess it's a big responsibility taking over the role of parents. Sounds to me like they've forgotten how to be siblings because they're busy being your protectors. Not that I'm criticising. I think you're very lucky.'

'I just wish they didn't feel the need to check in on me all the time. I wouldn't mind if it was because they thought my health was going to fail at any moment. I think it's more because I'm with you.'

'But they don't even know me!'

'Exactly. You're a stranger. They don't know if they can trust you.'

'This is the third time we've been out. Surely they realise I'll be delivering you back in one piece. I can meet them properly if you think it'll make things better?'

Chloe gazed along the riverbank, quiet for a moment. 'I'd rather keep you to myself, if that's okay? For now, that is. I feel like I need something that's just mine. Not that I'm saying you're mine.' She glanced at him through her thick eyelashes. 'More the time we spend together. Once they've met you they'll be inviting themselves along to join us.'

'I understand, and that's fine by me.' He hoped he understood. He was trying to be firm in what his goal was... He needed to reunite Mike's heart with Susan's. And he couldn't explain that to Chloe if her sisters were with them, so taking walks alone suited him.

At least if they were continuing on these daily walks, just the two of them, it would give Zack the chance to somehow explain himself. It was taking him much longer than usual to articulate what he wanted to say, but it wasn't easy when he wasn't sure it even made sense. 'My heart belongs to yours' would sound like a declaration of love that didn't exist. They were just friends. He didn't want anything more than that. Self-ishly, he realised, he was mostly here to make himself feel better. And for someone who'd given up selfishness years before, it was a hard realisation to have.

CHAPTER EIGHTEEN

MIKE

Every time Mike attempted to tell Susan, all words failed him. It was why he had a host of default responses and ways of shutting conversations down. It was because, in the latter years of his life, he was discovering he wasn't brave.

A brave man would simply explain that he hadn't retired early because he'd opted to. He'd been medically retired. And somehow, he hadn't been able to admit that to his wife. Perhaps because that would mean admitting it to himself and eventually everyone else.

Even now, at a table for two about to indulge in the buffet breakfast, he wasn't able to say it out loud.

'We need to decide on what to do today,' Susan began. 'I reckon we should do three things. One thing you enjoy, one that I enjoy, and something that we used to do together.'

It sounded like a lot to pack into a day when he wasn't even managing to do the one simple thing he'd been planning on doing. 'Busy day then,' he mustered.

'So what would you like to do? We can do that first.'

He needed to find a quiet moment away from all the other

passengers on the boat. 'I was planning on lying on a sun lounger. Maybe read for a bit.'

'That's not an activity. Or certainly not one we can really engage in as a couple.'

Mike sighed as he realised this would be another day that would pass without him managing to tell her. 'Do I have to decide now?'

'Well, yes, if we're going to fit it all in – it's only a short cruise so we might as well make the most of it. Here's the entertainment list if you need some inspiration.' Susan grabbed the info that she had stowed away in her handbag.

'Have you already decided what you want to do?'

'I'd like us to go swimming together. We haven't been in years and it's something I want to take up again, so I figure here's a good place to start.'

'At least we're not lost for choice,' he said, as he flicked through the leaflet.

'Exactly. We need to make the best of it.'

Susan was right. He had to stop mourning what he had planned. That was an abject failure and he shouldn't let it ruin what promised to be a good weekend. 'They have films showing in their theatre all day, right up until the live shows later. How about we go and watch one? We haven't been to the cinema for ages either.'

'Excellent. And for this evening, we can watch the show and maybe go and do some karaoke like we used to after a good night out.'

'Steady. We'll have to see how we feel by that point.'

'I plan to enjoy everything we can. We're not dead yet, dear.'

'You're right. So let's start with breakfast.'

Susan was right. They weren't dead yet. And even though he knew that was true, in recent months, he'd felt hollow. Unable to navigate his way. He knew that if he told Susan, much like how they'd got to the hotel, it would give her the chance to programme some coordinates into his personal satnav. Some direction to follow. She might be able to help bring him home. And he had a feeling Susan was all the home he'd ever need. Even on the days he didn't manage to convey that in the way he'd like to.

CHAPTER NINETEEN

CHLOE

With her hospital discharge almost two weeks behind her, Chloe had hoped her sisters would have released the reins slightly. Instead they were continuing to act as her at-home nurses.

They were keeping tabs on what she was eating and drinking, how regularly she was going to the toilet, how her heart rate increased when she exercised, and they administered her drugs as if she were still an inpatient unable to be trusted with her own prescriptions. They meant well. She knew that. But how was she supposed to point out that their good intentions were making her feel like she'd been discharged to a rehabilitation unit rather than her own home?

Fortunately, the walks with Zack were keeping her sane. It created a kind of harmony within her day and he was used to any grumbles from her siblings by this point. That didn't mean her sisters were any more accepting of the arrangement, though. Every day she was faced with the same questions, and here she was defending the situation once again.

'What do you know about him, though?' Alice asked as she pulled into a car parking space. It was another afternoon trip to keep her active. The walks were enough, but she kept saying yes to the additional outings in the hope it would appease them.

'I've told you. He's that gardener who's been helping with the care home revamps. He's been on the local news and everything. He's one of the good guys. I don't know what you've got against him.'

'Doesn't it strike you as odd?

'What? That he wants to do cardiac rehab together and spend time with me? I think you're odd for thinking that's odd.' She didn't want to get into an argument, but sometimes it was hard not to. The fact her sisters were being funny over Zack struck her as strange. It was almost like they were jealous.

'Well, if you put it like that then you make it sound like I'm being ridiculous. I mean, him bumping into you and you both happening to have had heart surgery... are you sure he even has? He might have just said that to get you on his side.'

'I've seen his scar, if that helps. What's making you say this? He's been a perfect gentleman. There's no call for this unless you know something I don't.' They stayed in the car for now, with the conversation becoming so heated.

'It's just... I've seen him about.'

'Seen him about? Where? You need to tell me a bit more than that.'

'In his car. Waiting when you're not out for your walks. It's... weird.'

'Where?'

'It's not always the same place, but in the streets surrounding our house. Leona spotted him the first time and we've both seen him since. I wasn't supposed to say anything, but I'm worried. It's a bit too stalkerish for my liking.'

'There could be all sorts of reasons for it.'

'But he has his own home to go to, right?'

'Yes. A flat.'

'Have you ever been there?'

'Well, no.'

'Don't. Unless he's living in his car, there's something not right about the way he's behaving. Let's go,' Alice said, putting an end to the subject before she hopped out of the car. 'Shall we walk to the pub and back? I parked a bit further away so we'd get a bit of exercise as well as some refreshment.'

Chloe nodded her agreement, but didn't say anything more as they wandered along the road, taking the scenic route. She didn't know what to say or what to think. If what Alice said was really true, what did it mean?

What explanations could there be? Was he making phone calls and had pulled over to make sure it was safe? Or perhaps he was able to make use of Wi-Fi somewhere nearby and his car was effectively becoming his office for parts of the day?

What really bothered Chloe was the fact that she thought he hadn't been driving yet. She was sure he'd said something about Larry living nearby and that he was going there after-wards. Immediately after any heart surgery it wasn't advisable to drive a car, and with a transplant it was only suitable to start again once a doctor had given the go-ahead. As far as she knew that hadn't happened yet, and it wasn't like he'd been parking outside when he arrived for their daily walk. That made her feel uncomfortable, as if maybe there was something strange going on. But perhaps he was keeping it a secret as he didn't want to rub in the fact he was a stage ahead in the recovery process. Something like that seemed more feasible than any of the concerns her sister was on about.

Alice led them to a pretty path that bordered the Oxford canal. It wasn't one that Chloe had visited before; at least the trips her sisters were taking her on meant she was seeing parts of the city she'd not been to previously. It made a nice change to be well enough to consider these kind of expeditions, even if it did always have to involve a tea break.

They didn't talk any further as they walked, instead taking

in the passing runners and cyclists and enjoying the breeze, which was cooler this close to the water.

Chloe didn't know what to say. She'd always got on with her sisters, so their new animosity towards someone who was being a much-needed friend was creating tension she'd not experienced before.

'I thought we could stop at the pub by the lock. If that's okay with you?'

'That's where you said we were going yesterday, remember? I expected the walk judging by where you parked.'

'Yes, I did tell you, didn't I?' Alice raised her eyebrow.

'That's what I just said.'

This conversation was becoming more strained and strange by the minute, and Chloe's unease increased.

After another ten minutes of walking, they reached the quaint pub that could only be accessed by the footpath or the canal. There was something special about the fact it couldn't be reached by more modern forms of vehicle. Chloe's laboured breathing meant she was ready for a seat when they arrived, and it made a nice change that they were able to sit outside with the sun shining.

'Oh, look,' Alice said, with more than a touch of sarcasm. 'What a surprise that Zack would be here of all places. I take it you told him that we were heading to this pub.'

Zack was occupying a corner picnic table and was busy reading a newspaper, apparently unaware of their arrival.

Had Chloe mentioned exactly where she was going? No doubt she had, as she'd had no reason not to. But what her sister had said about Zack's strange habits instantly had more weight now he was sitting in the pretty beer garden at a pub that wasn't on anyone's usual beaten track.

'What do you want to drink? Shall I get us a pot of tea to share?'

Chloe nodded, uncertain of what to do. She wanted to hide

from both Alice and Zack, to give herself some time to process what was going on. Could this be purely coincidental? Or was there no such thing?

As Alice had gone inside and was no longer in sight, and Zack hadn't moved from reading his paper, she took the opportunity to check her mobile phone. At least her messages would give a clear indicator. Sure enough, in the barrage of texts they'd sent each other in the past twenty-four hours, Chloe had clearly stated that she was going to the Dog and Duck by the canal.

The realisation made the heartbeat that she was supposed to be keeping in check thump a little faster. It forced her to get over her reservations, and she decided to go and speak to Zack directly.

'What are you doing here?'

Zack jumped, as if he'd been caught doing something he shouldn't.

'Oh God. You scared me. I just fancied a change of scenery. You made this place sound so appealing, I decided to check it out.'

'Why didn't you let me know you were coming here?'

'It was a last-minute decision. I thought there was a small chance I'd bump into you. I'm sorry if I've ended up gate-crashing. You don't have to chat with me, not after seeing me earlier. Just enjoy the time with your sister.'

'My sister said just before we got here that she thinks you're following me. Then you're sitting here waiting, so now she'll be convinced.'

'Why does she think I'm following you?'

'They've seen you waiting about in your car near the house apparently. Is it true?'

Zack adjusted his position as if he'd realised he needed to be on the defence. 'I sometimes have a nap in my car after our walk as it tires me out. Don't you think it's weird they're checking up on me?'

Right at that moment, Chloe didn't know what she considered to be stranger. Her sisters being so overly protective, or the fact that some of Alice's concerns weren't entirely unfounded. 'I don't think they've gone into full detective mode to find this out. I mean, you're literally sitting where I said we'd be coming. It's bound to raise questions.'

'Can I come and sit with you? Meet your sister properly and hopefully put some of her concerns to rest?'

Chloe's next move might prove to be checkmate, but there didn't seem to be many other options. It would be weird if she ignored the fact he was here, and what he'd said was a perfectly reasonable explanation. Hopefully her sister would accept it without cynicism.

'I don't see why not. Come and join me at the table. She can't say no if you're already there.'

If Alice was bothered by Zack's presence, she didn't show it. 'I've only got a pot of tea for two, I'm afraid. Did you need anything?'

'I'm good, thanks.' Zack raised his half-empty pint glass.

'Beer? I thought they advised you to steer clear of alcohol after the kind of surgery you've had?'

'Alcohol-free. They do an awfully good selection of fake brews these days.' Zack caught Chloe's eye with an expression that said, *What did I do wrong?* and as Chloe thought on it she felt as if there was very little, other than caring for her. Yet her sister was accusing him of all sorts, and rather than offering him a greeting she was analysing his lifestyle choices as if she were a healthcare professional.

Alice let the silence hang for an uncomfortable moment before remembering where she'd left her manners.

'Chloe told me you met when you bumped into each other at the hospital?'

'Yes, that's right. I know that rehab route well. Although my recovery was a bit quicker than Chloe's, by all accounts, coming out does take a certain amount of adjustment.'

'I'm sure it does. How come we've bumped into you here as well?'

'I hadn't known about this place until Chloe mentioned it. I needed a change of scenery. I didn't realise it would necessarily coincide with your visit, but I'm glad it did. It's nice to meet one of Chloe's sisters for longer than two seconds on the doorstep.'

The crackling tension buzzed between them and Chloe didn't know what to do. It was clear Alice (and therefore most likely Leona too) didn't trust Zack. So she had no idea what they'd think if they knew that she'd begun to wonder if he could ever be more than just a friend. Because despite their misgivings, she was beginning to develop feelings for him and she sensed it was mutual.

'It seems strange that we haven't met you for longer, considering how often you're in the vicinity. I've seen you a few times in your car and thought it was rather odd.'

'Ah, yes, Chloe said. I just find the walks tiring, so I like to arrive early and give myself a rest afterwards. I didn't think it was doing any harm.'

Alice took a sip of her tea as if she were considering his response.

Chloe had never felt so perplexed by her sister's behaviour. She'd been more welcoming to Logan, and he'd not been particularly nice to Chloe. So why was Zack getting the opposite treatment? 'It hasn't been doing any harm at all. And if you'd prefer to do that in the warm, you'll have to come inside next time and have some lunch. I hadn't realised you needed to recover before heading home, and you'd be more than welcome.'

'Thank you. If that's okay with you, Alice?' Zack arched his eyebrow slightly.

'I'll have to check with Leona. She's been worried too.'

'There's really no need to be,' Zack said. 'But I'll wait until you're all happy before taking up Chloe's offer.'

It irked Chloe that it was even a consideration. But of course he would wait. He was the perfect gentleman. It was one of the things Chloe really liked about him. So why were her sisters forgetting their own manners in how they were treating him? There had to be more to it, and Chloe vowed to find out what.

CHAPTER TWENTY

SUSAN

The Breakfast Club had ended up being their film of choice from the eighties selection that had been showing. They'd seen it before many moons ago and it had been fun watching it again.

Now Susan was in her swimming costume she was feeling self-conscious. The snug fit meant there were a few more pounds on show around her waist than the last time she'd had it on. Still, most of the people she'd never see again, so she didn't need to worry about what they thought. The only person she would see again was her husband.

Fortunately, his trunks were straining slightly more than the last time they'd been on too, so they were both in the same boat. And very soon they were in the same swimming pool.

Rather than both being self-conscious, they continued with some lengths of the pool, then tried out the flumes and played with floats as if they were kids again. By the end of the hour there, Susan was surprised to find she was actually enjoying her husband's company. They were managing to laugh in unison.

Later, when they were showered and changed and heading for dinner, Mike actually held her hand like they always used to.

They spent another evening with the same dining table guests, reminiscing about similar things before heading to the show.

'I've never really been one for thinking back on our memories,' Mike said.

'I like reminiscing about some things. Like when the kids were born or when we first met the grandchildren, but I don't see the point of doing it as a comparison. As in, we were so much better off back then compared to now.'

'What's your favourite thing about us that you like to remember?'

It was the kind of question she'd usually ask him. 'Our wedding day, of course.'

'And what else? Give me your top three.'

'I guess when you held our Isabelle for the first time. And when you got down on one knee.'

'Anything more recent?'

'Well, seeing Isabelle hold her Lily. That was special.'

'I mean between us. Any moments you reminisce on between us from lately?'

Susan blinked, wondering if it might be a trick question. Unless watching the back of his head retreating into his shed was a moment to embrace, most of her recent memories were very much lacking. 'Is having fun in the swimming pool too recent to count?'

'Certainly not. And we need to make more of those kinds of memories.'

'Does that mean if I ask you to dance tonight, you're not going to refuse?'

'I don't think I should refuse any opportunities on this cruise from here on out.'

This was quite the turnabout for the man in her life, and Susan embraced it as much as they embraced each other when the music switched to slower sets for the evening.

By the time they reached their cabin they were quite tipsy, and as they hadn't managed to navigate their way to the karaoke, they had a singsong on the balcony and sang all the way out to the ocean until someone a few balconies along told them to shut up.

Returning inside, Susan didn't rush into her cotton pyjamas like she usually did. Instead they held each other, helped one another off with their clothes, and basked briefly in each other's nakedness. There were years standing between them. Lifetimes had occurred since they'd first become a couple, and Mike was the most familiar thing in her life as much as the strangest. How was it possible to live together but get to a point where she no longer recognised the person she loved?

But here he was: familiar and squishy in the right places, and also hard where she hoped he would be.

It had been so long. And yet they knew each other implicitly. What caused pleasure. What caused pain. And so they rose together in a crescendo that might well have caused another yell of 'shut up!'

Susan fell into an easy slumber that night, exhausted from the day's activities and reassured that perhaps she would never have to ask *that* question. Perhaps she would never need to know what had changed if they'd managed to find each other again. Perhaps being in the arms of the man she'd loved all her life would be enough to fix the mess they'd found themselves in.

There were always so many unanswered questions in life. Perhaps this would just be another one of them.

CHAPTER TWENTY-ONE

ZACK

There was no doubt that Zack was going to have to be more careful from now on. It didn't help knowing that apparently both of Chloe's sisters were spying on him.

The thing was, he tried not to be near her for a couple of afternoons. And both of those afternoons he'd felt decidedly crappy. This afternoon, he'd joined Larry for lunch at the pub. It was the closest Zack had been to anything work-related since the accident. He'd been signed off for three whole months, which wasn't ideal given his self-employed status, but they were keeping the business running with the help of Larry's nephew. Zack was also very financially savvy so had saved carefully, meaning he wasn't having to worry now.

'Of course they think it's creepy. I told you it would come across like that,' Larry said, after Zack had updated him.

'I know it's odd. But what do I do?'

'Stop stalking her.'

'It's not like that and you know it. You've seen me when I'm not around her. Even now I can feel the energy leaving me.'

'Look, I'm going to say this as a mate, and I know that sounds shit so I'll come straight out with it.'

'Go on then.'

'Are you sure it isn't all in your head? I mean, you've become a bit fixated with the idea. Don't you think it might be that you like this girl and you're trying to convince yourself of this theory?'

'I don't like her, not like that anyway. You know full well I've been put off women for a while and that hasn't changed. She's cool and hanging out is kind of therapeutic, but I'm not hanging out with her because of any of *those* kinds of feelings. I'm hanging out with her because of the physical effect it's having.'

'Isn't your only option to come clean then? Tell her what you know? Tell her you think that the heart transplants you've had are connected somehow?'

Zack took a sip of his pint, which wasn't alcohol-free at all. He'd decided he needed to have a proper drink after getting judged when he wasn't having one. They were allowed on the odd occasion. 'I keep trying to tell her, but then I can't figure out what to say.'

'Tell me as if I was her. I'll tell you whether it sounds okay.'

Zack wasn't exactly one for roleplay, unless it was for one of their videos, and they'd given that up for now. But it might help to think about how to phrase what he needed to explain.

'Okay, so...' Zack glanced round to make sure there was no one in earshot. 'Erm, I, well, when I was recovering I learned of an accident that had taken place not long before my transplant date. I think that's where my heart originated from. When I visited the site of the accident, I learned it was a man and his wife that passed away, and instinct told me that I had his heart and her heart had gone on to help someone else. I think that someone else was you, and for some reason those hearts need to be back together.'

'Hmmm, not too freaky, but what are you proposing exactly? If they're meant to be together it sounds like you want to be her boyfriend, but from what you've said you'd rather be her flatmate?'

The heat in Zack's cheeks had risen with this short acting stint. He put his pint to one side, not loving the taste as much as he'd hoped. 'If it made sense maybe I'd know the answer.'

'I don't know either, mate. I was hoping finding her was the only answer you were going to need. I hadn't expected it to become a permanent arrangement.'

'Well, it isn't. At least, I hope it isn't. God, what I'd give to just up and leave. Go on our Ireland trip that we've always said we'd do.'

'Funnily enough, when it looked like we were going to lose you that was one of the first things I thought about. So, when you're better, we'll have to do it. But currently, all you can do is appreciate what you've got. And even if you do have a weird new obsession, I'm very appreciative of still having you about. I think you just need to talk to her. Be honest, even if it means your daily walks come to an end.'

Zack wasn't sure how he felt about that idea. Even if he wasn't about to profess undying love to Chloe, he had enjoyed her company. But he was less worried about no longer having her friendship and more worried about whether it was going to impact his own physical health. That didn't seem to be right by his standards, and he had to face the fact that coming clean was the only thing he could do.

The following day when he arrived at hers, he was greeted by the usual prickliness from her sister, Alice. He knew straight away that he wasn't going to be welcomed in, so he waited outside the porch as always.

Chloe looked different today. She'd curled her hair and he registered that she was wearing a lighter perfume. He drank in her pixie-cuteness for a few moments longer than was necessary.

'I thought we could head to my dad's garden today, if you

felt up to it? It's in a different direction, and it's a bit further, but it's mostly on the flat so we can stop whenever you need.'

Chloe nodded in agreement and they didn't talk much on their way there. Every step was an opportunity for him to say something, to explain himself. But all the way there he didn't manage it. He was waiting until he was at the garden, hoping that being there would give him extra strength.

Only, he found himself giving a tour before even starting to try and tell her the truth about their hearts.

'Growing vegetables was my dad's main love before he started to become unwell, so the raised bed allotment area was really for him.' After that he showed her how they'd made sure the whole place was wheelchair accessible, and how there was a sensory garden area that incorporated a fairy garden, which was much loved by all the visitors and the residents.

'It's beautiful. Such a lovely thing to have done. How many gardens have you completed now?'

They took a seat on one of the benches that had been installed. 'I've actually lost count. All I know at this stage is that there are five more gardens that want to have the work done and then our project is complete.'

'What will you do once it's over?'

'I just hope I get to the point where I'm well enough to see it through to completion. And after that, I'll enjoy having my weekends back. What about you? What are you looking forward to getting back to?'

'I can't wait to complete a painting without my sternum aching in response. I've started doing some sketching, but only very basic. I'm not sure I can endure the hours I usually spend on a piece yet. Seeing as you've welcomed me to where your work is on show, you'll have to come and visit the art gallery where some of my pieces are. It'll be another trip to enjoy, away from the house.'

'That would be amazing to see. I sensed the tension hadn't eased at home yet?'

Chloe shook her head, wafting her perfume his way. 'I asked Alice directly what her problem is and she said something about you having a reputation with women. I guess being a local celeb means the news that spreads isn't limited to your gardening skills.'

'Bloody hell. Do you think she's googled me?'

'That's normally her main font of knowledge,' Chloe said breezily.

'Oh, that's probably not good.' Zack shook his head, knowing he'd have to explain himself. 'Do you mind if we start walking back and I'll tell you what she might have found.'

There was something sacrosanct about the garden he'd created in his father's memory. He didn't want to utter what had happened to him before the accident here.

Chloe happily agreed and they started to head back to her house.

'The thing is, I got involved with someone and I shouldn't have. She worked at one of the homes and was really keen on me. We ended up, you know, and shortly after she was claiming I'd got her pregnant. Instinct told me it couldn't be true. I'd been careful, for starters, but she was insistent on it and practically started a forum calling for every girl I'd ever slept with to put their story up to support her case. Of course, none of that mattered because a DNA test was all that was needed to prove I was right, but I don't think the name-smearing was deleted so if anyone was looking, they might find that and come away with the wrong impression. That's not me, I promise you. I hope it won't make you think differently about me.'

'Do you think she knew she was pregnant when it happened?'

'I don't like to guess. All I know is that she told me so soon afterwards that it rang alarm bells. I knew something was off, but it took a while to confirm those suspicions. And during the wait my name got dragged – unfairly – through the mud.'

'And you think that's what Alice has stumbled upon?' Chloe stopped and Zack found himself looking into her hazel-brown eyes.

'I'm guessing so.'

'That sounds like quite an ordeal.'

'It was. And I hadn't fully recovered from it before putting a chainsaw through my chest.' He broke his gaze from hers, knowing this wasn't the conversation he'd been wanting to have, but he needed to clear the air all the same. 'If it helps your sister trust me, tell her I'm celibate these days. I'm waiting for someone special. Besides, I need to recover more before I think about anything like that.'

They'd arrived at the house, the return journey having gone quicker for all of the details of his life he was having to clear up.

'You should come in anyway. It's my home too. You're my friend. They need to respect that.'

So with that, they managed to smuggle him into Chloe's bedroom and ate some lunch there, sprawled across her duvet. But even then, he didn't manage to tell her the thing he really needed to say.

CHAPTER TWENTY-TWO

CHLOE

In the weeks since her discharge, the number of places Chloe and Zack had visited was increasing all the time. They'd been to several of the gardens he'd worked on, they'd been to the art gallery, they regularly occupied either his flat or Chloe's bedroom, and there hadn't been a day when they hadn't been in each other's company. Every day they still went on their walks but then also spent time just hanging out, much to her sisters' chagrin. They'd walked so much that Chloe had ordered some new trainers, having worn hers down.

The weather was beginning to turn to autumn after not having much of a summer, but Chloe hadn't minded the changeable cloud formations they'd been admiring each day. They were a reminder of how life moved forward, and she was at long last in a place where she was moving forward with them. She was feeling healthy. She was feeling happy. And having Zack by her side was adding to her glow.

When they reached their regular bench, Chloe sensed there was something different about Zack. He was rigid, not holding himself like he naturally did.

'I wanted to tell you something.'

Chloe had been waiting for this for weeks. With every trip out they'd been on, she'd known it was coming and she'd been hoping it would. But there didn't need to be words involved. Surely they could just kiss?

'What's that?'

'It's not exactly straightforward.'

'Is anything?' Chloe laughed like she did so often when she was trying to shift discomfort with humour.

'I love how you find everything funny.'

'Do you?'

'It's nice to know someone who smiles as much as you do.' Zack shifted closer.

It was the exact moment she'd been waiting for. She didn't need to hear any more. He loved how she found things funny. That was all she needed to make her brave enough to slide towards him and let her lips meet his.

It was uncertain at first, just one set of lips planted on another. They were so slow to move from that position: an artist could have come along and drafted out a composition sketch in the time it took them both to react.

Even without moving, there was a certain amount of magic to having finally done the thing Chloe had been dreaming of. And as it ramped up a level, becoming more feverish, it was everything she'd hoped it would be. His sensuous lips, his warm tongue inviting her deeper. It was the best kiss she'd ever had, right up until it stopped.

'We shouldn't be doing this,' Zack said, with more certainty than she'd ever heard from him before.

'I know we need the doctors to approve most of our lives, but I'm pretty sure kissing is okay.'

'But is it?' Zack stood up and put his hands through his hair, ruffling strands out of the ponytail. He looked as if he'd had the worst shock of his life.

'Is what?'

'I don't want to give you the wrong impression.'

'I thought we were…' Chloe's voice trailed off as the realisation dawned. *This wasn't what he wanted.* She didn't understand.

Zack paced to and fro, continuing to put his hands through his hair as if he'd been stung and was searching for the wound. 'I haven't been completely honest with you.'

Ouch. She thought they'd been totally open with one another. They'd talked about every aspect of their lives. She knew he'd had a bad encounter, but she was hoping she was the one to help get him over that. Even before hearing what he was about to say, she knew it was going to hurt.

'What do you mean?'

Zack continued to pace up and down the same path, making him appear as if he was in a locked cage. 'I'm sorry I haven't said anything before.'

'Have you even had heart surgery?' The nugget of doubt her sisters had planted in her thoughts was quickly taking hold. What if he was a stalker? What if they were right to be guarded and everything he'd told her was a lie?

Zack fell to his knees in front of her, a desperate pleading in his facial expression. Any onlooker might think he was about to propose.

'Yes, yes, I have.' Zack bared his sternum to her as if he were Tarzan, about to beat his chest.

It only confused her further. This wasn't the normal reaction she received when she kissed a man. She'd thought they were effectively dating with the number of walks and trips they'd been going on. Surely a quick snog or a handhold had been the natural next step? And what harm had it done? She couldn't understand why he was freaking out.

'And that's why we've been together.' Chloe nodded as if she had some understanding, but really she had no idea.

'Don't you see? Don't you feel it?'

Chloe stopped nodding. 'Feel what?'

'The connection.'

'I thought kissing was the connection? I mean, I figured that was the reason we were kissing.'

And she'd always heard that girls were supposed to be the complicated ones.

'Not that. Definitely not that.'

Ouch again.

'What then?'

'This is going to sound so mad, but I need to explain.' Zack took both her hands and sat next to her on the bench once more.

'I wish you would.' Generally speaking, Chloe had never been rejected directly after kissing someone. As rejections went, this was becoming increasingly awkward by the minute.

'Okay.' Zack released a hand to swipe away a sheen of sweat from his brow. 'The connection I'm on about is kind of like electricity. I think our hearts are connected. Like from before.'

'How?'

'I think, well, I kind of know, that my heart became available as a result of a tragic accident that I found out about inadvertently. When I went to the site of the accident, I knew that was where it had happened, and I also knew that my heart wasn't the only one that became available. I knew it had a partner.'

Even though Chloe was sitting, his words were making her dizzy, as if she'd been swimming against the tide all this time and she was finally out of breath.

'A partner?'

'Yes, as in, it's part of a pair. Ever since I had my accident, I've had this sense that there was something else. Or someone. So it made total sense when I found out that it was a couple that passed away in the accident. I kind of felt my heart wanted me to be reunited with the other and I've been drawn to it ever since. Drawn to you. Only not quite like that.'

Chloe's mouth was open, ready to catch flies. Every word that came out of his mouth made her more and more concerned. 'You're not supposed to know anything about your donor. How can you know any of these things?'

'I don't for certain. It's just that I do *know*. Surely you must have sensed it as well?'

Sense? None of this made sense. What Zack was saying wasn't computing in the slightest. All she'd wanted to do was kiss him.

'I just, I...' Chloe stood up. Staying still didn't seem like a sensible option.

'You do, don't you? You've sensed it too. That's why you were drawn to kissing me. Only it's not like that. It's our hearts that are drawn to each other. They're kind of reliant on each other to feel okay.'

'So that's why you've been hanging out with me? Not because you like me or that we're friends? It's because you think you have to be with me to feel okay because some kind of sixth sense told you this?' Chloe walked quickly in the direction of home and her sisters. Never had she wanted to be in their company more. 'And that's why you've been turning up and hanging about in your car? Because of this so-called electricity you think you require to stay healthy?'

'It's true, I swear. When I'm not in your proximity I just don't feel well. I'm sluggish and everything becomes a task. I realised when I had an appointment at the hospital that you must be there as I felt – I dunno how to describe it. I felt energised, I guess. So I started hanging around the hospital corridor in the hope that we'd meet, and when we did that I'd know it was you. And I did know. I knew in an instant. I was hoping you'd have felt it too.'

Chloe thought back to the moment, weeks ago, when she'd met Zack. Really he'd just been a guy resting on a bench. There had been none of the electricity he was talking about. She'd found a comrade, that was all. Someone with the same war wounds. Any electricity there'd been she'd put down to a chemical attraction, and she'd thought that had been growing ever since with every walk they'd taken. Every conversation they'd had. 'I don't understand,' was all she was able to vocalise.

'I hoped you'd know what I was on about.'

Chloe shrugged. What she'd thought was going on between them was obviously wrong.

'I'm not explaining this very well. Basically I was left with this need to find the heart that matched mine, and I didn't feel better until I found you. Being nearby made me feel better. I was hoping that once we met, it would go away. Like I'd carried out the heart's desire and it would be satisfied. But I was still feeling poorly at night time when I wasn't at the hospital, even after we met in the corridor. I knew we still needed to spend time together so that's what I've tried to arrange.'

Chloe's pace was faster than she'd ever achieved during any of their walks together. The need to get away becoming stronger with every word that passed his lips. But his pace was matching hers and she'd not managed to put any distance between them.

'Stop,' Chloe shouted. 'Stop talking and stop walking.'

To her surprise, Zack did. And rather than carrying on without him like she'd intended to, she stopped as well. How could she go home without fully understanding?

'What I don't understand is why you didn't want to kiss me? Say what you're saying is true. Say our hearts are destined to be together, why don't you love mine like I love yours?' Without meaning to, she'd said what she'd been secretly thinking. That she was in love – but here Zack was rejecting her in the strangest way possible.

'We're friends. I didn't ever mean to give any indication I wanted to be anything more than friends.'

'What? Other than coming to see me every day. Hanging around when we weren't together. Bumping into me at every given opportunity. Spending every moment possible together. Is it any surprise I thought you liked me?'

'I do like you. Just not like that.' Zack pinched the bridge of his nose and bowed his head, shaking it slightly. He couldn't look her in the eye.

'Just not like that,' Chloe repeated. The tears she was attempting to hold back were biting at the corners of her eyes. She'd just kissed a man and admitted to loving him, and his nonsense response was making her wonder if she even knew him at all.

'I should have said something sooner, explained myself, but I didn't know how to. I knew it would sound odd.'

'I think we should put our daily walks on pause. I'm not sure what's going on, but this isn't what I thought it was. I need some time to process it. I'd appreciate you not hanging around either. My sisters think you're strange enough as it is. Their opinion of you isn't going to improve if they find you lurking about when I've asked you not to.'

'Are you going to tell them?'

'I don't really have any secrets from my sisters.' Zack had been her only secret of sorts and look where that had got her.

'Can I call you?'

'I'd rather you didn't. I'll be in touch in a few days.'

'Right, well, I'm sorry. I didn't mean to tell you quite like this.'

'Like I said, I'll be in touch,' Chloe said, taking the opportunity to walk away.

The problem was, she didn't really understand what Zack had been trying to tell her. All she knew was that for weeks she thought they'd been skirting on the edges of that kiss and it turned out he'd only been interested in her heart. Only not in the way that she'd hoped. Because despite declarations of needing her 'electricity' to feel better, he'd not even noticed that he'd just made her heart shatter into tiny pieces.

CHAPTER TWENTY-THREE

SUSAN

It had been years since Susan had woken up in Mike's arms. So much so that when she found herself wrapped in his hold, she almost flinched. The alien position she was in, along with being in unfamiliar surroundings, set off alarm bells in her head that she didn't want to be there.

Once she'd adjusted to the fact she was on a cruise ship in the loving arms of her husband, she began to enjoy the sensation. Only a few days ago she would have thought this to be an impossible scenario. It seemed like they'd grown too far apart to be able to come together again and yet here they were.

It was some time before Mike stirred from his slumber. While she waited, Susan stayed present, trying to appreciate the moment for what it was, not focusing on how things had been of late nor worrying about how things would be in the future. In that moment, those things didn't exist. She didn't want to create those concerns by thinking about them, even though they were never far away.

Rather than dissolving the illusion, as she thought he might once he woke, Mike instead embraced her and wished her good morning.

'Isn't it just?'

'The best for a long while,' Mike agreed.

'Did you sleep well?'

'Like a log. And you?'

'The same. I think we both had a good reason to be more tired than usual.'

Mike sighed and squeezed her closer to him. 'It's funny. I know we've been living parallel lives. I mean, we live together, yes, but we haven't been together. I know that's been my fault.'

'I know exactly what you mean.' It was a very accurate description of the life they'd been living together. 'Together, but apart.'

'Indeed. Leaving the police force hasn't been easy.'

'I just wish you'd talk to me about it.'

'I know. But it's not that simple.' The shadow that so often passed through Mike's expression was there again.

'I'm always here. Waiting.'

'Yes, but I think being in the same surroundings, always having the same routine, socialising with the same set of people... The sameness of it all meant that I've not known how to act differently.'

'Always being in the same shed, you mean. I've felt like you've been avoiding me, not struggling to navigate your way back to me.'

Mike adjusted his hold, but didn't let go like she thought he might. 'I haven't been avoiding you. I've been happy, tinkering away at projects in the shed. If anything, I've been avoiding the house. To me, it's always felt too big since the kids moved away. As if you and I are rattling around in it.'

'I really hope, when we get home, there'll be more mornings like this.'

'Let's not talk of home yet.'

'You're the one that started it.'

'I know. What I mean is, let's concentrate on today. We

have one whole day of the cruise remaining. We need to make sure we make the most of it.'

'We do.'

'So, what would you like to do with today?'

'Is staying in bed an option?' Susan was enjoying being wrapped in her husband's arms far too much to want to think about moving.

'We can stay here as long as you like. Do they do room service in a place like this?'

'I think so. Although some things cost extra.'

'Let's do that. I think today we should do things we've never done before. Starting with breakfast in bed.'

As they slowly unravelled from each other and ordered breakfast to their cabin, the fear that had been gathered in Susan's stomach was replaced by a pleasant glow. If she'd have been able to choose how this weekend would go, she was now living her fantasy. This was beyond her wildest dreams, and when Mike wasn't looking, she pinched herself just to be certain she wasn't sleeping. Forty years was an incredibly long period of time to be with someone. There were bound to be times when the flow wouldn't follow the ebb. If they'd managed to get their mojo back, Susan didn't need to question it. She needed to enjoy it. And that's exactly what she planned to do.

CHAPTER TWENTY-FOUR

ZACK

Three days after Zack's confession, he was still waiting to hear from Chloe. It was hard to know how it could have gone any worse. He'd spouted incomprehensible information at her directly after their kiss while trying to explain that the kiss wasn't what he wanted.

The problem being that he really didn't know what he wanted. Not when so much of it didn't make sense.

If their hearts were dependent on each other like he thought, what arrangement could there be if romance wasn't on the cards? Had he expected her to invite him to come and live at the house like a pseudo-sibling that she didn't require?

The intercom buzzed and Zack was glad of the interruption to his thoughts.

'Are you going to come and supervise an honest day's work or what?' Larry said when he arrived.

'I'm not really allowed to do much so you have to go easy on me, remember? And no use of chainsaws unless you want me to have some kind of nervous breakdown.'

'This garden is an easy day's work. I promise.'

It wasn't long before they were in the van together and

heading for their usual cafe stop-off for brekkie, making it feel like an ordinary day.

'How's the care home project going?'

'We're nearly finished. One more Saturday should do it. You should come and see it once it's done. Check that it's up to the usual standards.'

'I'm sure it will be.' Zack found he wasn't in any rush to return to the place where he'd had his accident. 'Thank you for continuing on without me there.'

'I couldn't leave it unfinished. If you don't mind, I figure we'll hold off starting any more until you're better.'

'Of course. It's something I really want to see completed, but there's no point doing anything further until my sternum is fully healed.'

'Glad to hear you're planning on being sensible about it.'

'I am. So, what's on the cards today?' Zack asked, biting into his bacon roll, a blob of tomato ketchup escaping instantly.

'It's a basic garden clearance. Mostly brambles to remove. I've got some spare gloves if you feel up to doing anything, but mostly I want you taking it easy.'

'Thanks, mate. I'm looking forward to it. Even if I'm not going to be doing my usual workload, just going to work makes a nice change.'

'I've told the lady I'm doing it for that you're recovering from surgery so you'll mostly be there to supervise and will be taking more breaks than average. She's a lovely dot of a lady so don't be surprised if you get plied with tea and biscuits.'

'That sounds like exactly the level of work I can cope with.'

They'd both been self-employed since they'd finished school. They'd always enjoyed being outside and doing manual labour, and joining forces to become a landscaping company they'd landed on their feet. Zack couldn't wait to get back to it properly, but currently he had no idea when that would be. There was a possibility it would never happen, but hopefully with time and rehabilitation he'd get there. As that fear had been playing on his mind, he'd offered to do the odd day with Larry when the weather was being kind. Maybe, if and when he felt up to it, they'd be able to restart the care home project, but he certainly didn't think he'd be wanting to do a six-day week anytime soon.

The garden they ventured to was only a few streets away and they were both soon battling brambles left, right and centre. The lady who lived at the property had apologised, as if nature taking over had been her fault. She'd explained that she'd been caring for her husband for over a year before he passed away. He'd been the keen gardener before that and, when other things in life had taken precedent, the garden had been ignored.

'I want the space to enjoy again, but all that hard work is beyond me these days. I'm so glad I've got you boys here to make it nice. Now, what can I get you both to drink?'

True to what Larry had promised, she supplied a steady stream of coffee and biscuits throughout the day. Even though Zack stopped to have a rest about once an hour, he reckoned he wasn't far behind keeping up with Larry. Maybe Chloe was nearby and he didn't know it. Or maybe that kiss had resolved the issue.

The brambles were thick and darted off in every direction. They were a cunning weed that created patches of root as they spread. It was a good job it wasn't blackberry season, otherwise Zack might have spent half his time feasting on the goods. It was a wonder how something so damn prickly and troublesome produced what he considered to be one of the nicest fruits. By the time morning was over, they'd managed to clear the worst of them. It had been a bit like an archaeological dig. Because for every section they removed, they uncovered a part of the garden that had been there before. It was evidently made up of a well-kept lawn and garden beds in a previous lifetime. Zack's favourite discovery had been a pair of gnomes, and he'd been offered a slice of cake because the client was so delighted they were salvageable.

'It looks so much better already, boys!'

'It does, and it'll look even better after we're finished. We'll go and grab a spot of lunch and finish tidying up this afternoon,' Larry said.

Larry drove them around the corner to a local row of shops like they usually did when they took a break from work. Zack was surprised at how much he'd missed something as simple as that.

'I figured we should have a proper lunchbreak today. I guessed you might need the rest. There was more to do than I thought this morning.'

'It's been good doing something physical again. I'd forgotten how much I love being outdoors and being active.'

'Shame it's work, huh?'

'It doesn't feel much like work when you're with your best mate and have a constant supply of refreshments from a sweet old widow.'

'So, how are things?'

Larry didn't specify what things, which was obviously a deliberate move.

'Fine.'

'And... your walks? Are you doing them with Chloe still?'

'I'm going to grab a Diet Coke. Do you want anything?'

'Get me a can of Pepsi Max, and only come back once you're ready to tell me what's going on.'

Zack skulked about in the aisles for far longer than necessary. Avoiding the 'I told you so' for as long as possible seemed like a good option.

When he finally headed back, with Lion bars for both of them as a kind of peace offering, he confessed to what had happened.

'And you haven't heard from her since?'

'Nope. Not a thing. It's been nearly three days now and I thought she would have at least messaged.'

'Sounds like you've got it bad.'

'That's the thing, though. I haven't. We're just friends as far as I'm concerned.'

'And you told her this?'

'Yeah.'

'So let me break this down. You said you had something you wanted to tell her. She kissed you, which you briefly joined in with. Then you stopped her because the thing you wanted to tell her is you think both of your hearts became available because of the same accident, and because of that you think they're connected. But you then said you don't want to be connected like *that*, you just want to be friends. Is that more or less right?'

'Pretty much.'

'Bloody hell.' Larry bit into his chocolate bar as if he was actually trying to rip a lion's head off. 'No wonder she doesn't want to speak to you.'

'Do you think that's it? That I'm never going to hear from her again?'

Larry continued chewing for a while, washing it all down with his Pepsi Max in giant gulps. 'Do you want to hear from her again? You seem to be doing okay without being by her side all the time. Maybe what you thought was going on was down to an overactive imagination?'

'I don't know. It felt like it should mean something.'

'Maybe it did. Didn't you say you kissed her?'

'Yeah, but only briefly. I felt like I was promising her something I didn't actually feel, so I stopped it.'

'Didn't you tell me that you hoped that meeting her would be enough for whatever was going on to stop? But that didn't do it. It wasn't enough. So what if the kiss was? You seem to be doing okay now. Maybe that was what the heart desired. A goodbye kiss. And now that's happened you can move on and start living your life again.'

Zack's stunned silence was only interspersed by Larry guzzling more of his drink. He wasn't sure what he was more shocked by... the fact that Larry had had this realisation before he had or that his friend had taken on board what he'd told him, even though most people, including Chloe, would think he was mad for even believing the notion.

'You know, I think you might be right. I've been so worried about upsetting Chloe that I hadn't even thought about the kiss having been the answer.'

'And now you have upset her, where does that leave you? Other than us needing to get back to work in five minutes?'

Where did it leave him? He missed Chloe's friendship. She'd become his companion during one of the most difficult periods of his life. He didn't want to leave it how it was, but he also didn't want to pester her when she'd asked him not to make contact.

'Let's head back. Maybe more coffee and cake will help me on the road to wisdom.'

They were supplied with both almost as soon as they returned. As they worked, they pulled up as many bramble roots as they could see and neatened up the borders that were there.

'I'll have to get this back to a proper lawn. Might see about laying some turf. Is that the kind of thing you boys would do?' she asked, as she was busily giving the gnomes a bath over on her garden table.

'I'm sure we could. You've got my number. Give us a call if you need anything more doing in the garden.'

'Do you think a letter would be okay?' Zack said out loud to Larry. Ever since he'd got back to gardening, he'd been thinking about how to make things right with Chloe. If she wasn't going to message or call, he didn't want to contact her that way. Not least because it would be fairly obvious if he was being ignored.

'Oh, I love a letter. It's so rare to receive one these days. Why do you need to send one?' the lady asked.

'To explain to my friend Chloe that I still want to be friends even if I don't want it to be anything more than that.' The simplified version of events made far more sense than the earlier conversation in the van.

'Has she had her feelings hurt?'

'I think so. Well, I'm sure of it really. That's why I haven't heard from her.'

'Hmm,' the lady mused, while scrubbing her gnome at the same time. 'I'm trying to think how I'd feel. Has she very specifically said not to be in touch?'

Zack nodded. Those had been her exact instructions.

'Then I'd do exactly what she's asked.'

The lady nodded, as if very pleased with her short stint as an agony aunt.

'What if I was going away? Should I let her know that I am?'

'Are you going away?' Larry asked.

'I wasn't until a few moments ago, but now I've thought about it, I think I *need* to.'

The life Zack had been living since he'd got out of hospital wasn't the one he was used to. Before, he'd been carefree, spontaneous and always on the go. There had been many an occasion between garden projects where he'd booked himself onto a last-minute trip. Because he'd felt anchored to Chloe, the thought of doing anything beyond their daily walks hadn't even crossed his mind. But if Larry was right, and he no longer needed to be in her company, it was time to be bold and explore again.

'If you're going away on holiday, there's one condition. You take me with you,' Larry said.

'Oh, that sounds wonderful,' the old lady chipped in. 'And maybe just a small note to let her know you're going away and when you expect to be back would be polite. It does sound like she's a good friend and you're missing her very much.'

'I do miss her.' This realisation was a surprise to Zack. Of course, the reason he'd gone back to work today was because he was fed up of moping. It had been good to have someone who knew all the ways in which the post-surgical experience could be challenging. He'd missed chatting to her about life and goals and what the best films were on Netflix. He liked her creative nature and the way she was able to visualise things in the same way he did. He'd thought they'd have many mornings of chatter ahead of them, so the abrupt stop had jarred his system. He wished he could turn back time and tell her about his theory first, so there wouldn't have been a misunderstanding and the kiss.

'If she is the good friend that you think she is, she'll come back to you at some point. Even if it isn't this week, maybe she'll be waiting for you when you return. Where will you be heading?' their client asked.

Larry and Zack glanced at each other. The answer was easy. It was the trip they'd been talking about for weeks prior to Zack's accident. They were going to take Larry's van and they'd pinpointed all the places they wanted to stop along the route.

'The Wild Atlantic Way,' they replied in unison.

'The wild what? Where's that when it's at home?'

'Ireland.'

They'd always said they'd go there once the care home garden project was complete. And even though it wasn't finished, life had definitely indicated it was time to take a pause.

CHAPTER TWENTY-FIVE

CHLOE

Even though when Zack had asked, Chloe had said she would tell her sisters, as yet she'd not found a way to.

They were aware of his absence, of course. They'd jumped onto that fact as if it was the good news bulletin at the end of a broadcast. For now, she'd said he was on holiday. She didn't want further questions or to have to expand. Not yet.

The truth was that she was conducting her own little experiment in the hope of making some sense of Zack's revelations. When she'd thought back on her hospital stay, she remembered the nights when she'd felt like her entire recovery had reversed. If what he was saying held any truth, then anytime now she was going to end up feeling horrible. While in hospital, there had been definite moments when she'd felt okay and others when she'd felt like her batteries had been unplugged without warning. Whether those two states of being were related to Zack being close by or not, she had no way of knowing. Not when she hadn't been included in this silly theory at the time. So far, she'd been feeling okay, which put paid to Zack's suggestion. Unless he was continuing to lurk in a street close by.

The other thing she'd like to investigate more was his theory that their hearts had come from the same accident. That the hearts had previously been man and wife. She wasn't certain how he could ever have found that out when those details were kept confidential. But without contacting him for more information, she wasn't sure how she'd ever know. All she knew was what he'd explained but he hadn't given her any specifics, not even the names of the couple. There were alarm bells going off about the whole thing. It reminded her of the scams where someone was seduced by a holiday romance and then subsequently paid out large sums of money, never to see the person they'd fallen in love with again. In a similar way, she felt she'd been duped. She'd been led along a path with unsaid promises that had been strong enough to make her fall in love, only to find it was a mirage at the end.

However tempting it was to find out what the truth might be, Chloe wanted to get her life back to some sense of normality. But after having spent so long at hospital in recent months, she'd forgotten what that might look like. She'd visited the art gallery to see her friend Rowan, but hadn't filled her in on the details of what she'd thought was her latest romance. Instead she tried to concentrate on the different aspects of her recovery.

In a week, she'd be past the three-month post-surgery mark. That was the stage at which her sternum should have healed enough to do more physical activities. Perhaps heading to the local swimming pool to find out when the quietest periods were so she would be able to go at her own pace would be a start. It would give her something to aim for at least that didn't involve sitting in her bedroom. Though she was no longer isolated to a hospital side room, she sometimes felt like she was still there, especially when she was avoiding answering any more of her sisters' questions.

Sold on the idea of walking to the swimming baths to see how much that would tire her out, Chloe grabbed her hoodie, ready to head off.

She was standing by the coat rack when the letter box rose and fell, an envelope with her name on the front suddenly flapping to the floor.

In her chest, there was a kind of blooming, like when a flower finally reveals the colour of its petals. Without doubt it was Zack on the other side of the front door.

But how did she know? It wasn't as if she knew what his handwriting looked like. It was just a feeling. A sixth sense. And she felt better knowing he'd been there.

Perhaps she'd been too quick to dismiss his strange theory. Because right now her heart tingled as if it had been brushed with nettles. A tingle that was hard to explain and only noticeable now she was aware of the ways it was responding to his presence.

Chloe picked up the letter from the doormat and retreated to her room. She didn't want either of her sisters to stumble across her while this melody was dancing through her very being.

Because before she even opened the envelope, she knew this wasn't going to be good news. Not for her anyway. She was already regretting being so stubborn in not contacting him.

Dear Chloe,

I had hoped to speak to you. For there to have been one more walk. But I understand why I haven't heard from you. I understand why I might never hear from you again.

I've stayed away, like you asked, up until dropping this note off. I didn't want to leave without saying goodbye and this felt like the right way to do so. Larry and I are off on the travels we'd planned before I had my accident. I'm feeling okay. Now seems like the right time for a break.

Anyway, I hope this finds you well. I might not be in the

country, but if you ever do find yourself wanting to keep in touch, my number will be the same.

Sorry to have made you think I'd wanted something more. I hope we can still be friends.

All the best,

Zack

Before she'd managed to stuff the letter back into the envelope, she heard the letter box go again, and in an instant she moved from her bedroom back to the front door in the hope it was him. Now she knew he was going, she felt compelled to say goodbye.

When she opened the door, it was an unfamiliar figure struggling to open the garden gate.

'Can I help you?' Chloe said.

She'd not even picked up whatever had been placed through the door to see what it was.

The figure turned and it wasn't as unfamiliar as she first thought.

'Just delivering something.'

'You're Larry, aren't you? The other gardener?' She recognised him from the news just as she had Zack, but more than that because she'd heard him spoken about so often in recent weeks.

'Er, yeah, that's me. I just wanted to add to Zack's message and check you got his.'

'I did.' Chloe indicated the crumpled-up letter in her hand.

'Grand.' Larry peered awkwardly at his feet. 'Well, I'd best be going.'

'Have a great holiday,' she said, not sure what else to add.

'You look after yourself.'

'Tell Zack to do the same.'

Chloe waved a goodbye before retreating back inside after the strange moment. She picked up the second letter from the doormat and returned to her room. There she read over Zack's letter again and held it to her chest as she buried her head in her pillow. She wasn't sure why it hurt, but it did. To know that the past few months hadn't been what she thought they were. Knowing that she wouldn't be bumping into him anytime soon. She wasn't sure whether to be pleased or horrified. At least this would mean she wasn't lying to her sisters. She'd told the white lie that he was on holiday and now he really was. Not that she had a clue with regards to where or for how long. She should have asked Larry, but she'd been too surprised at seeing him there.

It would seem she didn't have a clue about much of Zack's life. He was an enigma. He'd come into her life, but now he was out of it, she was going to try and forgot all about him. For all her determination though, she wasn't able to lower the letter away from her chest. Nor did she act on opening the second letter, knowing it wasn't from him. It was as if her heart wanted to be close to only Zack's words. And while her head told her one thing, it truly did feel as if her heart belonged to another.

CHAPTER TWENTY-SIX

MIKE

Spending the equivalent of a lifetime with someone came with certain guarantees. Habits that used to be endearing become more of an endurance. There will be something minor (like not unloading the dishwasher) that will end up multiplying itself into something major. A harmonious routine will be achieved and that becomes hard to move away from. All of these things were true of Susan and Mike. They woke up at roughly the same time each day, ate similar breakfasts, discussed safe subjects (the weather, events on the local Facebook page, what to have for dinner), then went into their day with exactly the same tasks, usually avoiding each other until dinner time.

When Mike thought on it, he knew it had been deliberate. Not only had he not known how to tell Susan, he'd also not wanted to. When they'd woken, it had been on the tip of his tongue. It was the closest he'd managed to letting her know, but he'd not wanted to break the spell they'd found themselves under. Instead he was rolling with it in the hope that at some point today he'd find the moment to be brave.

'I'm really not sure why we haven't done this before,' Mike said, with a lightness in his voice he'd forgotten was possible.

They'd arrived in Amsterdam, their one and only stop on the cruise, with a determination to do something different. The advantage of being somewhere that wasn't home was the many new activities on offer.

The first choice had been Susan's, and she'd opted for a taste of Amsterdam life by hiring some bikes for an hour, giving them the opportunity to whizz by the beautiful canals, admire the architecture of the tall buildings, pass the blossoming flowers by the water's edge, and the various shops that flew by in a blur, some of which they were both glad they didn't get the chance to focus on for too long. They hadn't had to venture far to make their bones rattle and there were plenty of places to stop for a drink. They'd ended up at a pub, having a cold beer with a cheese platter that they certainly didn't need given the food on offer on board, but they both decided to indulge all the same.

After all, who was to say when they'd do this again?

Having returned the bikes with all their limbs intact and still a few hours in the city to spare, it had been Mike's choice next for what new activity they should try.

What he'd opted for had surprised Susan. Initially she was slightly averse to the idea, but as he'd rallied over her desire to ride a bike through the capital, she was going with it. He'd hoped it might help him find the bravery he required, but instead rambling thoughts were tumbling though his head.

The first spliff of his life was a good one. Not that he had anything to compare it to. But as they had with the beer and cheese, they'd gone for it knowing this was a taste of Amsterdam they weren't likely to get again anytime soon.

'I'd love to do things like this more often. A little adventure and spice in life,' Susan said.

Should cannabis be classed as a spice or a herb? Spice was an entirely different drug in America. Having seen the effects of drugs in his line of work, he usually steered completely clear, but this mellow feeling that was encompassing him was like a welcome hug.

'More days like this,' Mike said in agreement.

'We should start a plan. Kind of like a bucket list, but not that. More like an adventure list. I can think of five or six places I'd like to go without even flexing a brain cell.'

'Do you think you'd actually be able to flex a brain cell at the moment?' Mike made himself giggle, but the sound came out more like hiccups.

'Don't be so cheeky!'

'List them then. These five or six places.' Seeing as he had planned to whisk her away, knowing where she wanted to go would be helpful.

'The Lake District. You know I've always wanted to go there. And Paris. And Venice. And I've always fancied seeing the pyramids. Oh, wouldn't it be wonderful?' Susan had another puff on her cigarette, and coughed as she had every time previously.

'That's only four. You said you could name five or six?'

'Trust you to be counting. Now I am going to have to use a brain cell.' Susan coughed a little more and took a sip of her coffee before giving her final suggestions. 'New Zealand and Cornwall.'

Mike chuckled. 'Could you choose two places further apart?'

'I'm not planning on doing them in the same week. What about you? Where would you like to go on your adventures?'

'What about the things we've never done closer to home? We could get an English Heritage membership. Go to Stonehenge, visit some castles, watch a medieval duel.'

'Wow, okay.'

'You don't sound impressed.'

'It has to be said, I did come up with a more impressive list.

Yours are the kind of things we could do as day trips at the weekend. Mine would be actual breaks away.'

'I'm sure English Heritage have places near the Lake District. We can combine our big adventures. Anyway, I'm not sure we have the finances for such grand plans. We're better off doing things closer to home.' He should just tell her what he had planned now, but somehow he didn't feel like he should mention one without the other.

'Why? Isn't this better?' She waved her hand, spraying ash without intending to.

'I'm not saying it isn't, but we can't be getting stoned in Amsterdam every weekend.'

'But we could do more than we do now. Much more. We haven't done anything like this in years. We can't be leaving it that length of time again. This holiday has to mark a change.'

Susan stubbed out the cigarette. It was another occasion where his inability to say what he should actually be voicing was going to cause an argument. 'It has marked a change. You know that. But you know me, I never like to be too far from my shed.'

'Are you ever going to tell me what's so exciting about that place?'

'I just like to get on with my projects.' Why did generic sentences like that trip off his tongue so easily when it wasn't what he meant to say? Why couldn't he say it was his safe space? It was where he'd found distraction from the memories that had crowded him far too often.

'What projects? It's not like a self-build has sprung up in the back garden since we last discussed this.'

'I've just been...' Mike hesitated, not certain how to form the sentence even though in his head he'd said it a hundred times before.

'Have you been having an affair?' And just like that, the

question she'd been holding on to was out in a street in the middle of Amsterdam.

And Mike's tongue was still tied so tight that he wasn't able to answer.

CHAPTER TWENTY-SEVEN

ZACK

The drive to Ireland had been long so they'd taken it in turns, and slept on the ferry when they'd crossed the Irish Sea. They'd both been thankful for a smooth crossing. Once they'd driven as far as Tipperary the roads became decidedly narrower, and for some time they followed a series of country lanes as darkness fell.

Their plan was to follow the Wild Atlantic Way that would take them 2,500 kilometres along the west side of Ireland. Originally they had wanted to do it as backpackers, choosing to hike or bike different sections. They'd planned to record various parts of it and share it on their TikTok account. That plan had been revised and now they were following the driving route, stopping at different locations and joining in with activities as Zack's physical health allowed. It was one of Larry's more sensible suggestions. And as far as they were both concerned, coming up with content for the sake of anyone but themselves was over. They were doing this because it was something they'd been talking about on and off for ages. After what they'd been through, it felt like they owed it to themselves to be here doing this even if it didn't involve quite as much exercise as originally planned.

When they reached West Cork it was too dark to really appreciate the beauty of Allihies, but the stars twinkled in the sky, void of clouds, with the moon glistening over the bay.

'Ye boys must be lucky,' their host had declared when they'd checked in, clarifying that she'd not seen the bay that calm in years.

As Zack got ready for bed, popping his now regular pills as he went, he wondered if she was right. Because ever since the accident he'd felt like he was riding entirely on luck. He'd been lucky to have his life saved with the heart transplant. He'd been lucky to find Chloe and to have been granted a kiss he didn't deserve that seemed to have dissolved whatever spell he'd been under. He was lucky to be here with his best friend by his side, about to set out on the adventure of a lifetime.

As he laid his head on the pillow, knowing he'd been free of someone else's dreams ever since the kiss, he realised how strange it was to know that he was lucky, but to somehow not feel it. For it not to reach the parts it was supposed to. There was a disconnect. One that he'd felt ever since he'd woken up after splicing his chest open with a chainsaw.

The following morning greeted them with the biggest blast of fresh air they'd ever known. The B&B they were staying in had Seaview in its name for a very good reason. From the moment they woke up to the point they were full of breakfast and on the beach, the sea air had tantalised them with its promise that all was right with the world.

'So what do you want to do with the day?' Larry asked.

'Stay here. This feels like perfection.'

'You're not going to be sunbathing all the time, surely?'

They'd not long sat down. The soft, dark yellow sand sank slightly with their weight. Zack picked a handful up and allowed it to fall like an egg timer without the glass. It made him realise what was bothering him. He was on borrowed time. This wasn't a life he should be living, but here he was. That fact made him want to appreciate it. Every second of this new life should be cherished.

'No, but I'd like a slower day today. Don't go calling me an old man or anything, but the reason we brought the van is because I'm not able to run around as much. I've also realised I don't want to live life at one hundred miles an hour anymore. We need to enjoy every moment of this holiday. Even moments like this where we just get to be.'

The need to rush was so present in everyday life it could be hard to switch off, and Zack recognised it in Larry. The need to be doing something every minute of every day. But this was just as important, sitting here and taking in the stunning view: the ocean that stretched for miles, the mountains crystal clear in the distance, the small harbour towns it was just about possible to spot along the coast. This was the most rural spot they'd ever sat in and Zack was in no rush to move on to the next thing, even if his best buddy was.

In the end, they came to a good compromise and that involved swimming trunks. Larry was desperate to be in the water in whatever form that took, so today they were going in for a dip, knowing Larry would be in for much longer than Zack. Larry had also agreed to go fishing, to give Zack some of the rest he needed.

For the first time, Zack realised he was conscious of his wound site. He hadn't been in any situation to date where he'd had to have his top off in front of others. It was a hidden part of his life, one that he could chose to share if he wanted to.

Rather than worry about it more than necessary, he opted to keep his T-shirt on when he joined Larry in the sea. The roaring waves came at them until they were far out enough to avoid the breaking surf, and instead they bobbed up and down with each swell of the ocean. The extra layer was a welcome move with the initial cold as they stepped in, but once they were immersed, with the sun shining, the temperature became balmy.

'Do you miss her?' Larry asked randomly, as they both floated on their backs admiring the sky, only the odd flight of a bird breaking the canvas.

'Who?' Zack knew. Of course he knew.

'Chloe.'

A bigger swell of water took them both closer to the shore, preventing Zack from answering immediately.

He missed his mum.

He missed doing things without thinking about his scar and his new heart.

Did he miss Chloe as well?

'I just wish we'd parted on better terms, you know? It has that sense of being unfinished business.'

'She didn't respond to your letter then?'

'Not even an acknowledgement. There's nothing more I can do.'

'Not going in for a grand romantic gesture on our return then? Given that you miss her?'

'Don't you start. We've barely been here a day. That's not long enough to miss anyone.'

'But you do, though. I can tell.'

The waves continued to lap them towards the coast, until they had to quit floating and swim further out, ready to be pushed back in again.

'The thing is, it was never about me and what I wanted. I was doing what my heart led me to believe was the right thing to do. And however crazy that sounds, it's true. So, yeah, I'm curious to know how she is. I'd like to know if she's okay and if it all works out for her, but I only ever wanted to be friends. I just wish I'd realised she saw things differently earlier on.'

As they bounced in the waves of the Atlantic, Zack realised

that if his new heart had sent him on a quest, he'd completed it. He'd been a fool in how he'd behaved – he realised that and he did miss her – but his heart was happily bobbing on the current of the ocean, not asking anything more of him. The crushing exhaustion he'd been experiencing had lifted. After weeks of obsessing over where Chloe was and what she was doing in an unhealthy way, it was time to start living his own life once again. It was time to restore some balance.

CHAPTER TWENTY-EIGHT

CHLOE

Not for the first time in her life, Chloe had been summoned to a family meeting. She wouldn't mind, but she was never the one calling them and, on the whole, they tended to be about her.

She'd much prefer it if they were able to discuss things over breakfast like a normal family. Instead, there was always this formality, making it sometimes feel like they were acting more like a management team than her sisters.

It was only because they cared, Chloe reminded herself, as she prepared a coffee for herself and left enough in the cafetière for anyone else who might want to help themselves. One thing she had learned in the years since her parents had made their departure was that these kinds of meetings required caffeine.

Without realising, she was the last one to join the gathering in the lounge. She obviously wasn't very awake this morning if she hadn't twigged that they were both waiting.

'Right, now we're all here... Shall we get started?' Alice said.

'Is there a set agenda?' Chloe joked, but she was met with a stony response.

'Not an agenda, no, but we wanted to discuss redecorating the house now you're well enough.'

'Oh.'

'We just didn't want to suggest anything while you were still poorly at the hospital.'

Chloe tried not to dwell on the number of conversations that tended to take place without her present. They were bound to occur given she hadn't been here.

'Do we really need to change anything? I know the decor is old-fashioned, but it's so old now that it's coming back into style.' The whole house had a very seventies feel. There were lots of browns and muted oranges. Even the plates and mugs they all used were from the same era. They might not have their parents here anymore, but they had their house and the things within it. Somehow it seemed like sacrilege to change it entirely.

'There are certain parts of the house that are becoming decrepit. If we wanted to sell it at any point in the future, we need to make sure we get as much for it as we can rather than selling it as a DIY project,' Leona said. She was sitting stiffly in the brown leather armchair that had seen better days.

'We always said, once you were well enough, we'd look to sell so we can all branch out. I sense you've had enough of us clucking around you like mother hens. We're not in any way thinking about that immediately, but we all thought as the house is looking tired we should do something about it sooner rather than later,' Alice said.

'Are there any new boyfriends I need to know about?'

'No new boyfriends, or girlfriends for that matter. But you're home and well, so it makes sense to start. We'll all have a big nest egg to leave with, like Mum and Dad would have wanted.'

'Do either of you know where you'll go?'

'We're not going anywhere yet. Getting this place sorted is going to take months, possibly years, and we're making it nice for the here and now as much as anything.'

'Right,' Chloe said, even though her chest felt hollow.

'Then, in a few years, if you're still doing well, we can sell up and find places of our own.'

It was hard knowing that her sisters' plans so often pivoted on her. That her health, or more often than not the lack of it, was the reason they were all still here living under one roof.

'I suggest we go about it by tackling a room at a time. The communal rooms that create the least inconvenience first, and then the kitchen and bedrooms last,' Alice said, in a way that demonstrated she'd clearly been thinking about this for some time. 'I figure if any of us don't want to camp out in the front room while our bedrooms are decorated, we can go and stay in a B&B for a while until that room is finished.'

'How are we funding this?' Chloe asked, knowing she didn't have much money to contribute. She'd be able to put enough together to decorate her bedroom, as long as it didn't extend to more than a new carpet and a lick of paint, but she wasn't able to contribute, say, a third of the funds for a newly fitted kitchen.

'There are the emergency funds we kept back from the inheritance from Mum and Dad. We've always kept them for a rainy day, but if everyone's happy, we could use them to get the house sorted?'

'Emergency funds?' Chloe repeated blankly.

'Yeah, we always kept some over in case we needed them for whatever reason.'

'I don't remember this?'

'You were poorly at the time. We probably didn't call it that, but we did discuss it with you. I'm not surprised you don't remember, given how unwell you were.'

'Was I the emergency?'

'Well, not necessarily, but it seemed prudent to be cautious.'

'So I was the most likely emergency?'

With sudden clarity, Chloe realised this was the first time in her life that her sisters weren't waiting for her to die. That they'd been keeping money aside for funeral costs knowing there had always been a possibility it might be needed. For years now they'd been dancing around her, making sure she was okay, doing all they could for her. And far too often she hadn't been thankful. For some reason, she'd often felt crowded rather than cared for. In a way, she knew this was because it wasn't the natural order of life. A pair of sisters in their thirties shouldn't find themselves in the role of carers. But they'd done it and they'd done it without question or complaint. They'd done it because losing their parents was enough loss for a lifetime.

'We don't like to think about it like that, but Mum and Dad did bring us up to be pragmatic if nothing else.'

'Did any of you bring Prosecco for this family meeting?' Chloe said.

'Why?'

'Because what a celebration this should be. I'm... well! Or well enough at least for the next era to come into play. I was beginning to worry you'd all be spinsters forever, when you insist on doing nothing other than looking after me. Getting the house sorted shows the tides are turning. You lot have decided to do something that means you're planning for your own futures as well. And I honestly don't know how to thank you all enough. For everything.'

Of course, over the years of being in and out of hospital multiple times, Chloe had thanked her sisters whenever the opportunity had arisen. But even those multitudes of words weren't enough. It was hard to think of a way to show her gratitude completely.

'You know you don't need to thank us. We're your sisters. It's what sisters do, however clichéd that sounds.'

'How far have you got with your planning, Alice?' Chloe asked.

'There aren't really any plans as such, other than having a rough idea of what rooms we'll do first and what our budget is. I thought the downstairs toilet was the obvious place to start. We'll just have to cope with the queue for the family bathroom.'

'How would you all feel if I project managed it? I haven't been doing my art pieces like I normally would and this would be another way to flex my artistic muscles. You've both got jobs to carry on with. It makes sense while I continue to recuperate that I have something to do, and rather than get rid of all of the original features, I'd like to make best use of them. A kind of vintage revamp.' It ticked all the right boxes. It was something she would be able to do from home. It would be a way of saying thank you to her sisters, providing the opportunity for them to spread their wings at a later date. And it would fill the time she was no longer spending with Zack, which she now occupied with thinking about him instead.

'Wow. That would be amazing. And we can all muck in to help so we can keep the costs low where possible. I know we'll need to get experts in for some parts, but we'll be able to strip walls and paint them.'

'I've got nothing but time these days. I can create a plan for each room and work out schedules. Set you all tasks depending on your skills. We've all got things we'll be better at and I can lead the overall project.'

Her two sisters glanced at each other and nodded their agreement.

'I don't see why not. That's it then. Are we going to make a start as soon as we can?' Alice asked, and both Leona and Chloe nodded once again.

'I'll start to make a plan this afternoon. I'll make a general to-do list to start off with and then research labour costs and parts for the bathroom, including working out what we can do ourselves.' Chloe's mind was abuzz with what would need to be done. She'd have to run the colour palettes and tile choices by her sisters, but if she was able to present a mood board for each of the communal areas she was sure they'd like her ideas.

'That sounds great to me,' Leona said. 'I was worried it might drag on for ages, but if you're spearheading how things go it should be much quicker.'

'That's agreed then. I'll fill you in on the plan once I've got it all down on paper.'

It would take a few days to have a solid idea of the timescale and at what junctures they'd be able to save a penny or two by doing the work themselves, but the thought of being the one managing something for her sisters rather than it being the other way round was empowering. Already it was filling her with a sense of purpose that had long since been absent.

For once, she was going to be the sister in charge, and it marked the success of her surgery in a way nothing else could.

CHAPTER TWENTY-NINE

SUSAN

The question had wafted out of her like a smoke trail. And once it was out, there was no getting it back.

Rather than answer, at first Mike said nothing and stood silently. It felt like a full minute before he spoke. 'I'm not going to sit around while you make accusations like that,' he finally replied, before walking away.

Susan should follow. There were parts of her that wanted to. But the parts that were too mellow to care won over, so she remained in her chair with half a coffee for company.

And however relaxed her response was compared to her usual demeanour, she couldn't help but notice he'd not answered the question. There had been no firm yes or no.

For so long she'd wondered and had never been brave enough to ask. Because surely, *surely*, something was going on that didn't have anything to do with projects. And now that nugget of doubt was out there, and it wasn't a small one. It was a huge nugget of doubt that wasn't going away.

Even though the trickling feeling of overwhelming relaxation was still with her, it didn't stop her from realising what time it was. Not only had he not answered what she really needed to know, he'd also not mentioned that they needed to get back to the cruise ship ASAP.

Abandoning her chill-out zone, Susan had to orientate herself and hoped she wasn't too late, rushing along the unfamiliar streets and swerving to avoid the occasional cyclist.

Fortunately it wasn't too hard to work out where she needed to head. The vapour trails of calm left her as she pounded along the pavement. How dare her husband abandon her in a strange city! What if she ended up being late to the ship? Would she end up stranded here? And all because she'd asked *the* question. She'd deserved an answer rather than this, surely?

By the time she made it to the cruise ship, she was out of breath and no doubt dishevelled. The cabin crew didn't seem to pay any attention to that though and greeted her with their usual warmth, while taking her name at the same time.

The wind still in her sails, Susan rushed to their cabin to see what he had to say for himself. But, of course, he wasn't there. She shouldn't have been surprised that he wasn't lying in wait ready to get an earful from her, but now she had no idea where he was.

Suddenly aware that she had made the boat and he might not have, she rushed back to the welcoming crew members to check.

'Yes,' they said, he had checked in, and they all agreed he would likely be entertaining himself somewhere on the ship, and for her to contact a member of staff if she continued to struggle to locate him.

Susan opted not to look for now. If he was here, he wasn't stranded. She wondered if he'd do her the same courtesy and check she was safely on board.

Instead of searching, she headed for the bar. A glass or two of the free house white wine would go down very well right now.

'Lovely day, isn't it? Did you get to see much of the city?' A lady of about her age was also nursing a glass of wine.

'We did, and then I misplaced my husband.' It was the start of a long conversation where they both divulged most of their life story to a stranger. Susan's travelling companion was widowed and this was her first solo outing. She'd decided that she couldn't remain at home indefinitely by herself. So this was a taster cruise and if she liked it, which she did, she planned to go on a longer cruise next time.

Susan explained that she'd booked it as a surprise, also fed up with being at home and alone far too much, despite a husband living with her. She'd confessed to the fact there was an element of make or break to this holiday and that the dial was switching from one to the other with far too much fluctuation for her liking.

'So what's caused the rift this time?' Joy, Susan's new friend, asked.

'It's crossed my mind far more times than I'd care to mention, and I've always held off asking. But this time it slipped out. I asked if he's been having an affair.'

'What did he say?'

'He didn't answer. He just told me he wasn't going to put up with accusations and walked off. I've not seen him since.'

What had started off as a glass of wine had soon dissolved into sharing a bottle between them.

'Say he has or had been... would you forgive him?'

Susan finished her glass and poured them both another as she thought on her answer.

'I don't think I could. What is it they say about a leopard never changing its spots? I think I'd spend the rest of my days waiting for it to happen again.'

'And is it possible that he really has just been attempting to finish projects that never get finished? I know plenty of men who could add that to their résumé as a skill.'

'I guess so. It's strange, though. Even that feels hurtful. That he'd opt to have screws and planks of wood for company rather than me.'

'Men are a funny breed to comprehend at times. My husband adored books. Constantly had his head in one. Collected them and claimed they were all keepers. My house is still full of them. I'm rather afraid that if I get rid of them it might turn out they're supporting the structure of the building. I know I need to tackle it at some point, but I'm scared that's where his essence belongs. And even though it wasn't a love we shared, it was his love. It was part of who he was. Anyway, what I'm trying to say is we all have to be individuals even when we are in a couple. I was never a bookworm in the way my husband was and, at times, the ever-mounting collection irked me more than it pleased me, but I miss that passion of his now. I miss him coming home with another three books from the charity shop. I miss spending an hour looking through his shelves because I was convinced he'd bought a duplicate. I even miss moaning at him about it, although I sometimes chat to the books as if they'll pass the message on.' Joy broke into a sad smile, taking a sip of wine before continuing. 'The shed might be your husband's way of remaining an individual within your marriage. It gives him time to just be. We all need that.'

'I just wish he'd talk to me. The only memory I'll have to dwell on once he's gone is a closed shed door.'

When Susan did depart from her new acquaintance, having discovered she lived less than an hour away back home, they'd already vowed to meet up for another drink once they'd returned. It would give her at least one thing to look forward to if Mike was still being antsy.

The conversation had left her in a philosophical mood. Could it be that Mike had only ever been striving to have some space of his own? Was she so worried about what he was up to that she'd forgotten to find hobbies of her own? She wished it was that simple, but somehow it didn't feel like it was. Because she'd tried to talk to him about it before and even then she'd been fobbed off with no definitive answers.

Wandering back to her cabin in a slightly more unsteady fashion than usual, Susan decided if he still wasn't there she'd go and dine alone. She should perhaps call him and see if he was okay, but they were in another country and she didn't want to rack up a huge phone bill unnecessarily. And why should she chase him when he was the one in the wrong? Walking off hadn't helped anything.

The hope that he might be back in their room was quickly lost when she opened the door and only the breeze from the balcony met her.

In a second her heart stopped as she spotted a note on the dresser. He wouldn't have left her, would he? They'd not long been talking about the places they'd like to travel to. They'd started to mend a little.

A tear rolled easily down her cheek, the emotion of the day beginning to catch up with her. She should have run after him. She should have shown him that she still cared.

She banged her knee on the side of the bed in the tight cabin space as she rushed to read the note.

There is another woman. But it's not what you think.

    I'll tell you about it over dinner. I've headed down to our usual table. I hope to see you there.

Love Mike x

CHAPTER THIRTY

ZACK

For every kilometre they travelled along the Wild Atlantic Way, Zack's energy became a little more lacking. He didn't want to get up early to be the first to hit the waves. He didn't want to travel miles off-route to visit the smallest house in Ireland. He didn't want to soak up every single viewpoint on the way.

Larry was making up for Zack's lack of enthusiasm with gusto. He wanted to see all the places, do all the things, not miss out on a moment.

Zack stayed in the van as Larry bounced out to try and see another mountain view that was clearly covered in cloud. He wondered whether these opposing energies were part of the problem. Anyone spending twenty-four-seven with Larry in his current state of wild fervour was bound to end up exhausting themselves. It was like a child going mad in a sweetshop and living off the sugar high for days on end.

'Can we stay longer at our next stop?' Zack asked once Larry had returned to the van.

'You should have come out, man! I know the mountains are clouded over, but you can see the sheep grazing down in the valley. They're clinging on to the edges like you wouldn't think was possible.'

Zack attempted to smile, but only managed a grimace. He should be loving the idea of sheep defying gravity and the wind, embracing the toddler spirit that had overtaken Larry, but a sheep was a sheep, wasn't it? Once he'd seen one on the edge of a mountain, surely he'd seen them all? His tiredness prevented him from getting too excited about more of them. 'So, next stop. A few more days?'

'Is this so you can lounge about in bed more?'

Zack peered at the clouds. 'Yes, it is. I don't know if you remember, mate, but I had major surgery less than six months ago. We're doing this in the van to make it easier on me, but I think you might have forgotten that.' He didn't want to be angry with Larry. After all, this was his holiday as well and he was doing the majority of the driving. But all the time Larry was doing a good impression of an excitable ping-pong ball, Zack didn't intend to try and keep up.

'I'm sorry, mate. You know me, I don't want to miss out. But I don't want to wear you out either, especially if it ends up making you grouchy. We'll stay in Dingle as long as you need to feel a bit more refreshed. There's plenty there for me to do to keep myself amused.'

'Thanks. I appreciate it.' Zack realised his friend was right. He had turned grouchy in recent days, his need for rest outweighing any enjoyment. 'I know the scenery is amazing but if it's okay with you, I'm going to snooze on our way there. Exhaustion has caught up with me.'

'Of course, mate. Hopefully it'll put a head start on you beginning to feel better. That and making sure you pop the pills at the right time of day. And you must know you're not going to miss out on anything. Not with the amount of photos I'm taking.'

'I'd rather you didn't while you're driving.'

'There's plenty of viewpoint stops along the way. Don't you worry.'

He was waiting in a queue for a rollercoaster ride and for the first time he realised that his teenage son had outgrown him. It may only be millimetres at this stage, but it made him sad that it seemed like only yesterday they'd been checking if he was tall enough for the ride, and now the boy had taken over his dad.

The flashback made Zack do nothing other than worry. After kissing Chloe, he'd had a hiatus without them. But as they'd got further from home, they'd started to happen again. The reprieve from them was only temporary, apparently. He should be having the time of his life. Instead, the old feeling that had plagued him since his surgery was creeping back. It was inexplicable and yet it was beginning to take up every pore of his body. The reason he was feeling so washed out was because his heart was beginning to fail. He sensed he needed to see Chloe but, without a doubt, Chloe never wanted to see him again.

CHAPTER THIRTY-ONE

SUSAN

Susan felt like someone had thrown a bucket of ice over her. She'd gone from panic at seeing Mike's note to a crushed acknowledgement of knowing that she'd always been right. There was another woman. And even though she didn't know what he meant by 'it's not what you think', it still hurt.

The problem now was there was no escape. What if she didn't want to face up to the secret he'd been keeping? Susan certainly didn't want to learn about it over a black-tie dinner where angry shouts and screams would be frowned upon. She could of course try to keep away from him for the rest of the journey. There were certainly enough places to hide onboard the ship. If she didn't want to attend dinner, she could order some bar food or head to the buffet restaurant. She could stay up late watching films then discreetly grab some sleep on a sun lounger. There were lots of options that didn't involve going to a formal dinner meant to mark forty years of being together, which would now be the occasion when Mike let her know exactly what she was dealing with.

Rather than back out like she desperately wanted to, Susan decided she was going to go into this with her head held high.

She hadn't done anything wrong, after all. She put on the red sequinned dress she'd packed especially for the occasion. She did her make-up perfectly to mask the fact she'd been crying. She put products in her hair so it wouldn't become flyaway like it so often did. All of these things she was doing for herself. She wasn't doing it to grab her husband's attention. She was doing it because she respected herself above all else and she didn't mind who knew that.

Even so, the confidence over how she looked didn't make the walk to the dining hall any less daunting. Especially in heels.

Sadly, they weren't on a table for two. They hadn't been for any of the sit-down dinners on this cruise. They were with the same three couples, none of whom Susan had seen at any other point.

She heard murmurs of 'Hasn't it been wonderful?' as she took her seat, not looking up in the hope she could avoid making eye contact.

'Everything okay?' Mike whispered quietly in her ear.

Seeing red was the only option. Everything was so far removed from okay he could shove the question up his backside. Why hadn't he waited in their cabin so they could discuss this in private?

'Who. Is. She?' Susan asked as quietly but as scathingly as possible. There were a few possibilities that had passed through Susan's mind. A neighbour. A friend. A stranger.

'I'll explain once we've had dinner.' Mike gave Susan's knee a squeeze as if he hadn't shifted the axis of her world.

'Tell me *now*.' All eyes were on her now she'd given up the pretence of lowered voices.

'It's... complicated.'

'No, it isn't. The only thing that is complicated is the way you've told me to join you here, rather than just telling me all the other times I've asked what's going on. The way you thought doing it here would be better than waiting for me in the cabin. It's not my fault that your dirty laundry is going to have to be aired in front of a bunch of strangers.'

'Is everything okay?' the woman who had been talking about nightclubs the previous evening was brave enough to ask. She was the second person who could shove that question up her backside tonight. Quite frankly it was none of her business, but that wasn't going to stop Susan from explaining herself.

'My husband has been having an affair. I'm just hoping to find out who with before the starters arrive.'

'I haven't been having an affair!'

'What then? Your note said there was another woman! Even if you've only been kissing, it still counts as an affair.'

Cheating was cheating as far as Susan was concerned. He might only have gone as far as a dalliance, but that was far enough.

The whole table was agog and Susan wanted nothing more than to be doing this in a private space, only her husband had had other ideas.

'It's a bike. A motorbike. Her name's Bella.'

'A motorbike? That you've named?' Susan's throat dried up in an instant.

'There's never been anyone else.'

They were words she should have been glad to hear, but instead she got up and walked away. She couldn't face the humiliation of the pitying looks from their fellow diners.

'Susan, don't go.'

'I'm not staying.'

'Well, let me come with you.'

Susan's red mist matched her dress as she made her way out of the dining hall without looking back to see if Mike was following. There was a strong chance he wasn't, but she was beyond caring.

It was only when he went to grab her wrist that she stopped.

'I don't see why you're so upset. It's not like there is another woman. As in an *actual* woman. Surely a motorbike doesn't count as cheating?'

'Do you know how humiliating this has been? Why couldn't you have told me in private? I've been worrying about you for months. Ever since you finished work. And I've lost count of the times I've asked you what's going on. Why couldn't you have just been honest with me? Instead you write a note declaring there is another women and invite me to dinner among strangers to talk it out. It's just *not* okay.'

They were standing outside the closed duty-free shop. The wide, empty corridor echoed their words.

'I'm— I don't know how to say this. Can we go and take a seat somewhere?'

They traipsed to the bar and it gave Susan a chance to process what she'd been told. All those hours of pottering. All those times she'd felt ignored. All because of a bike?

'There is something I haven't been telling you.'

'So the bike's not it? Is it really another woman?' Susan had spent far too long joining the dots without guidance.

'No, definitely not. And I don't ever want you to think that there has been. It's always been you, Susan.'

'What then?'

'When I ended up retiring early, it wasn't out of choice as such. It was because of the trauma involved with our last case. We saw such horrendous things, things that I'm not able to talk about. I wasn't the only member of staff to end up suffering with PTSD. Because my retirement was on the horizon anyway, I was offered to go early. I took it in a heartbeat to spend more time with you, but ever since I haven't found a way to tell you what's been haunting me.'

'I would have understood.'

'It's just... it's been so hard when so many things trigger

what I've been trying to forget about. I've been trying to block it out and I realised the only thing I've blocked out is you.'

Susan pulled her husband towards her, gripping him harder than she usually would have, and for a while he cried into her shoulder and she could feel that he'd been needing to do that for a very long time.

'I'm glad you've finally felt able to tell me,' Susan said, when Mike eventually found his way up for air.

'Me too. And all my tinkering, it was to distract me, but I was doing it for us. I didn't say anything because I was planning it as a surprise. The idea was that our anniversary would have been spent travelling around the UK after I'd managed to fix Bella up. She's a Triumph Bonneville, a real classic, and I thought I would be able to bring her back to life, but I never managed to get her working. A bit like our marriage. It looks like I've made a hash of both.'

'You haven't made a hash of anything. It's me that's been impatient with you.'

'I'll get us a drink,' Mike said.

The place seemed like a museum when there was no one else around. All gold trim and plush pink coverings. Susan wondered how many couples had shared moments like this here, where they faced either the beginning or the end.

'I ordered us some bar snacks as well, seeing as we're missing dinner. Call it a peace offering.'

'I think we're both due to give each other one of those. I knew you'd put up a metaphorical brick wall but I had no idea how to get it down.'

'I know, I know. The bike was my way of trying to fix things, and when it wasn't working it just made me feel like even more of a failure. None of this is quite what I hoped we'd be doing, but I didn't want to tell you that when I'd failed.'

'What would we be doing, then? If your plan had come together?'

Mike smiled broadly. 'We'd be in Margate right now. I'd planned out a trip to take us right around the coast of the UK. We were even going to stop in the Lake District.'

'So why didn't you tell me?'

'Because I didn't want you to be angry or disappointed.'

'Why would I be angry?'

'Well, I always seem to do a good job of getting you into that state. Present circumstances included. The thing is, I spent a fair bit of money on the bike. I wanted to make it as travel-worthy as I possibly could. But that doesn't count for much when the engine still won't start.'

'How much did you spend exactly?'

'I've already said I don't want to make you angry.'

'I think it's a little too late for that.'

'Probably about the same amount that you've spent on this cruise, which makes us even really.'

'I'm not sure why we're worrying about money. Going away was always about finding each other again, and hopefully we've come some way to managing that.'

A member of staff delivered the food Mike had ordered: dirty fries covered in cheese and bacon, and the biggest hot dogs Susan had ever seen. She tried not to dwell on how she was going to eat one of those without adding dots of mustard to her red dress.

'It has. And don't forget... we've got another adventure waiting to happen. Once I've fixed the bike, that is.' Mike took hold of Susan's hands and looked longingly into her eyes. 'I know I'm not great with words and I'm sorry for the confusion I've caused. And not just today. For all the times you've reached out and I haven't been able to connect. For all the times you've been the one holding the fort and I've been along for the ride. I've felt lost ever since I finished work, and Bella was my way of finding myself and my way back to you. I'm sorry I didn't tell you. It seems foolish now when we could have made those plans together. But I wanted to surprise you because normally it's the other way round. Then when I knew it wasn't going to work and you'd come up with something to do, I felt like a miserable failure. I was a bit of a grumpy git over it, but I still didn't tell you because then I would have been admitting defeat.'

'She's... I mean *it*. It's not called Bella. Naming vehicles and talking to them is the epitome of uncool, if you ask me.'

'Referring to her as a woman certainly hasn't helped my case. But that doesn't mean I'm not cool. Ask Lily.'

Susan would have laughed, but she wasn't quite over the rollercoaster of emotions tonight had presented her with.

'I'm not sure you've helped your case at any point really.' She grinned at him to let him know he was forgiven, especially as it wasn't anywhere near as bad as she'd been left to imagine. In fact, it was a darn sight better than any of the scenarios she'd come up with. It was something they'd be able to work through... together.

'Is there any way I can help my case now?'

'Tell me more about where we would have been heading. Which other places would we have stopped at?'

'I still plan for us to do it. I don't want it to be theoretical. I'd planned it so there was only ever an hour or two between each stopping point. I figured we'd go for a mix of camping sites and B&Bs. We were going to start at Margate and Broadstairs, then on to Hove. We could maybe pop over to the Isle of Wight if you fancied it, followed by a stop in Devon. I thought maybe Sidmouth, and then we'd travel into Cornwall before starting to head up the west side of the country.'

'Wow. Is there anywhere we aren't exploring?'

'Not really. You only live once, right? I know that hasn't always been my attitude, but I've realised we need to do more to appreciate each other. This was my way of helping us to do that.'

'That was the idea behind this cruise too. At least it sounds like we're singing from the same hymn sheet.' Susan helped herself to one of the dirty fries, the temptation being all too much.

'That is a relief. This means we have a lifetime of adventures to continue enjoying together.'

'It certainly does,' Susan agreed, as they both started to tuck into their meals.

And it might not have been the grand formal dining affair that they'd been booked in to enjoy, but their hot dogs for two in an empty bar was as perfect as it needed to be. Because sometimes love wasn't perfect. Sometimes it was stretched across so many years it felt as if it had lost its elasticity. Marriage at times could be a saggy pair of pants that felt like they needed replacing.

But as Susan and Mike went to bed together for the second time on their weekend voyage, they discovered once again that it was possible to pull those pants up (or off in this case) and learn to love all over again. All was not lost.

CHAPTER THIRTY-TWO

CHLOE

Considering it was the smallest room in the house, redecorating it was taking much longer than Chloe had wanted it to.

Booking a plumber to do the required work in the downstairs loo had been more of a palaver than she'd accounted for. Apparently everyone and their uncle wanted their bathroom refurbished at the moment. Three weeks later than planned – and with a workman who wouldn't have been her first choice, but needs must – the work was starting.

For the next week, Chloe intermittently offered cups of coffee and watched progress from the sofa while peering at colour charts as her new kind of therapy.

They'd already chosen the tiles for the bathroom. They were a deep teal colour and would give the room the updated feel it needed while still playing into the seventies vibe that the house was never likely to shake.

Next they were opting to tackle the hallway and landing. The evidence of years of comings and goings was far too evident, with the colour of the once-mint-green wallpaper now faded, plus scuffs and marks too pronounced to even try and cover. The swirly-whirly carpet was also outdated by decades and not in keeping with the overall sleeker look they were going for.

'Would you like another coffee?' Chloe asked the plumber.

'Would I? Without a doubt. It's tough work here.'

The way he responded always made her feel like she was being a lazy couch potato. As they were paying him good money, she wasn't about to get up and offer to be his apprentice. Making him coffees on a regular basis was as good as it was going to get.

Because of the work, Chloe had given up her daily walks. There was something about having a stranger in the house that made her feel like she should remain on the premises. So walking to the kettle at regular intermissions was the grand total of her current exercise regime.

Perhaps it was the lack of fresh air or the significant reduction in her daily step count, but it was clear her fitness levels had plummeted since the redecoration project had begun. The short distances she was travelling were wearing her out and each time she waited for the kettle to boil, she had to take a seat on one of the dining room chairs.

Her sisters were coming and going at different times of day, as they usually did, keeping a casual eye on proceedings but happy to leave Chloe in charge. When they asked if there was anything she needed from the shop, her answer was more coffee and toilet rolls. The plumber seemed to be going through an unexpected amount of both.

For the hallway, Chloe was hoping to get Alice and Leona to agree to panelling on the lower half of the walls painted in a darker grey with a lighter colour at the top. It was on the grand side, but she'd seen it in enough interior design magazines for her to have fallen in love with the idea. That and the fact that it was very on trend would hopefully have them all signing up to the plan.

Chloe spread out the assortment of colour swatches she had

in shades of grey. There were so many to choose from. It was as if they'd depicted every cloud colour that had ever existed and some of the names reflected that fact: Stormy Grey, Dark Clouds Grey, Clear Sky Grey.

She preferred the ones that were named things like Pebble, but it was difficult to know where the balance was between too dark and too light.

After making yet another coffee (she wasn't able to keep up with that much caffeine so had switched to water), she took the three colours she had narrowed it down to into the hallway, hoping the light there would help make the final decision.

Holding them up against the wall, it was hard to tell the difference and, for a moment, her world swam. She had to place both hands on the wall to steady herself.

As soon as she did, everything righted itself again. That dash of dizziness was gone.

Nothing to concern herself with. It wouldn't be the first time in her life that she'd been faint. Having an issue with her heart meant it had been a regular occurrence. *Had* been. Not now. It shouldn't be now.

Before peeling away from the wall, Chloe glanced at the pieces of cardboard and realised the Pebble Grey matched her hand. The light grey swatch matched the pallor of her skin. And it was certainly more of a pallor than a colour. When had that happened? When had she become so busy getting the house refurbished that she'd missed the fact she was beginning to lose all colour?

Giving up on making decisions for now, Chloe returned to the sofa where she would be safe again. She didn't feel unwell as such. Just washed out.

Until then, she hadn't realised that she needed to concentrate on the colour in her cheeks rather than the colours they'd be putting on the walls.

CHAPTER THIRTY-THREE

ZACK

When Zack wasn't in bed, he'd quickly come to the conclusion that Dingle was the nicest place he'd ever been to. It was picture postcard perfect with many of the buildings painted different colours. Along the water, there were shops and cafes busy with tourists, and over the road, on the water's edge, there were numerous boats and fishing vessels, many waiting to give tours of the beautiful surroundings.

Even though he'd slept a lot, he was beginning to think that he was okay. That perhaps everything had just caught up with him in the way things did sometimes.

'I figure we'll get something to eat when we're back,' Larry said, as they headed along the sea wall and joined a queue ready to officially become tourists themselves.

'Definitely. I'd much rather go out to sea on an empty stomach. We don't know how choppy it'll be. It is part of the *Wild Atlantic Way*, after all.'

'I'm going to film this, if it's all right with you? We've had lots of enquiries about whether we're both okay. I guess if we let people following the project know that we're having a break and a short holiday they'll understand. We can share that without the local media finding out about your accident. Turns out we have a fan base of sorts.'

Zack hadn't even thought about the TikTok account they'd been running for some time, which signalled the changes that had occurred over the past six months. He wasn't spending his time thinking about securing sponsorship and even though he wanted to finish the garden project, it hadn't been on his mind either.

'We can do some videoing, but maybe we should just save it for Facebook, for our friends and family.'

'I don't mind where we put it, but if we see any dolphins or other marine life I want it on camera.'

Zack wasn't about to stop his friend. But he for one was no longer intending to live his life through a camera lens. That was all everyone seemed to be doing these days. Concentrating so hard on capturing the moment that sometimes they ended up missing the point entirely. He felt maybe that's what he'd been doing. With his mind only on the project for years, he'd lost focus on being him.

On the journey out, Zack stared back at Dingle. He loved the little harbour and the backdrop of the colourful buildings, with mountains in the distance and boats bobbing about in the foreground. It was the kind of image that artists would try to get down on canvas.

Apparently, if they were lucky they might see Fungie the dolphin, who'd been dancing in and out of the harbour for nearly forty years. He had quite the celebrity status in the town, including a statue dedicated to him. As well as Fungie, they were told they might see seals, puffins, and all sorts of other wildlife if they kept their eyes peeled.

As the boat chugged further out, Zack stayed firmly on the padded seat at the side. The stronger waves were making the vessel lurch up and down in a way that he really wasn't keen on. Nor was his stomach.

When they arrived near some rocks and Larry got excited, Zack braved getting up to see the two seals that all the tourists were snapping and videoing. One woman was even talking to the camera as if she were doing a news report. It was bizarre to see her facing the wrong way so as not to be able to see the seals herself, making out that she was presenting the Channel 4 news.

With a jolt from the waves, Zack gave the girl an accidental bump.

'Do you mind? This is live!'

'I'm sorry. I didn't realise I was going to interrupt your eight viewers.'

Zack hadn't meant to be mean, but it did seem a bit much to get told off when she wasn't paying any attention to the other people around her. The only ones that mattered were on her phone.

'Eight? More like eight thou— Sorry about that loser, guys.'

The screen definitely said eight – Zack checked discreetly over her shoulder – and then the boat lurched again.

This time he didn't just bump her. This time he vomited his full Irish breakfast, white pudding and all, over her shoulder.

'Ohhh. Myyyy. Gawwwddd.' For a moment, the girl didn't know whether to be more worried about the sick dripping down her coat or the fact her recording was still live.

Zack laughed inappropriately at the absurdity of it all. 'Sorry about that.'

'You're laughing? How are you finding this funny? It's dis-gus-ting.' The tang of an American accent was drawn out more with every sentence.

Another lurch of the hull made Zack's stomach turn once more so rather than argue, he perched on the bench and concentrated on not heaving again.

'God, are you all right, mate?' Larry said, when he caught up on what the source of the disruption was.

Zack closed his eyes and tried to remember what he was supposed to concentrate on when feeling sick. Did he need to focus on a spot? Or squeeze his nose? Or put his head between his knees?

'Is *he* okkkkaaay?! What about me?'

'You're not the one who is ill at the moment,' Larry said, matter-of-factly.

'Ay. You can al'ays go for a dip in the sea and take that camera with ye,' a crew member advised the young woman.

When Zack opened his eyes, it was almost as if he hadn't. A black veil remained there with only dots of light for company. He blinked in the hope they would go away but, rather than that happening, he was sick a second time just as he'd been trying to avoid.

That cleared his vision for a moment and he was able to see, far in the distance, the tranquillity of Dingle harbour. It was the most beautiful scene to take in as he realised it wasn't his vision that was stopping. It was his heart. And for the second time that year, he landed on the floor quite certain that he was about to die.

CHAPTER THIRTY-FOUR

CHLOE

For the next few days, Chloe didn't concern herself with how the bathroom fitting was going. She didn't even offer coffee; instead she waited to be asked. What she occupied herself with was comparing the colour of her skin to the charts she had. She was Dove Grey at best and Lost-at-Sea Grey at worst.

Even her sisters were beginning to notice, clucking around her with their notes of concern.

'Can I get you some breakfast, Chlo?' Alice offered, even though she should be setting off for work.

Normally she would decline, not wanting to disrupt her sister's day, but today she required energy. 'Yes, please. Could you fix me some peanut butter on toast?'

Alice made the best peanut butter on toast. It cured all evils as far as Chloe was concerned. It had to. She didn't want to be going backwards rather than forwards.

'Do we need to get you a GP appointment?' Alice asked as she delivered breakfast. 'You're not looking as spritely as you were.'

It was a polite way of saying she looked like death warmed up.

'If I'm no better in a day or two, then yes. I haven't been eating much. It might just be that. This is going to help.' Chloe bit into the toast to prove it was all she needed to make her feel better.

'I'll get Leona to check in on you today. She can make you some lunch if you're not feeling up to it yourself. Is today the last of it?' Alice glanced towards the downstairs toilet.

'Apparently so. And I'll be very glad when it's done. I want to get back to my daily walks. I think that's part of the problem.'

Chloe wanted that to be part of the problem, but as she said goodbye to Alice and worked her way through what felt like a mountain of toast, she wondered if it was linked to something else. She wondered if she could afford to ignore Zack anymore.

She'd hoped by not making any contact, the heartache that she'd felt over her unrequited feelings would go away. She'd wanted to dispel his idea that their hearts were effectively fuelling each other, keeping each other well. And for a while, the idea that they weren't linked seemed to have been true. It might still be, but with each passing hour she was beginning to think Zack might have been right. Because the worse she felt, the more she thought of him.

Letting the plumber in, hopefully for the final time, and putting her plate in the dishwasher, Chloe went to retrieve the letter she hadn't parted with. She'd written Zack's telephone number on there rather than storing it in her phone. She would have messaged him a hundred times over if she'd kept it there. Even though she'd been trying to get over Zack (because it did feel like she was getting over him and that kiss) by wrapping herself up with the renovation project, it hadn't worked. Because even before she was past the first room, here she was back to thinking about him.

Because if she was ill, did that mean he was too? Was the synchronicity he'd told her about real? Checking in with him was the only way to find out.

Keying his number back into her phone, Chloe sent a WhatsApp message for the first time since they'd kissed and he'd filled her head with what she'd then considered to be nonsense.

Hi Zack! How are you doing? I'm missing having a rehab buddy.

Chloe stopped herself mid-message. 'Missing' sounded wrong even if it was true. She didn't want to come across as anything other than cool as a cucumber.

Hi Zack! How are you? I haven't been doing my daily walks and need to get back to it. Let me know when you're home and maybe we can be rehab buddies again. Chloe x

The kiss was how she always signed off and after overthinking it for longer than necessary, Chloe left it in. She wasn't about to start changing who she was because of what had happened between them.

The overthinking only intensified with every passing hour after that. Rather than the usual notification of it being read, the two grey ticks meant it hadn't been opened. So she fretted about leaving it too long to contact him. She shouldn't have added the kiss on the end of the message. To him that might seem more like a threat than a habitual pleasantry. She should have been more casual and only asked how he was, not suggest they meet up again straight from the outset. All of these thoughts and more ping-ponged around in her head until she decided to go to bed. Leona was spending the afternoon working from home so she would be able to bid farewell to their plumber.

An afternoon nap would cure her. From what she wasn't sure. Because for all the hours she rested, her heart continued to long to hear from Zack, even though there was a chance he'd make her wait as payback for the time she'd stopped communicating with him. That would mean weeks of waiting and, given how she was currently feeling, she wasn't sure she had that long.

CHAPTER THIRTY-FIVE

ZACK

If it was possible to get a degree for waking up unexpectedly on hospital wards, Zack was about to earn himself a 2:1 at the very least.

'Shit, man. Not again,' he said to no one.

Or at least he thought there was no one about, until Larry leapt up from a chair and a member of the medical staff joined him by his bedside.

'I'm so glad you've decided to wake up!'

'This is my bad karma for laughing at an influencer, right?'

'If that's what caused it, don't ever do it again.'

'What happened?' Zack wasn't 100 per cent sure he wanted to know, but then it couldn't be as bad as the last incident that had landed him in hospital. Not when there had been seal pups involved. Or had he imagined them?

'You hit the deck, Zee. I mean that as literally as it gets. You passed out. Because of your medical history they sent a chopper. If you ever want to recall the tale, I'm pretty sure your Insta friend can hook you up. She forgave you for puking all over her once you were unconscious and giving her the best content she's ever managed to put together.'

'There I was thinking I'd managed to keep my medical woes off social media.'

'I think you're straight out of luck there, my friend.'

A nurse flitted about taking Zack's vitals, a dance he was far too familiar with. The ECG leads were back in place, carrying out their monitoring, and even though he'd not long been awake, the beeping was already beginning to drive him insane. 'So do they know what caused it yet?'

Zack hoped it wasn't as bad as he'd been imagining at the point he passed out.

'You fainted, but they haven't ruled out the fact it might be related to your heart. So you won't be going anywhere for a bit. They want to keep you here for observation.'

'Where are we anyway?' For a moment Zack had forgotten they weren't in their home town of Abingdon.

'You're in Kerry General Hospital in Tralee. The good news is it was in the right direction of travel at least.'

'There'll be no travelling for ye for a while. Not until the doctors say so,' the nurse interjected before leaving them to it.

'Killjoy,' Zack said. 'It's not like I put a chainsaw through my chest this time.'

'How are you feeling anyway?'

Zack hadn't been awake long enough to carry out a true assessment. Before he'd passed out he'd been a seasick jumble: hot, sweaty, nauseous, flustered. That side of things had evaporated, but he was left with the general fatigue that had been plaguing him for days. 'I've improved from how things were when I was on the boat, but I can't lie... I don't feel right. It's surprising, but I'm glad to be here.'

Hospitals weren't Zack's natural habitat. In fact, they were as far as could be from where he'd ever expected to spend large portions of his life. But right now, he was happy to be in the presence of people who understood the human body far more than he did.

'Me too. And you have to swear you won't put me through any more medical emergencies. I'm not cut out for it.'

'How did you get here?'

'I got driven by the Gardaí. Everyone was brilliant. The van's still in Dingle, but I'll pick it up once I'm happy you're okay. They've even made sure I have somewhere to stay tonight.'

'God, I can't believe this has happened. I don't want to bugger up this trip more than I already have. Promise me, if I get stuck here or have to go home, you'll continue on without me.'

'I'm not making any promises with the amount of adrenaline that's still buzzing through me. The only thing I'm going to manage is a spectacular crash, preferably into bed, very soon.'

'How late is it?'

'We're cracking on for midnight.'

'Have I really been passed out that long?'

'You did knock yourself out good and proper. Gave yourself a head injury for them to observe as well as your heart. Getting yourself a proper meal ticket.'

Zack shook his head at the thought, but that hurt so he quickly stopped. 'Honestly, mate. I'd do anything to not be feeling like this. Hopefully they'll fix me up soon and we'll be on the way for the rest of our journey.'

'I'm gonna keep everything crossed. If you don't mind, I'm going to go and find where this accommodation is and get my head down. I think this has officially been one of the longest days of my life.'

'I'd probably agree if I could remember most of it. You go and get some rest, and I'll try to do the same.'

Larry chatted with the nurse before leaving, and Zack rested his head back on the pillow.

What. A. Day.

It was hard to imagine that he'd been on a helicopter for the first time in his life and couldn't even remember it happening. He should have known that if he was feeling ropey, he shouldn't have pushed himself. It was hard not to though, when he was on holiday and wanted to enjoy his time. A boat trip to see some wildlife had seemed harmless enough.

'Is there anything I can get ye before lights out?' the nurse said, interrupting his musings.

'Do you know where my bag is? I had a rucksack with me on the boat. Did it make its way here?'

'I think it's in the cabinet. Let me check.' After a moment of rifling, the nurse produced his bag. 'It seems to have got wet on its journey. Not surprising really.'

'Thanks,' Zack said, accepting it despite the dampness.

'You get a good sleep.'

'Hopefully,' he said, knowing he wasn't feeling sleepy at all. It would seem being knocked out for hours was all the rest his body needed for now.

Left alone, Zack was able to see how bad the damage to his bag was and, more importantly, his phone. Parts of the bag were sodden, making Zack think it might have landed on a very wet deck at some point. Not having any memories of the event didn't help. He'd have to ask Larry for more details when he felt up to hearing about them. Although, it might end up being like his first accident where he was never going to be brave enough to face the full account.

The book that he'd been carrying around and reading was ruined. The pages were too waterlogged to even contemplate saving. Zack said a prayer for his phone as he scrambled to find it in the side pocket. It was slightly less damp, but the screen was blank. Without a charger to check if the battery had gone, it was hard to know if it was that or the fact it was also waterlogged. As it wasn't exactly urgent, he'd have to wait to see if a charger or a bag of rice would be enough to fix it. For now, he needed to get some rest and concentrate on getting better. Everything else could wait.

CHAPTER THIRTY-SIX

CHLOE

After far too many days of avoiding it, Alice had at long last brought up the subject of Zack with Chloe.

'Is he really on holiday?' had been her first question.

They'd gone on to have a long conversation, initially about why Alice hadn't trusted Zack (she had indeed looked him up on the internet and discovered the sordid, but not entirely true details of his sex life), and Chloe had gone on to tell Alice, as best she could, why she was no longer in touch with him, but now wanted to be again.

'Do you really think there's any truth to it?' Alice asked.

'Look, until he came out with this theory, I didn't have any reason to think he was untrustworthy. It just sounded really irrational at the time, but now that I don't feel great it's making me wonder if he's right. Plus there's almost a sixth sense that's hard to explain. As if it's not my instincts, but my heart's.'

'And do you really think getting in touch with him again is a good idea after how he's treated you?'

It was a fair question. The kiss that he'd rejected sometimes left her in tears when she thought about it. But she was the one who'd ignored him after that, not the other way round.

They could still be friends. That could be salvaged, and perhaps it might extend to their wellbeing if what he'd told her was true. 'I've already tried to get in touch. That's why my last resort is seeing where Zack thinks it happened, if you'll take me.'

Alice seemed as curious about the whole notion as Chloe, so it wasn't long before they were in her car ready to set off.

Chloe stared out at the passing countryside. There were some beautiful views across the local areas. She often thought how nice it would be to own a cottage out in one of the villages they'd passed through.

'I thought perhaps going to the crash site might help me understand what Zack's been telling me.'

'How do you know where it is? It's a pretty obscure place you've made me put in the satnav.'

'I don't really know where it is.' Chloe didn't understand the numbers she'd been given – the coordinates from Larry, Zack's friend. The letter he'd delivered barely an hour after Zack's had held the information. At the time, she'd not read the letter, and it wasn't until she'd fetched Zack's letter out again that she'd remembered the odd encounter with his friend. The details it held had been basic, and she read them again now to see if they gave any more clarity.

Hi Chloe,

The concept that you are somehow connected with Zack started at the following coordinates. If you ever want to see if it gives you the same sense of what he's been telling you, it might be worth a visit.

See ya round, Larry.

'Zack's friend gave me the coordinates,' Chloe clarified. 'I've not looked into it any further. I was worried I might find out more details than I'd want to know.'

Like Zack's letter, at first she'd ignored it. She'd wanted it to go away like a bad dream should. But as her energy had continued to leave her, she'd wondered if it would give her an answer. She'd put if off as long as possible, but when she'd messaged Zack, it had also cracked open this possibility. And as she hadn't heard back from him, this was the only option remaining.

'Look, sweetie...' Alice briefly took her eyes off the country lane to glance in Chloe's direction. 'I just want to say, it's probably not wise to get swept up in his theories.'

'It's not just Zack's theory if Larry believes it as well. He said it was the place Zack began to believe we were connected. He thought it might help me if I knew where that was.'

'O-kay. Well, I really don't know what to believe, but you know I'll do anything to make you better, even this. We're nearly there anyway. If at any point you decide you want to go, you just let me know.'

Chloe had no idea what to expect, but soon Alice entered the forest and shortly afterwards pulled into a layby.

'This is it. Pretty much the exact coordinates. Are you sure this is where you're meant to come?'

Chloe shrugged. 'I'll go and take a look and see if any of it makes sense.'

'I'll be waiting here if you need me.'

'Thank you.'

Chloe left the comfort of the green Nissan Micra that had taken them on many journeys. Normally she was glad when it wasn't being taken to a medical appointment, but today she wasn't so sure.

With nothing obvious to see, Chloe put the exact details into Google Maps on her phone. It told her she was in the right place, but needed to move a few metres down the country lane.

As she did, her heart pounded. It struck her, whether because of the location or the things Zack had told her, that she was at the final destination. The one Zack seemed to believe linked the pair of them. It didn't take long to locate the only place of note. A tree that must have stood there for hundreds of years was now dented and marked by a floral tribute.

There were two displays laid on the ground. They'd survived, Chloe realised, because they were made of plastic. One said Mum and the other Dad.

They'd said their vows and her new husband was pushing a wedding ring onto her finger. They both secretly knew that they were already expecting, but that hadn't been the reason why they'd rushed the wedding. They were in love. Totally and utterly. The kind of love that would last in this life and the next.

Crouching down, she placed her hands on the ground as she let out a silent sob. *So, it's true.* She'd had a sense of something ever since the surgery, but she'd been able to blame it on other factors. Now she knew that her heart had a story to tell. All at once, she knew it was true and her pulse throbbed with the impact of it. Everything Zack had told her. Everything that didn't make sense. Everything that was too far removed from real life.

She dug her nails into the ground, as if holding on to the earth where it had happened would help her.

A part of her *had* been here in this spot. Her heart had given its final beats in this place. Life had stopped right here where she was clawing the ground.

And for a moment she couldn't breathe. For a moment everything was too hard and the world was closing in on her. The soil underneath her hands wasn't enough to ground her. Because how could life possibly continue? How were there cars still driving along the road? How did life continue to pass by while hers had stopped? And yet here she was... Living. Breath-

ing. Given a second chance. All because of what had happened
here.

The pain and the agony that were coursing through her
were almost too much to bear. And it was so hard to decipher,
what pain belonged to her and what belonged to the previous
owner of her heart. What agony belonged to the woman marked
out by the word 'Mum'? Because the connection was
undoubtably true, just as Zack had said it was.

For a while, Chloe had to let those emotions wash over her,
staying in her crouched position on the floor. It was all too much
at once to even consider standing up. The weight of two lives
was crushing down on top of her.

No wonder Zack had tried to find her if he'd come here and
felt this. The heartache. The absence. The loneliness. All of
those things were hers now. The things that had driven him to
find her. They belonged to her and it was now her turn to find
him. To work out what it was they needed to do to make this all
okay again.

Because even with all the heartbreak that was present, she
sensed there must be a way to fix it. She knew, without doubt,
that second chances existed. She knew, because she was one.
The phrase 'in this life or the next' had new meaning. This
heart wanted a second chance. And she was the only person
that was ever going to be able to give it that chance. The question was, how did she do that? It meant finding Zack. Soon.

CHAPTER THIRTY-SEVEN

ZACK

His mobile phone had to spend a day sitting in a bag of rice before it kicked into life again. Even then it was patchy, not finding a clear signal.

When Zack's emails, voicemails and messages did come through, they did so in a barrage. Fifty-eight red notifications that were so alarming Zack opted to ignore them for now. It wasn't as if he had any family to notify that he was here. Larry was his family these days, and he would have kept Kathy up to date. Everything else could wait.

Twenty-four hours passed before he did finally check his messages, and when he read the one from Chloe, his heart monitors virtually danced in response.

'She knows it's true,' Zack said, as soon as Larry arrived on the ward.

'Who does? What are you on about?'

'Chloe. She's back in touch.'

'What has she said?'

Zack showed Larry the message on his phone.

'Have ye replied?' Larry said, already demonstrating an Irish lilt.

'Not yet.'

'Don't you think you should?'

'What do I say?'

'That you're in hospital, and if your theory is right you probably need to see her.'

'I'm going to bet that will scare her off, and I don't want to do that again.'

'Then just act normal. Or be casual. Whatever you do, don't ignore her. If she's reached out, it might be because she's ill like you are. She might have realised your mad theory is true.'

Zack deliberated over his words for far too long. It was as if he was writing down a marriage proposal and every syllable needed to be carefully chosen.

Hi Chloe. How are you? I haven't been so good. Currently in hospital in Ireland. Hoping they'll decide what to do with me at some point. Would be great to see you when I can. Take care, Zack x

After typing the message, he read it out to Larry. His face said everything.

'Is that the best you can come up with?'

'What else am I supposed to say?'

He'd tried so hard before and Chloe hadn't believed him then. He wasn't sure what more he could say now.

'Tell her you've missed her. Tell her you want to see her. Make the whole situation more appealing so she wants to see you.'

'But I don't want to give her the wrong idea. Not after what happened before!'

Larry rolled his eyes. 'Are you still trying to tell me that you're not interested in the girl you've been obsessing over for months?'

'I've sworn off women. You know that and I haven't

changed my mind. If you don't understand that, then it's no wonder she's got confused with signals that aren't signals.'

'You're definitely confusing me. Send your message then. If there's one thing I do know, that text doesn't have signals in it. It's so boring it'll be like watching paint dry for the girl.'

'How many Irish ladies have you managed to chat up now with your new accent?'

'What are you on about?'

'Zero, right? So don't go giving me advice on how to talk to women. Not until you've got it right yourself.'

'If you need advice on how to chat a woman up, then I'm completely your man. But it seems to me it's exactly what you don't want to do.'

Larry had a point. Zack was being crabby with the one person who was there for him again. 'You're right. Sorry, mate. I didn't mean to diss your chat-up skills. This just feels important. Like I need to get it right having messed up before.'

'Apology accepted. But it still sounds very much like you're talking about a girlfriend if you ask me.'

'Humpf,' was the only noise that came out of Zack. He wasn't about to respond and go round in circles once again. Instead, he pressed send on the bland message, hoping he'd get a response and that at some point soon, she'd see that they needed to be reunited.

CHAPTER THIRTY-EIGHT

SUSAN

Being back in the car was a bit like being home already. The adventure was over and it was beyond thrilling to think that it was only the start. Susan had booked the cruise in the hope of fixing their marriage and it had worked. This was going to be the second phase. A new era. One for them both to enjoy, even if the first juncture was going to be getting the house on the market.

Over breakfast before they'd departed they'd laid out a plan, and downsizing had been the first thing they'd agreed on. It would free up some money for them to go on their travels, and they didn't need the number of rooms they had now that the children were grown. They'd pinpointed several things they could do to help each other. Along with selling the house, getting Mike to see the doctor and booking some therapy was their priority now he was no longer hiding his PTSD.

When they returned, Mike's first trip to the shed would be with Susan in tow. He was going to introduce her to Bella, although Susan had been teasing that she was going to call her Bert.

'I still can't believe you haven't got any pictures of Bella on your phone to show me,' Susan said, as they passed another field that was getting them closer to home.

'I didn't want to risk you finding out.'

'It's not like I go prying into your phone.'

'I know. But I'm always sending you the ones I've taken of the grandkids. It would be just like me to go sending over an extra by accident.'

'Well, I'll just have to look forward to meeting her in the flesh.'

'And I'll look forward to introducing you. I think we should take a stop at the next services. Maybe get a bite to eat before we get home.'

'We can pick up some milk while we're there as well.'

They both decided on a burger with fries when they saw what was on offer and, as the sun was shining, they opted to eat outside, under some trees.

'I'm glad this isn't a one-off. I feared I might be waiting another ten years before you wanted to go away again,' Susan said.

'Little did you know!' Mike grinned, the bite pattern in his burger producing a matching grin. 'But in all seriousness, for far too long I've been putting my foot in it by not saying much. I love you, Susan. I want you to know that. In this life and the next.'

There were plenty more romantic spots in the world. But it didn't always require the perfect setting to be a perfect moment. Sometimes a service station with a takeaway meal and the sun shining was all it took. Sometimes it was just the right person saying words that were strong enough for a heart to absorb and carry until the end of time.

CHAPTER THIRTY-NINE

CHLOE

With no word from Zack yet, and in an effort to get over the effects of their roadside trip, Chloe had thrown herself into planning the decor for the hallway because she didn't know what else to do with herself. Discovering that panelled-effect wallpaper existed made Chloe feel like she had reached the peak of Google search skills. It would save them time and money. That smugness soon wore off though when she found herself on the floor at B&Q waiting for an ambulance.

The message from Zack had done it. As soon as she saw his name on her phone the wind was knocked out of her, and that was before she'd even had chance to read what he'd written.

It turned out her skin colour turning from Pebble Grey to Azure Blue was a definite indicator that all was not okay. Needing to sit down on the floor immediately also set off alarm bells for both Alice and the store staff, who swooped into action.

Chloe wasn't able to stay present for much of the time between collapsing on the floor and being blue-lighted to hospital. It was several hours later that she began to feel slightly more with it and able to draw all her attention to the same thought for more than a moment.

'Rest. You don't need to be trying to get up. Alice will be back soon. She just went to get us some drinks,' Leona reassured her.

Chloe hadn't been aware she'd been trying to get up. And she'd gone to the DIY store with only Alice in tow. When had Leona arrived?

'What's going on?' Chloe asked, woozy from the whole episode.

'Your heart isn't functioning as well as they'd like it to be. They're going to try various things to help.'

'Zack.' She said the name of the one thing that she knew would help.

'Pardon?'

'Zack. I need to see him.'

'I'm not sure... given the circumstances...' Leona mumbled two incomplete sentences.

'Can I have my phone?' Clarity worked its way towards Chloe's consciousness.

'The screen smashed when you fainted. Fortunately it seems to be the only thing broken.'

'Is it usable? Does it switch on?'

'I'm not sure, to be honest. Alice has it, and I have a feeling everyone was more worried about you. I don't think the phone has been a priority.'

Alice returned with a tray of hot drinks.

'You're awake again. Amazing! How are you feeling?' Alice asked.

'I got a message from Zack.' Chloe tried to implore Alice with her eyes. They'd not had the chance to tell Leona about their field trip and she'd only explained her flashback experience to Alice.

'What did it say?'

'I never got to read it. I collapsed before I had the chance.'

'Damn. I'm not sure your phone is in the best shape after

landing on that concrete floor.' Alice passed the hot drinks to
Leona and rifled through her handbag. 'It's as dead as a dodo.'

'That doesn't look like it has a good prognosis,' Leona said.

'Not good at all.' Alice showed Chloe the cracked screen
that had a hundred fracture lines. 'I'll take it to a phone shop
tomorrow and see if there's anything they can do. I think that's
the best I can do for now. The message might get deleted if we
just take the SIM out.'

'What am I going to do if I need to get in touch with either
of you?' Not having ready contact with her sisters was more
worrying than not having read Zack's message. They were her
lifeline and always had been.

'You can borrow my phone for tonight. We'll get you a
temporary one tomorrow if nothing else,' Leona offered.

'Thank you.' Chloe wanted to cry. It dawned on her that
she was about to face something she'd hoped wouldn't happen
again: an overnight stay in hospital. And if history was keen on
repeating itself, it was unlikely it would only be for the one
night.

For a while, Leona provided a tutorial on how to operate her
phone. Given that it wasn't that different from Chloe's it
shouldn't have been too difficult, but as soon as she was told
something it was quickly forgotten, so Leona resorted to writing
down the basics. With her skin still a pale grey, lessons in phone
use were a bit beyond her.

Once that was done, Leona and Alice finished their drinks
and made murmurs about having to be on their way.

Even though she tended to bump heads with her sisters
more than she wanted to most days, she also wanted to cling to
them closely right now. She didn't want them to leave. If they
did, it would mean that this was more than a fainting episode.
That this was more than the heat in the store getting to her.
That the problem she'd been trying to ignore wasn't going away.

And her problem now was that nobody here was going to

believe her medical cure was actually a person. Because how could they ever believe that when she hadn't believed it at first?

When Leona popped out to wash up their reusable cups, Alice held back. 'I'll make sure we get hold of Zack somehow. I don't want you sitting about here worrying. We'll get you reunited, whatever it takes.'

Chloe held on to her sister's arm, briefly curling into it. 'I'm so glad you came with me. I'm so glad you understand.'

'I'm not sure I do fully understand, but I'm here for you. I'll see you tomorrow, and I promise I'll do everything I can, so you just spend the evening relaxing. We need you home.'

Chloe liked to pretend she was independent from her sisters. That they were the clingers-on. But here she was, not wanting to let go. She didn't want to be on the same ward, getting to know new nurses and ordering meals she was never wildly keen on. She wanted home. She wanted to continue making dubious wallpaper choices. She wanted to spend the emergency fund and live in the belief that they no longer needed that pot of money put to one side.

But here she was back at square one. And she didn't know if she was better or worse off knowing that the cure wasn't in the hospital.

CHAPTER FORTY

ZACK

For over a week now, the format had remained the same. Towards the end of the day, a gaggle of doctors would appear at the end of Zack's bed and repeat similar sentences to the previous day. They would say that they needed 'to continue monitoring the situation'.

When he pressed them for more answers, they'd all be a bit flummoxed by exact details. They didn't know why this had happened. His general heart health seemed to be good with some elements that didn't make sense, occasional blips in his monitoring causing concern. That's why they wanted to watch things more closely for a bit longer. No, he definitely wasn't well enough to return to the UK while they considered him to be medically unstable. The expectation being that what had happened before could happen again.

'I don't know, man,' Larry sighed after Zack had told him about his brilliant idea. 'It sounds too risky.'

'It'll only take half a day. I'll either be in a passenger seat or a cabin bed. I won't be doing anything more arduous than I am now.'

Larry scratched his head as if he'd suddenly developed a

bad case of nits. 'Yeah, but who gets in trouble when it all goes wrong? Effectively, I'll be kidnapping you from your hospital bed.'

'It's not kidnapping if I've consented to it.'

'Keep your voice down. You might have agreed, but the hospital haven't. They're the ones that'll be letting the authorities know if you end up disappearing.'

'They can't hold me here against my wishes.'

'Yes, but you can't head off and cause them more expense than you already have. I'm pretty sure your travel insurance isn't going to cover a second emergency helicopter ride. Especially if this one is self-induced.'

Larry had a point, but surely it wasn't going to come to that if they were taking the relatively easy route, as far as he was concerned. Larry would be doing all the donkey work and Zack would be able to chill out. His biggest concern would be taking his pills at the right time.

'The thing is, no one is ever going to believe my theory. And why would they when it sounds ludicrous?'

'Have you heard back from her? Have you actually spoken to Chloe yet? Because if you haven't, it seems like a big risk. What if we do get you back to the UK and then she doesn't want to see you? The risk will have been for nothing.'

Zack picked up his phone to check it again. It had recovered to full function after its run-in with the ocean, but there hadn't been any further messages from Chloe. He'd been certain there would be a response. The fact there hadn't been was sending alarm bells off in his head. The piece of invisible lace that strung their two hearts together was telling him something was wrong. And the only way he'd find out would be if he went to see her. To find out why she hadn't replied. 'It won't have been for nothing. I'm certain of that.'

'Okay, well, let me think about it. We can't just up and leave. I'll need to do some preparation.'

'We just need fuel for the car and fuel for us, and then we're set.'

'So you say! I need to check the tyres, book a ferry and get a decent night's sleep, so you can add those to the list as a minimum.'

Their voices had been gradually rising and a nurse came into the bay, which soon shut them both up. Not suspicious behaviour at all. They waited until she'd checked on all the other patients too before talking again.

'I'm going to head off and research some things. I suggest you sort out some kind of go-bag with everything you need so we can head off at any given opportunity. And call Chloe at the very least.'

'Thanks, man. You don't know how much this means to me.'

'It's only because, strangely, I really do think it'll make you better. And if I'm the only person able to assist that, then that's the way it has to be. But please try not to let it develop into an emergency. If you feel unwell, we'll have to get medical attention, so don't go keeping it to yourself.'

'Promise. I'll let you know if I hear from Chloe.'

After Larry had left, Zack tried to call Chloe. He hadn't quite had the energy to do so before.

At the other end, the ringing constantly chirped but with no answer. No instant words of reassurance were there waiting for him. It only deepened his concerns.

He spent the rest of the evening pottering about his bed space and making sure his bag was packed. Most of his things were still with the van, but he had his essentials here. He stowed away the biscuits he was given with his tea so that he had a snack for the journey. Not that he knew when the journey would be, but as they were going to be doing it in stealth mode, he was doing as Larry had suggested and getting prepared.

All the while, he was monitoring his phone, willing it to come to life with a notification. Only, there had been no messages or phone calls from the one person he'd been hoping to hear from. It was no wonder Larry thought he liked Chloe when he'd been acting like a lovesick teenager, not wanting to be the one to make the next move. This wasn't about securing another date or planning to go to the movies. This was far more important than that. This was the start of trying to work out why they only seemed to be well in each other's company and hoping that it was still true. Because if it wasn't, he didn't know where that left them.

Happy the bag was as ready as it was ever going to be, Zack tried his luck one more time, but there was still no answer from Chloe.

Soon it was time for another sleepless night on the ward. All the thoughts running through his head were designed to keep him awake and if they didn't, the strange noises from the ward certainly would. This wasn't where he wanted to be. He might be in one of the most beautiful countries in the world, but they didn't have the magical formula that was going to make him better. That was hundreds of miles away, and if the doctors weren't going to discharge him, he had to hope that Larry was going to come up trumps.

When the phone did buzz, it was Larry, doing exactly that.

Be ready to leave at four in the morning. That's five hours from now. Let me know you've received this message and try to get some sleep. I'll meet you out the front. I'll message you once I've arrived.

In the circumstances, sleep was very hard to come by, and Zack only drifted into a snooze with one hand on his phone. They had planned on going on the adventure of a lifetime. It had certainly been eventful and as for adventures, they might not know it yet, but the biggest one was about to begin.

CHAPTER FORTY-ONE

SUSAN AND MIKE

It's a shame we don't know how every chapter and verse will go in our lives. If we knew what the next part held, would we do things differently? Would we change things? Or would we be content knowing things are just so?

Because as Susan and Mike made their way back to the car, they didn't know this would be their last journey. They had plans. They were going to do things. They knew, in their future, they had further time to repair. There would be another ten, twenty, thirty years of being together. They would see the places they'd been wanting to see.

Only, life can change in an instant. It changed in the moment the speed limit switched from thirty to fifty. It changed in the moment Mike put his foot on the accelerator and their song came on the radio. He'd not heard it in years and it was as if the universe had a message for him, but not the one he'd expected.

A brief glance in Susan's direction and a smile as they both recognised the tune at the same time. *Their tune.* The one that had brought them together forty years ago. The song that had sealed the fact they would go on to bring three children into the world. The song that meant their grandchildren had come to be in existence.

The song that made them both indulge in a glance towards the person they loved. The person they'd been in danger of losing, but now held their love anew.

The song that made them miss the deer.

The deer in the middle of the road as Mike accelerated to fifty miles per hour.

The deer that registered as a foreign object, possibly even a human, in that split second of life.

The deer that he tried to avoid with a yank of the steering wheel, but instinct, or perhaps destiny, made him pull left towards the trees, rather than right into the empty lane. His brain had told him not to drive into oncoming traffic, without registering that it was clear in that direction.

The deer that meant they ploughed into a tree so fast that neither of them would remember this moment. Instead they would remember the one before. The one where they'd glanced into each other's eyes and known they'd fixed what had been broken. That they had everything to look forward to. That their love wasn't ordinary, it was extraordinary.

The deer remained unscathed and sauntered away so that minutes later, when the crash was discovered, the cause was nowhere in sight. And the journey of their lives was over.

CHAPTER FORTY-TWO

ZACK

Considering the time of night, the hospital was more alive than Zack would have liked. It made his escape less inconspicuous than he would have preferred. Any explanation about getting some fresh air would be met with raised eyebrows when they saw his bag. Fortunately, he'd had the foresight to hide it further off the ward, so when he used that excuse with one of the night staff, they were too busy to question it in any depth.

Using a public toilet further along the corridor, he changed into his outside clothing so his hospital-issued pyjamas wouldn't give him away. He made sure his hospital band was removed as well so it also wouldn't give the game away.

After navigating two stairwells and another corridor, the outside air hit him like a welcome greeting. He was going to miss Ireland and he vowed to himself that he would come here again. He just had to hope that next time round he would be feeling much better. That he wasn't left experiencing this weird in-between where he currently was, as though he was lost somehow.

Larry beeped his horn to get Zack's attention, which was

undoubtedly the stupidest thing to do when they were attempting a stealthy escape.

Horns did not equal stealth, but by the time Zack made it into the van, he was too out of breath to tell Larry off.

'Let's get out of here,' Larry said, doing a suitably fast wheel-spin that pinned Zack to his seat.

'Could you be any less subtle?'

'You're the one who wants to be kidnapped.'

'I thought we agreed – you can't be kidnapped if you're willing to leave.'

'True, true. But when we tell this tale to our kids and grand-kids in the future, I want you to remember that I was the hero.'

'You make it sound like I'm going to misremember some-thing. I'll only ever need to tell them the actual tale for them to know you *are* my fucking hero.' Zack's breath was beginning to calm now. That returning sense of tranquillity needed to remain with him. It needed to travel all the way across the Irish Sea and get them safely to the UK. They couldn't afford for there to be any further medical emergencies on their way home. Especially as they weren't supposed to be on their way there.

'What's the plan then, hero?' Zack asked, realising he didn't know completely. It had gone from Larry making a plan to suddenly being ready in the early hours of the morning. The fast turnaround was enough to confuse even Zack.

'I figured if we were going to do it, it was best to do it without overthinking and over-planning. We're due to be on the ferry at eight this morning. I'm hoping that by leaving early, the hospital staff won't even notice you're gone until at least handover time. And by then, we should already be on our way. If we're really lucky, we'll have made it to Wales by the time they realise something is amiss.'

'Can we go any faster?'

'Getting there early isn't going to make the ferry arrive sooner. And this is going to get me in enough trouble without being done for speeding as well. You just put your head back and try to get some sleep. Your only role today is to rest.'

'Shouldn't be too difficult,' Zack said, without wanting to admit that his heart was beating harder than usual. And as he rested his head back, as instructed, his heart refused to take the same relaxed stance.

It hammered as if it wanted to make its way out of his ribcage. As if it knew the route they were taking and wanted to lead the way.

When they arrived at the ferry port and waited in the queue, the pounding reached a peak. Having not experienced adrenaline on any scale for some while, Zack's body was now responding to that rush of fear, leaving pins and needles in his limbs as if his blood supply no longer knew which part of the body to go to. All equilibrium was lost and the sensation was making him dizzy.

Rest back. Relax.

Rest back. Relax.

That was the mantra going through his head on repeat in an attempt to make his body respond and not keep up the drumming that felt somewhere close to a cardiac arrest. Zack dreaded to think what his heart rate was but, whatever happened, they had to get on the boat. They had to get out of the country. They had to be on their way to Chloe. He'd never been more certain of anything.

'You got your passport handy if we need it?' Larry asked, as the dormant row of cars came to life.

'In my pocket.' Zack gestured to his shirt.

'Great. Pretend you're asleep. The less suspicious we look, the better.'

Zack shut his eyes and continued his mantra – *Rest back. Relax* – as they trundled closer towards the ferry.

When they were stopped to show their paperwork, Zack kept his eyes closed as instructed.

It was only when he heard the words, 'You're grand,' and the van started to move forward once more, that he finally felt his heart begin to relax.

They just had to hope that the rest of their journey home was plain sailing.

CHAPTER FORTY-THREE

CHLOE

Chloe waited for her sisters to arrive with an impatience she'd never experienced before. It was beyond frustrating to feel as if, once again, her destiny lay in other people's hands.

She had to remind herself that looking after her health had to be the number one priority. Being fed up with people who only had her best interests at heart was never going to get her anywhere.

When her sisters didn't arrive on time, though, it didn't help her mood. They were never late, which made her worry in that jaw-grinding, nail-biting way that was never pleasant.

Half an hour after they were supposed to arrive and still hadn't, Chloe called Alice using Leona's phone after her text messages had gone unanswered.

There was no reply.

As she was more mobile than she had been on her last stay here, she wandered to the nurses' station to see if they knew any more. Perhaps they'd have left a message.

'No, they've not left any message,' the kind nurse told Chloe, 'but you know your sisters are never away for long. They're probably caught up in traffic.' The rational reassurance was what Chloe needed, but it didn't untie the knots in her gut.

Something was wrong. But she had no idea what or how to find out.

In the circumstances, there was very little to be done other than wait. Waiting should have been a speciality of hers given that her life had been spent in hospitals and appointments waiting for the next test or the next check, but it turned out this kind was much harder. It gave her a small insight into how it must have been for her sisters over all these years. The waiting. The not knowing.

Ten minutes late was forgetting a set of keys.

Half an hour could be blamed on traffic.

An hour was a road block they'd struggled to get around.

Two hours was unheard of and hard to explain away.

It didn't help that Chloe's skin was still a dishwater grey and she wasn't up to starting a search herself. She hounded one nurse enough for her to check what other numbers they had on Chloe's file, but they all went unanswered.

When lunch was delivered, Chloe couldn't stomach a morsel. How could she when she didn't know what was going on? When the stable certainty of her sisters' frequent visits had come to a sudden stop. It wasn't even like she could blame getting the time wrong when it was a given that when visiting hours started at least one of her sisters would arrive.

At 2.43, a full forty-three minutes into afternoon visiting hours, at last, Alice made an appearance.

'Where have you been? What's going on?' Chloe didn't try to hide the panic from her voice.

'Nothing to worry about.'

What was it about that kind of statement that made every neuron she had go into total overdrive? 'What do you mean, nothing to worry about? I've done nothing but worry.'

'I've been sorting out your phone. You know the phone

signal is rubbish in the shopping centre, otherwise I would have let you know.'

'What about Leona? Why didn't she come instead or at least let me know?'

'I'm sorry. I'm here now. Panic over.'

Chloe wasn't sure about that. The sense of panic hadn't left her yet. And what Alice was saying didn't quite ring true or explain everything.

'You've never been late before. Not without letting me know what was going on. And Leona's phone was left with me so I could be contacted. What's going on? Is one of you ill?'

'Honestly, it's nothing I want you to worry about. Do you want to know the good news?'

'What?'

'They've managed to switch your information onto a new phone while the other one is sent off for repair. Good job you had insurance for it.'

Despite being left with the distinct sense she still wasn't being told everything, Chloe had one other pressing matter she wanted to ask. 'Is the message from Zack still on there?'

'Yes, the guy said he managed to transfer everything over, so all your messages and photos and things have been saved.' Alice passed Chloe the phone.

It was identical to the model that had broken, so it was easy to navigate and find her way to the message that had partly been responsible for her ending up here.

It confirmed what she'd been dreading. Zack was also unwell but, worse than that, he was in Ireland, hundreds of miles away and with a sea dividing them. She shared those facts with her sister.

'Do you believe me when I say seeing Zack is the only thing that's going to make me feel better?'

Alice glanced towards the window. Outside the clouds were an ominous grey colour, not unlike Chloe.

The fact she was unable to look Chloe directly in the eye sent further panic through her system. 'Is everything okay? Has something happened to Zack?'

And if something had, did that also spell the end for Chloe?

'I'm not sure what to believe anymore. I think I believe it because I want to believe it. Because if I do, then I don't have to worry about the real reason you're here.'

'Have you spoken to him?'

'No.'

'Then what's changed? After visiting the crash site, you were on my side.'

Chloe knew the whole theory seemed impossible. She'd not believed it herself until she'd been to where the crash had happened. Now it made total sense and she understood what Zack had been on about. She thought Alice understood too.

'I just... I don't know. Why don't you ring him? Find out how he is? Establish some facts and we'll go from there.'

Chloe did as suggested, but with one eye on her sister. She couldn't place what was wrong, but something definitely was.

But it wasn't possible to establish any more facts when the call went straight to answerphone. 'No answer,' Chloe said.

'Maybe try again in a while?'

They sat in silence after that. Chloe didn't know what to say to her sister when the answers were all rebuffs. And she didn't know what to do about trying to find Zack when she hadn't even managed to speak to him.

All she knew was that they were both back in hospital in two different countries and her sister, who wasn't known for being dishonest, was definitely not telling Chloe the whole truth.

CHAPTER FORTY-FOUR

ZACK

Having made it onto the ferry and into their cabin, Zack was now battling every nautical mile.

Prior to his ferry trip in Dingle, he'd never been one for being seasick, but life was now making up for that fact in abundance. So much so that he hadn't been able to rest in his bunk bed as planned. Instead, he'd not been able to leave the tiny confines of the ensuite toilet.

Other than the loo, there was nowhere else to sit, so he'd bunkered down on the floor, its industrial lino glinting at him when he tried to stare at somewhere other than the toilet pan. He filled and flushed it three times before his nausea even considered subsiding slightly.

Larry had already headed off to see if there was anything available on board that would help with seasickness.

It left Zack with only a sink as a friend, and even he was sensible enough to know that if the only way he could get up would be by pulling on that, then maybe he was safer on the floor until Larry returned.

The small room had no external light. There was a small space with a shower and, with the sickness fading, Zack shuffled himself over there, using a towel as a pillow, resting against the wall. This was not how he had envisaged this journey going, and it didn't bode well with them barely half an hour into their trip. They didn't want to have to draw any attention to themselves, and retching up the contents of his guts and then some was only unproblematic if he stuck to the cabin.

'Everything all right in there?' Larry asked on his return.

Zack must have nodded off as he jerked awake at the question, nearly knocking his head on the shower taps.

The brightness of the artificial lighting danced before his eyes in a way that was blinding, while his brain slowly adjusted into some kind of understanding of where he was and what he was doing there.

'I've been better.' The gruffness in his voice was evident and there was an acid sting at the back of his throat.

'I got you some water and a seasickness band. Not sure how much good it'll do at this stage, though.'

Zack accepted both with an appreciative nod. He slipped the sickness band onto his wrist and pressed on it like the instructions suggested, hoping for a miracle. Perhaps if he concentrated on doing this and only this it would distract him enough to not hurl again.

'Do you think you're done being sick? You can't sleep down there. You'll end up with a damaged spine if nothing else.'

'I just didn't want to risk trying to get up without you about.'

'Blimey. Does that mean you were being sensible for once?'

'I guess it pays to be on the odd occasion.'

Larry offered his hand and Zack gladly accepted it as he levered himself up and took a moment or two to check that the world wasn't swimming as badly as it had been just minutes before.

'Is it a bug, do you think? Or just being on the ferry that's done it?'

Moving towards the bed was creating a new kind of dizziness that Zack really didn't want. When he'd been at the hospital he hadn't felt as bad. Not great, but well enough to sit and be bored. He'd hoped that travelling would have been the same. Well enough to sit, only without the boredom because he was on his way home. It turned out that sitting wasn't even an option at this stage. He didn't have the energy within him to do anything other than lie down, pressing the small button on his sickness band again.

'It might be a bug.' A bug sounded like a good option. A bug was transient. It might not be great now, but it would be gone in twenty-four hours.

'It's not a bug though, is it?'

Zack would love it to be, but his hammering heart told him different. 'I'm not sure. We'll blame seasickness for now. It's settled a bit. Hopefully I can get some sleep.'

'You're not going to sleep without this by your side.' Larry plonked down the waste bin, which held a flimsy bin liner.

The noise of metal hitting the floor put Zack's teeth on edge and made the nausea sweep through him once more, but he was too empty for any further vomiting sessions.

Instead, for the next few hours he fell into a half-sleep where his dreams were far too vivid. He was back at his flat, only the layout was different and, as he went in, all of his ex-girlfriends were lined up ready to greet him. Only, at least 50 per cent of them weren't happy to see him. Next he was at his mother's graveside, and that sense of loss for a moment was as acute as the day it happened. Next he was at Larry's parents' house for a roast dinner as he'd so often been since they'd taken him in, and continued to treat him as if he were one of their own. Then there was the chainsaw that was able to cut through flesh and bone. The one that carved its way into his chest and should have killed him. The memory he shouldn't be able to recall because it should have finished him. Instead, here it was terrifying him with its accuracy and detail.

'Zack. Zack. You okay?'

The voice was hard to trace, to know where it should sit in amongst everything that was going on in his head. It was familiar yet far away.

'Zack. Come on, man. We need to get back to the car soon.'

It was someone he knew. He was certain of that. Opening his eyes was going to help. When he did, the brightness was blinding, so he closed them again.

A hand on his shoulder gave him a gentle shake. 'Jeez, man, you're burning up.' The same hand landed on his forehead and, once again, he was reminded of his mother. 'Shit!'

It couldn't be his mother, though. She never swore, no matter the circumstances.

'Zack, bro. I'm gonna need you to sit up for me and take some tablets.'

Another shake of the shoulder brought Zack back to whatever senses still remained.

'What's going on?'

'Do you know where we are?'

It looked as if they were in something like a prison cell. 'No, I don't,' Zack said, as he wondered if their antics had landed them in jail.

'We're going to arrive in Pembroke port soon and then I'm taking you to a hospital, where you should be.'

The penny very gradually dropped and clattered around his headspace, much like the sound of the metal bin. They'd been in Ireland and they were trying to get home. Zack needed to see Chloe and everything would be okay again.

Very gingerly, Zack managed to haul himself to sitting, every inch of him hurting as if he'd done ten rounds with Mike Tyson.

'That's the ticket,' Larry said as he gave him a hand. 'I want you to take some paracetamol. You have a temperature, so hopefully these will help bring it down and buy us some time.'

Larry offered a packet of pills and a bottle of water.

It took some fumbling to release two tablets from their foil. It took even more effort to place them on his tongue and swallow them down with some water. Once they were down the hatch, Zack cupped his hand and filled it with a dash of water to splash over his face. It only made him feel fractionally more human.

'What's the plan now?' Zack's head needed some clarification.

'When they give a shout-out on the tannoy, we need to head for the van. We can take the lift to make life a bit easier. Once we're in there, you just need to stay well and I'll drive for as long as I can. But if I'm worried about you, we'll be stopping at the nearest hospital available. And, as things stand, that might be the first one we come across.'

Now Zack was upright, certain things were clicking into place. What Larry had just told him wasn't the exact plan. The plan had been to sail smoothly back to the UK to be reunited with Chloe. That was what they should be doing. 'What about Chloe?' His voice trailed off at the realisation he was being irrational.

'Chloe's going to have to wait. I was hoping this was going to be an easier trip and the doctors were just being overly cautious by keeping you in. But so far you've chucked up enough to fill the Irish Sea and you're spiking a temp. Both things that I am in no way, shape or form qualified to deal with. Especially if they're a sign of anything else being wrong.'

It was almost as if Larry knew, like Zack did, that his heart was unravelling. That the things that were happening weren't the sort that would come and go. That this was to do with the heart he was holding on to. Barely. And now, by its own malfunctioning, it might deprive them of ever completing the journey they'd set out on. They might make it back to the UK, but they weren't going to make it to Chloe. 'If I manage to get back to the van, just promise me you'll get me as far as you can. If it's not Chloe's doorstep, then the nearest hospital to her.'

'Let's just stick to getting you into the same country first, before we get all fanciful.'

As expected, the tannoy buzzed with instructions about passengers returning to their vehicles.

'That's our cue. Are you going to be able to manage it?'

Zack found he was orientated enough to know he was in a cabin, but not strong enough to stand up without a great amount of effort. When he did manage to get upright, he might as well have been a dandelion head about to get blown away by the wind. With some grit and determination, he made it along the corridor to the lift, leaning on Larry on the occasions no one was watching.

Finally reaching their destination, it was a great relief to flop into the passenger seat of the van. Now, the main concern was getting past the customs staff. They had to hope that in the hours Zack had been missing, no one had put out an alert. It wasn't as though leaving hospital was breaking the law, even if it wasn't sensible. With a brief look at their paperwork, they were waved through. Having breezed through, they were on the home straight.

But it didn't take long for the effects of the paracetamol to wear off, and even Zack knew his temperature was on the rise when he started to sweat profusely from every part of his body. The dreams followed soon after. At first they were his own, then they switched to Mike's memories, before becoming a mishmash of the two that felt abstract. There were ones where the colours in the picture were all mixed up. Where things that should be blue were red and the greens were yellows. Where the voices didn't match the faces. Where everything was confused, and a room became the size of a box and stairs became a forest. Until nothing made sense. Nothing at all.

Because Zack was no longer able to draw a line between what was real and what was imagined.

So when he saw the sign saying Accident and Emergency, he had no idea what parts of that were real. Or if it was anywhere close to the place he needed to be.

Because the cure for this heart wasn't going to be found in the medicine cabinet of any A&E department. There was only one place it would be found and, in the confusion of his delirium, he had no idea how far away that was.

CHAPTER FORTY-FIVE

CHLOE

'Are you sure you're telling me everything?' Chloe asked Alice before she left for the night.

'Of course. Your phone just took longer than I thought it would. No need to worry.'

Chloe should have been reassured by Alice's words, but it was the way she couldn't look Chloe in the eye that had her questioning what was going on. Alice might have been saying all the right things, but the mannerisms going with them weren't the ones Chloe was used to.

With her replacement phone in hand, and Leona's phone returned via Alice, Chloe knew the only detective work she could do was to contact Leona. She was supposed to have visited with Alice today, and the fact she hadn't gave enough cause to ask the question.

> Hi. What were you up to this afternoon? I thought I was going to see you. Hope all is okay? Love Chlo xx

She thought the tone of the message was about as right as she was ever going to get it. Not too accusatory or uncaring. But it asked the question that might give her a bit more information about what was going on.

It was after pressing send and while she was waiting for an answer that she noticed the change happening.

If she had a colour chart, she was now blush pink. In a matter of minutes, she watched as she went from the grey she'd become used to, to this new shade as her capillaries filled in the way they should.

She'd never believed in miracles, but here she was watching one.

And it could only mean one thing. It meant Zack was *here*.

CHAPTER FORTY-SIX

CHLOE

Chloe ran. In a way that hadn't been possible only minutes before, she ran as if life itself depended on it.

Because without a doubt she knew. There would be no hanging around on benches for weeks on end for her, because she knew the only place that Zack would be headed was A&E. She'd never had such conviction about anything else before in her life.

'Should you be...' a nurse from her ward said as they passed in the corridor.

But Chloe's pace stopped her from listening to the rest of the sentence. The only thing she should be doing was finding Zack. It was no longer enough to be in the same vicinity. She knew she needed to see him, even if going at this pace was going to finish her.

But that was the thing... she felt fine. Nothing like she had felt over the past few weeks, since he'd been gone. But the sudden change gave her a sure sense that something was wrong. This felt different from the buzz of being near him that she usually felt. This felt as though she'd been given the strength of two people and if she had, what did that mean? All she knew was that she had to find out.

The two flights of stairs and the endless corridor she had to navigate felt like the longest journey of her life. The impulse to see him overtook everything, and even that didn't make sense. She was running towards the man who had hurt her. The man who had turned her down and walked away. But now, it was different. Now she knew he hadn't been making it up. That the heart inside her chest had once belonged to the heart inside his. And for whatever reason, they needed to be together again.

When she reached the internal entrance to A&E, the colour of the doors changed to red. It gave a clear indication that this was where the most urgent cases were dealt with. It was where the severity of a patient's condition was assessed.

Chloe charged in. Only to find an empty corridor.

There were no people going back and forth here. Instead it was filled with a static anticipation. Of what had been and what was to come. She wondered if this static energy could point her in the right direction.

When the corridor did come to life with people, they all headed in the same direction, not even looking her way.

Their faces told her that wherever they were headed, it was urgent. As she drew closer, above the room was the word RESUS.

Then she saw him. Zack.

Zack had a tube in his mouth and his tongue looked blue.

'Clear!' someone said, as she followed through the door.

Chloe didn't clear, not wanting to move away from him now she'd found him. Instead, she stepped closer. This couldn't be real. If she was feeling better, he should be too. That was how it worked. That was what he'd told her.

'You can't be in here,' a member of staff said.

She didn't know which one. The only person she was paying any attention to was Zack.

'Chloe!'

Someone saying her actual name got her attention, so she turned in their direction.

Cowering against the wall was Zack's friend, Larry. He appeared to be half the man he had been when she'd briefly met him, but as he was watching his best friend die for a second time it wasn't surprising.

'No pulse. Charge again.'

'I don't understand.' She had to say it out loud to someone who might comprehend what she was on about.

Larry wiped a hand over his face, his tears evident. 'He told me I needed to get him to you. I don't understand either. This was meant to fix things.'

And it had. For her.

A hundred thoughts rushed through her head. What if they weren't connected? What if his energy had only made her better? What if none of this mattered? What if none of it was true? What if it was true, but it had gone wrong somehow? All of those things and more pushed through her as Zack's body convulsed with another surge of electricity they were putting through him.

And then there was only one thought.

Stay alive.

Be alive.

Alive.

She willed it so much in her head that the word became strange, as if it wasn't spelled right or it had some other meaning that no one had ever told her. Because no matter how much she thought it or wondered how it was spelled, it didn't work. Zack's tongue was still blue. His limbs were mottled. And even though they were shouting the word 'clear', she still stepped closer. She needed to see him. She wanted to tell him it would all be okay like her sisters so often did, and even though she didn't ever know if it was true, hearing those words was a comfort itself.

But would they ever be enough when someone was dying?

Even if it wasn't enough, she still wanted to say them.

Another step closer as his body convulsed once again.

'You shouldn't be—' a nurse said.

'It's okay. Chloe knows him. She's his girlfriend,' Larry said from his position pressed against the wall.

'You still can't be here. We're doing everything we can. We need you to wait outside. Perhaps you could take her.' The nurse gestured to Larry.

Neither of them moved straight away.

Leaving Zack here felt like the last thing Chloe should be doing. Not when she knew they should be together. Till death do us part might not have been a vow they'd made between them, but the previous two owners of their hearts had. She was sure of it. She'd *seen* it.

'If you don't leave now, I'm going to call security.'

The words made Chloe want to cry. They were hard to hear, although the nurse was only trying to act in Zack's best interests. They went against everything her instincts were telling her.

'Okay,' she said, turning reluctantly, not wanting to look away.

The repeated ritual occurred behind her: checking the heart rhythm, determining what it was, deciding what dose of electricity to put through him, and the noise of his body moving but his heart still not responding.

Even though she'd been warned and forced to go, the longing to tell him it would all be okay was stronger.

It was irrational and stupid, but she made a one-eighty-degree turn, looping by the nurse that stood in her way. She wanted him to be able to hear her, and that wasn't going to happen if she was at the foot of his bed.

The rest of the medical team were too intent on Zack to notice what she was up to. She wasn't even sure what she was up to. All she knew was that she wanted to be closer to Zack. She wanted to say hello and that she'd missed him before it was too late for him to hear those things.

More medics or possibly security guards came into the room, and while everyone peered in the direction of the newcomers (apart from the nurse, who looked ready to rugby tackle Chloe), she took her moment to advance.

Zack's face was Pebble Grey. He was the same shade she'd been on her colour chart, only the added dashes of blue made it all the more telling. Where she had been close to death, he was so much further into his demise.

'It's all going to be okay,' she said. Those words that, despite their instant reassurance, had often seemed empty on reflection, devoid of truth when the world felt like it was tumbling. But they were the best words she had. And the best ones she'd heard the many times she'd been in hospital. They were the essence of comfort and sometimes that was exactly what was needed. Like tea and buttery toast on a cold blustery day.

She touched his bare arm in the hope he would know it was her. That her comforting words and this small connection wouldn't be missed, even if he was as close to being gone as it was possible to be. And with the touch came a flash.

A bright light filled the room. Not like the electricity from the defibrillator, which was steady and controlled. This was lightning from a storm, flashing bright. Then it was gone.

Everyone in the room remained still for a moment, trying to mentally calibrate what had happened.

'What was that?' someone asked.

'Is everyone okay?' a doctor tried to clarify.

'Do we carry on? What was it? An electrical surge? Are we safe?' a nurse said.

'It was her.' The rugby-tackle nurse gawped. The one who moments before had been calling for security.

'It was Chloe,' Larry said.

No one spoke then. Instead, everyone looked to Zack, who was dusky pink and trying to get up.

CHAPTER FORTY-SEVEN

ZACK

The scene before Zack didn't make sense immediately. He was in a room full of medical people he didn't know, and they all looked very confused.

'Did the defib discharge? Is it faulty?' someone said.

Zack hoped the questions weren't directed at him. The last thing he remembered was arriving at the cabin on the ship they were taking home. Nothing about what was happening now made sense until he saw her. *Chloe*. They'd made it.

'Chloe,' he said, spitting the piece of plastic out of his mouth so his words weren't inhibited.

'Everyone step away from the bed. I'm going to turn the defibrillator off to make sure we're all safe. We'll get another machine if it's needed again. I'm not sure if this one is safe, but at least we have a good outcome.'

Chloe had a hold of Zack's hand and she didn't move anywhere, despite the instructions about stepping away.

Rebel. He knew there was a reason he liked her.

'It's all going to be okay,' she said, as if it were a mantra she'd been repeating all her life and wasn't able to let go of.

'The defibrillator is neutralised. Can I get an okay from

each of you if you're unharmed? We'll start with me and go clockwise. Okay.'

'Okay.'

'Okay.'

They continued around the room until all ten people had chanted the word. Zack had never been more confused in all his life.

The circle of okays stopped at Chloe.

'Are you okay?' someone asked her.

'How are we defining okay?'

'You've had no ill effects from the electrical pulse that occurred?'

'Okay,' she laughed. She laughed so hard it was almost a sob. 'What did I tell you, Zack... Everything's going to be okay, and here you are with a roomful of them!'

'I'm okay,' Larry's voice said from the back of the room. He was crouching down on the floor. 'Thanks for asking, everyone.'

'What is going on?' Zack finally ventured to ask.

The doctor who'd headed up the chorus of okays turned to him. 'When I write up your medical notes today, I'm going to record that what's happened is nothing short of a miracle. Now let me do some checks on you to make sure we're not all hallucinating.'

'A miracle?' Zack queried.

The doctor nodded. 'The closest I've ever been to seeing one.'

'I didn't think you were supposed to get more than one in a lifetime,' Zack said.

'This isn't your first time then?'

'No, but I'm very much hoping it's my last.'

CHAPTER FORTY-EIGHT

CHLOE

Nobody, least of all Chloe's sisters, was keen on the idea of Chloe and Zack being on the same ward. With it being a specialist heart unit, there were four different wards they could be admitted to and they'd previously been on different wards, but this time Chloe wanted them to be together.

There weren't many things that Chloe was insistent on, but this was one of them. Having seen Zack at death's door, she now wanted him as close to her as possible.

Eventually, because Chloe had refused to leave his side otherwise, they'd admitted him onto her ward in the bay next door. It was close enough for her to be happy. At any moment, if she was worried, she could go and check he was okay.

The following morning, as soon as visiting hours started, Chloe was met by both of her sisters.

'We need a family meeting,' was the first thing Alice said.

'I'm in hospital. We can't all have a cosy chat in the lounge at the moment.' The fact it already sounded like she was being told off didn't bode well for Chloe.

'They've told us we can use their office.'

'What's this about?' Chloe suddenly found herself on the defensive.

'You running off the ward, for starters,' Leona said.

'I haven't been out of the hospital. It's hardly running away.'

'Can we go to the office to continue talking?'

'No.'

'But we need to talk.'

'So let's talk like civilised adults here. I'm not going anywhere.' She hadn't argued to ensure Zack was close to her only for her sisters to drag her away. If they'd been there yesterday they'd know why.

Alice and Leona glanced at each other, saying nothing.

'What? What is it that you can't say out loud? It can't be about interior decorating choices, that's for sure.'

Chloe crumpled onto her bed. The past twenty-four hours had been so tiring and she wasn't able to make complete sense of everything that had happened. She was so well now in contrast to how she had been feeling, she wouldn't be surprised if discharge was mentioned soon. She wanted to talk to her sisters about what had gone on and not feel like they were about to scold her.

'She needs to know,' Leona said.

'I know, but I can't force her to come with us.'

'Is it about Zack?' Chloe asked, knowing her sisters had never approved of their friendship. The reunion certainly didn't seem to be going down well.

Alice looked at her properly for the first time. 'No, not exactly. It's about *your* heart.'

That piqued Chloe's interest enough to engage. 'I'll come and have a private meeting if you'll tell me what's going on.'

Once they were all gathered in a room normally reserved for ward meetings, both of Chloe's sisters wore the same expression: one of reluctance.

'What's going on? You're being odd.'

'I wasn't sure whether to tell you. I'd thought perhaps it was best not to,' Alice said.

'Tell me what?'

'I think you already knew something was amiss when we didn't all turn up like we normally would the other day.'

'What's up? Is one of you ill?' All sorts of scenarios went through Chloe's head, but then she remembered Alice had mentioned it was to do with *her* heart.

'Nothing like that. It's to do with what you told me.'

'I'm not following.'

'About your heart and Zack's and how he seemed to think they were connected.'

'Right? And?'

'I hope you don't mind, but I told Leona.'

It was a little too late if she did mind. 'That's fine. What I don't understand is why you both look so upset?'

Surely their reunion was something to celebrate?

'I also told her about the fact you know where the crash site is. The place where you both believe this all started. I said that when we were there, you became overwhelmed and to me it was almost like you were reliving the accident, you were so upset. I also told her how it had affected me at the time, and how I'd reached a point where I wasn't sure if it was the place itself giving me that feeling or just seeing you so upset that did it.'

Throughout Alice's short speech, Leona nodded and uh-huhed in all the right places.

'I thought being there helped you see it was true as well.'

'It did, at the time. But it was like one of those weird memories that you want to hold on to, but it fades. It became less tangible with time.'

'So I suggested she went back to see if she still sensed the same thing without you there,' Leona said.

'Oh. So did you?'

'We both did. We figured if one of us sensed it and if Larry had sensed it, then Leona would too.'

'And did you?' Chloe knew it didn't make sense, but she wanted her sisters to believe it as much as she did.

'That's the thing. We didn't really have the chance to, because we met someone else who has.'

'I'm not following.'

'It's why we thought it was important to get you by your-self,' Leona said, a small smile reaching her features.

'We thought it was better to tell you without you being influenced by Zack,' Alice said.

'Why would you worry about that?'

'Because he seems to have had an effect on you, but it's important that you make your own decision without any pressure from elsewhere. Not even your sisters.'

'Pressure over what?'

'When we arrived at the site, there was already someone there.'

'Who?'

'Her name's Isabelle. She's the daughter of Mike and Susan.'

'What did she say?'

'That the family had been continuing to visit the crash site as they felt some kind of connection there, like you had. She'd like to meet you. All of their children would.'

'Just me? What about Zack?'

'We didn't tell her about Zack. I think the fact we were there was overwhelming enough at the time, and we didn't know Zack was back.'

'Are you upset that he's back?' Neither of them seemed to be pleased about it, as far as Chloe could tell.

'We're glad that you're feeling better, but we don't want you hurt again. You might say that he's made you feel well, but all we remember is him breaking your heart.'

'So that's why you didn't mention him to Isabelle?'

'We didn't mention him because we want you to make this decision on your own. Speaking to the family would be a big thing. Especially as it wouldn't be through the usual channels where you'd have more guidance. They might have certain expectations. They might want to listen to your heart. They might want to work out why we've all circled back to the spot where their parents died.'

The thought of making her own decision almost made Chloe laugh out loud. For so much of her life, decisions had been made for her. It was either the doctors or her parents and then her sisters deciding what was best for her. She much preferred choosing what colour scheme to go for over whether to meet the family of her donor. With what she'd witnessed yesterday, she wouldn't put it past her heart jumping outside of her chest to get what it wanted.

'If I do, I'll do it with Zack. Now he's back, I don't think he's running away again anytime soon. I'll talk to him about it.'

'Just be careful.'

'Careful about what?' Her sisters were making it sound like they were practising unsafe sex.

'Just, you know.' Leona shrugged.

'I don't.'

'This connection that exists, hasn't Zack always been after finding a way for you to disconnect? Meeting the family may be the thing that makes that happen. It's a big thing and we wouldn't necessarily encourage it if we didn't think it might help you. We just don't want him to end up breaking your heart again, no matter what happens,' Alice said.

'I'm not sure why you all keep going on about him breaking my heart. It was never like that.'

But as her sisters exchanged their usual knowing looks, Chloe knew that it *was* like that. Her heart had been broken. It had been broken in every sense, far too often. And now she didn't know what would happen, because even though Zack was back, she was pretty sure nothing between them had changed.

CHAPTER FORTY-NINE

ZACK

In a quiet moment in the middle of the night, Zack did something that patients weren't supposed to do. He was becoming quite excellent at doing things that patients weren't supposed to do, and it was hard to gauge whether this was better or worse than self-discharging without letting the staff know and running off to another country. Once again, he wasn't sure whether what he was doing was illegal or not, but he was quite certain it would be frowned upon.

When the staff had been occupied, like a ninja he went and grabbed his notes before returning to his bed space with them pressed against his chest. They weren't the thick bundle that were stored in patient records and yet to make it to the ward. These were the notes solely created for this admission. He wanted to find out if reading them would help fill in the blanks, between falling ill on the ship and waking up in the hospital, peering at the strangest scene he'd ever been a part of.

The paper crinkled far too loudly for the time of night, but he figured it was better to do this quickly. That way he was less likely to get caught.

The doctor's scribble was hard to make out. It told him

about being an emergency admission and it mentioned having been in hospital in Ireland, in relation to his heart. There were mentions of limited signs of life and the need for immediate resuscitation intervention.

Even though he'd known it was true, seeing it in black and white was bringing it home.

Next there was information about the medications they'd used to try and save him. The drugs they'd pumped into his body. And alongside that, the voltage levels they'd used to try and revive his heart. After each, it stated the outcome.

Unsuccessful. Unsuccessful. Unsuccessful.

Not one of them had resulted in successful resuscitation, which begged the question: how was he standing here?

It was the note after that, confirmed with various different pieces of handwriting and signed with initials for each one, which gave him his answer.

A notable flash of light was witnessed by all members of staff present not long after a discharge from the defibrillator. The paddles were not on the patient at this time and a charge had not been dispensed. Shortly after this, the patient's sinus rhythm was noted to return, along with consciousness. As an unplanned discharge occurred from the defibrillator, the safety of everyone present was checked. All there were unharmed, and our joint conclusion of the event is that despite the paddles not being in situ, the shock that it created caused the patient's heart to restart.

All the initials and short sentences followed the statement, obviously noting they were in agreement. One of those stood out as Zack browsed through them. It said: *Satisfactory outcome and nothing short of a miracle.*

After trying to digest the information, he managed to

successfully return the notes to the desk without anyone noticing they'd been gone.

For the rest of the night, Zack had strange dreams, and the following day continued in a daze. He was reunited with Chloe. He was better. He had everything he wanted, but that didn't explain why he was feeling hollow.

It was nearly lunchtime when he first saw her. She was wearing dungarees with a pink shirt underneath and if he didn't know better, he would have thought she was a visitor, not a patient. She looked so well and full of life and lovely. Like a flower that had grown unexpectedly even though it hadn't been tended to. Zack felt as if he were seeing her for the very first time. How had he missed how beautiful she was? And what strength she had?

'How are you feeling? You're looking so much better than yesterday,' Chloe said.

Zack realised he was staring. The reunion they'd had hadn't been the one he'd wanted. He wondered if they could redo it right now. Whether he could embrace her in an attempt to scratch away any awkwardness that might be gathering between them.

'If I'm honest, I feel like I woke up on another planet and I don't feel quite like my feet are planted firmly on the ground yet.'

'I'm not surprised really, given the circumstances.'

'What did you make of the flash of light?'

'How do you know about that? I thought you were unconscious.'

'I sneaked a peek at my notes. Wondered if they would tell me a bit more than the curious discussions some of the doctors have been having.'

Chloe sat on the bed next to him and glanced around to see if she'd be heard. 'The thing was, I didn't just see it, I *felt* it. I touched your arm and, even though it's implausible, it gave you life again. Just like you always said. That our hearts need to be together. It turned out that yesterday you really did need mine to be there.'

'Does this mean you believe me now?'

'You have to admit that it sounds mad. And yet, here we both are... alive, because we are together.'

'Together, huh?' The idea didn't scare him now like it had before. He'd been letting the past determine how he should act and that had been wrong. Now he saw Chloe for all she was and realised she was exactly the kind of person he wanted in his life.

'Not like that. I know not like that. But we both know that for now, until we've worked out how to be okay, we're going to remain in close proximity.'

'I thought we had worked it out for a while. After we kissed, I thought that might have solved everything. But there's a scene in a resuscitation room that's missing from my memory that tells me different. We weren't okay being apart at all. So tell me... what do we do next to work out how it'll be okay?' He was surprised to find he wanted kissing her again to be an option.

'Funnily enough, I've just been listening to my sisters giving us an option.'

'And what's that?'

'I'm not sure if he told you, but Larry left me the details of the crash site. Visiting there made me realise what you'd said was true. Alice took me, but Leona wanted to go as well to see if they got the same sense of some kind of energy being there, like we'd felt.'

'Did they?'

'I'm not sure if they got close enough to work that out, because someone was already there.'

'Who?'

'Mike and Susan's daughter. Apparently she'd felt a sense of something there so kept returning. When my sisters spoke to her, she wanted to meet us. Well, me. They didn't tell her that you and I had met in real life.'

'Do you want to meet her?'

'If it'll give us some answers. If it'll solve this riddle we find ourselves in.'

Zack understood. Because no one wanted to live their life attached to a stranger. Even if that stranger had become a friend. And even if his feelings had changed, it wasn't fair to muck Chloe about any more than he already had. They needed to see this through, and if this was the answer then he was all in. 'Then let's do it.'

Chloe nodded. 'I think we should. I'll set something up once they've let us out of here.'

'Right. Good.'

After that, a silence lay between them, with only the sounds of the ward continuing. Zack didn't know what to say. He'd strived to get here, feeling like it was the most important thing in the world, and now he was lost for words.

'I'm sorry for upsetting you.'

Chloe waved a hand in the air, dismissing it with a gesture. 'You don't need to apologise.'

'But I want to. It took being away to realise how I'd treated you. I used you like an object. My only regard was for your heart and being close to it. I'd been so intent on that, I'd forgotten to think about the bigger picture.' For someone who'd been lost for words, Zack now found he had verbal diarrhoea. He knew that if he carried on in this vein, he'd dig himself a hole so big he wouldn't be able to get out. 'Look, I don't want to start off on the wrong foot. How about we go back to our daily walks, starting today. If they see we can waltz around the hospital without any problems, they'll discharge us sooner.'

The hospital grounds were nowhere near as scenic as the walks they'd previously encountered. They weren't as breath-taking as the Wild Atlantic Way where Zack had been. But there was the odd tree and a couple of benches to stop at that made it more familiar territory.

'I feel like I'm starting over again. I'm no fitter now than I was when I was last discharged from hospital,' Chloe said.

'Don't go comparing your past self to your present self. Your present self will never win.'

'That's true.'

'It's easy to do, though. I mean, I'm dishing out great advice, but I do it all the time.'

'So what would your past self advise your present self to do?'

Zack ruffled his hair. 'That list is going to be longer than I'd like!'

'I've got time.'

They reached a bench and without even having to check with each other, they both took a seat. They weren't up to long walks without pit stops yet.

'First up, I'd tell myself to never attempt to do a safety video for chainsaw use because that really didn't turn out like it should have done.'

'That really was bad luck. I'm glad you're here to tell the story.'

'Me too. I know I don't talk about it much. It gives me horrendous flashbacks of that moment that could have ended so differently.'

'It is solid advice, at least. What else?'

Zack pushed his thoughts away from the scene that saw his heart in a state of disrepair. 'I'd tell myself not to be an idiot. To be honest with you right from the start about the connection we have.'

With that sentence, he realised he wanted to hold her hand. Not as a friend, but because he wanted more. To be closer to her. But he'd lost that opportunity before he'd left for Ireland.

'I don't think that was a flawed decision. We may never have become friends if you'd told me that straight away.'

'So we're still friends?' They had that at least, even if he'd lost the chance of anything else because he was an idiot.

'Of course. How could we not be?'

'Let's walk some more.' Zack held out his hand to help her up and when she took it, he felt electricity. Only this wasn't the type that he'd felt before. This was the type that stemmed from a desire that had been lying dormant before their reunion. The one that had awoken and was making him see Chloe in an entirely different light.

'I just hope we work out what's going on.'

Zack agreed in every sense. Because it was very hard to know what to do with his heart saying one thing and his head saying another. It was hard to know if they would ever align. And he knew no matter what, he never wanted to hurt Chloe again and really wished he'd never managed to in the first place.

CHAPTER FIFTY

CHLOE

Chloe and Zack had to wait patiently for five days until the hospital finally consented to discharging the pair of them. The staff hadn't been able to completely explain away their speedy recoveries, but they stopped scratching their heads when a theory was put forward that increased medications had done the trick.

They'd agreed to see how they both felt on discharge and, if necessary, Chloe could move in with Zack. Only, she wasn't sure if that was what she wanted. In the aftermath of Zack returning, she'd not had much of a chance to evaluate how she was feeling. He was back, they were both well, but what they did going forward was a puzzle she didn't know the answer to.

Because of that, she'd been concentrating solely on arranging to meet Isabelle and her siblings. It had to hold the solution. Because if it didn't, she didn't know where that left her and Zack. Flatmates for life so neither of them went into cardiac arrest?

The siblings had invited Chloe to their family home the following day, and like with so many things at the moment, she didn't know how to play her cards. Did she go alone? Did she take Zack with her? Did she tell her sisters?

Because she didn't know what to do, she decided to treat it as if she were redecorating a room and started a mood board for herself. Right now, she didn't feel like she was living her own life. Not when so much of what she was doing was anchored to what her heart wanted her to do. And the problem was, she knew that wouldn't make sense to anyone else. But wasn't it true of so many people... that often we try to meet other people's desires before even thinking about our own?

Chloe wrote small notes on all these thoughts and added them to the board. In the centre, she put her own name. She thought about all the things she liked to do... of her days at the art gallery and the paintings she liked to create and the time she spent with her sisters outside the hospital. On a separate piece of paper she wrote the name 'Susan' enclosed with a heart bubble. But working out its position wasn't easy. If it was at the centre, where a heart should be, did that mean Chloe was meeting its desires above her own? Or were they now aligned and that's what she needed to accept in order to move on? What she was coming to realise was that the discussions about moving in with Zack weren't what she wanted. They were being forced into each other's company and that was Susan's desire, not hers. She saw that now.

It made her realise that she needed to go and see the family, taking Zack with her in the hope that getting the hearts home once again would be enough to break the spell they were under. Because she really had to hope that something finally would.

CHAPTER FIFTY-ONE

CHLOE

The house was a suburban detached Georgian property. It looked as if it would have been the perfect family home, something both Susan and Mike would have worked hard towards to welcome their growing family. There was an arched porch over the front door. Before even reaching for the doorbell, every single doubt joined Chloe's anticipation of what they were doing.

This was an important meeting and it was nerve-racking in the sense that they only had one shot at this. To say the right things and give the family the comfort they no doubt needed.

'Are you ready?' Zack said, by her side.

'I just want to make sure they gain some comfort from meeting us.'

It felt like they were here to solve a riddle and that made the whole thing more disconcerting. Chloe didn't want to be neglectful of the donor family's feelings but also had to listen to her own. She'd been on the receiving end of that from Zack and wasn't about to inflict the same on other people. Not when their primary purpose today was to say thank you. Without the gifts they'd received, neither of them would be here now.

'They will.' Zack rested a reassuring arm around her shoulders. 'Remember, one step at a time.'

Pressing the doorbell was the first step, and Chloe did her best not to be nervous about those that would follow.

Isabelle opened the door, her eyes glistening as if they were ready to fill with tears at any moment. 'Hi, Chloe. It's so wonderful to meet you.'

'It's wonderful to meet you as well. This is Zack.'

As soon as they made it into the hallway, they were introduced to Isabelle's brothers, Phil and Stuart. It was strange how they all felt familiar. That even though Chloe hadn't seen pictures of Mike and Susan, she somehow was able to recognise that these were their offspring.

'We didn't bring our children as well. We thought it might be a bit much for them to understand, especially the younger ones,' Isabelle said.

'Of course.' Even though she was listening to what Isabelle was saying, Chloe couldn't help but take in the surroundings. There was a fortieth anniversary banner over the mantelpiece and on the table were lots of red sequins saying the same.

'We haven't had the heart to take it all down,' Isabelle said, noticing where Chloe's gaze was hovering. 'We'd organised a surprise party for when they returned. Dad knew about it, but it was a surprise for Mum.'

'Forty years,' Chloe whispered, her voice taken away by the impact of seeing the sign.

'Yes, they'd just been away on a cruise to celebrate. We were all waiting here when we heard the news.'

Chloe closed her eyes briefly, imagining the pain despite trying not to. 'God, that must have been so hard.'

'It was the worst party I've ever been to,' Phil said with a dry sense of humour.

'It wasn't the easiest time, but we were told about the important decision they'd made to become donors and how those wishes were going to be carried out. Because of that, a part of our mum is here in the room.'

'It's not quite the party we planned, but we do have cake. Mum would tell us off if we didn't greet visitors with high standards of hospitality, so we definitely have to treat you to tea and cake at the very least,' Stuart said. 'I'll get the kettle on.'

'Wait!' Chloe said. She didn't want to say what she was about to without them all there. 'I need to tell you something.'

'Okay, the tea can wait.'

'What is it?' Isabelle asked.

'I know that my sisters didn't mention this to you, and I thought long and hard about when to tell you, but I thought in person and soon was best.'

'Is everything okay with your heart?' Isabelle pressed a hand on Chloe's wrist.

'Yes, it is now.'

'It's not *her* heart she wants to tell you about,' Zack said.

Isabelle glanced from one to the other and a look of realisation began to wash over her. 'You?'

'As far as I can be certain, I believe your father was my heart donor.'

'You're both... You know... How did you find each other?' Isabelle's glisten turned into real tears now.

Both Phil and Stuart took Zack into a hug complete with back slaps. 'My Lord, we never thought we'd get to meet both of you, let alone have you in the same room. Let me make us all a drink and then you can tell us how you met.'

Chloe had a feeling making tea was a distraction to let them all get a hold of their emotions once more. Even she was on the edge of moving into floods of tears.

'I hope you didn't mind me telling them,' she whispered to Zack while their hosts were busy.

'It's why we're here. Any longer would have felt like we were deceiving them.'

Before long, they returned with drinks for everyone and a cake already sliced. The pile of napkins on the tray would help with any further tears.

'So, if you don't mind us asking, how did you meet? We didn't think that was possible.'

'It wasn't through any official channels,' Zack said. 'This might sound a bit strange, but my friend stumbled across an article he thought might be related, so I visited the crash site. It gave me a sense that there was more to it. That someone else had also received a heart. Later, when I was in close proximity to Chloe at the hospital, I instantly felt she'd had the other transplant. I'm sorry because I know that sounds a bit unfeasible, and we don't have any proof to confirm it for certain. We just both had a sense it was true. If I'm being completely honest, I've been seeing occasional memories that weren't mine. You three and the love your dad had for you have featured heavily.'

'It's true,' Chloe added, worried they might think they were charlatans.

'It's okay,' Isabelle reassured. 'We've all had a sense of something whenever we've gone there. The fact you've experienced memories is beyond anything we'd ever imagined. I have to admit, in the past, I always thought it was morbid when relatives would visit the spot where a loved one died. I figured it wasn't the best way in which to remember them, but then when this happened, I understood. We've had that same sense there. Like there was an unfinished sentence they wanted us to hear. It was as if it was echoing there. None of us could help visiting now and again, in the hope we'd catch what it was. That's how I met your sisters.'

'We figured that was the echo when we heard from Chloe,' Phil said. 'That they wanted us to meet you. We thought inviting you here was the best thing to do. To help finish the journey they never completed. We never thought for a moment that the echo was strong enough to bring both hearts here.'

Chloe glanced at Zack. Maybe this was it. Being here would be the thing that would complete the circle. And it was strange, to be looking at him and knowing there was love there, yet not knowing if it was her love for Zack or Susan's love for Mike.

'It would seem their love was strong enough to make that happen,' Zack said, giving Chloe a brief knee rub as he said it.

After that, Chloe didn't know what to say next or what to do, so she concentrated on her drink and eating the slice of cake she'd been given. There hadn't been any fireworks like she'd imagined there might be. All that hung in the air was a sense of sadness. This wasn't the party the siblings had planned for their parents. That party remained under a layer of dust on the sequins they never got to see.

'This might be a strange request, but can I feel your pulse? Both of you?' Phil asked.

Chloe glanced at Zack for reassurance again. This was proving to be harder than she'd ever considered possible. The want to fill the gulf of sadness and the inability to do anything other than live was something she was struggling with.

'Of course. Is that okay, Chloe?'

Zack offered his wrist over the coffee table and Chloe did the same.

Phil located Zack's pulse using two fingers on his radial pulse point. Once he was satisfied he'd located it, he did the same on Chloe's wrist using his other hand.

It was an odd moment to settle into: a stranger feeling for her pulse, while she glanced from Zack to Phil.

'Amazing,' he said, while continuing to feel for both heart-beats. 'They're completely in sync. Not a beat out of place.'

'Are they?' Chloe asked.

'I'm no expert, but your pulses don't have any difference between them.'

'Can I feel?' Isabelle asked.

Zack and Chloe both nodded their consent, and Isabelle

took her turn at feeling for both of their pulses and holding on to their wrists for a couple of minutes, followed by Stuart doing the same.

For all the monitors and tracing of their heart rhythms they'd both undergone, this wasn't a method they'd ever experienced. They'd never been in the same room while their heart activity had been charted at the same time.

'I can't believe it, but now I've felt it I know it's true. We know they're together again, wherever they are,' Isabelle said.

The three siblings comforted each other with hugs, wiping away tears, and it made Chloe realise that coming here had been the right thing to do. She might not have a clear sign that this had all meant what she'd been hoping for, but perhaps this was it... knowing that Susan and Mike's children had found the comfort they'd been after.

'I'm going to go and get some fresh air, if anyone wants to join me,' Phil said.

They were all obviously overcome with emotion. It was as if the house was too small to contain all the feelings that they were releasing and everyone, Zack and Chloe included, decided that moving outside was the right thing to do.

'I want to feel it,' Chloe said to Zack as they headed outside. 'I know they've all said our pulses are the same, but I've never felt yours to know that.'

'Same. Wouldn't it be bizarre to find out they are?'

The back garden was well kept, apart from the grass being longer than it should be. In one corner was a large shed that had been treated to regular creosote layers. Even though the garden had a pretty display of flowers, Chloe's gaze was drawn to the shed, as if she was familiar with its structure and knew what it meant.

Mike, who was so often venturing into the shed, was coming out of it, his arms wide open. After he'd squeezed her tight, he asked her if she was ready for an adventure. One where they'd

*create memories so big they wouldn't be able to squeeze them
into this lifetime. She agreed, and even though she hadn't packed
a bag, she hopped onto the bike knowing that she wanted to go on
this last journey with her soulmate.*

'Shall we then?' Zack asked, an expectant look on his face.

Chloe shook off a vision that wasn't hers, the weight of it
almost overwhelming her.

'Here?'

'Unless you want to wait and do it somewhere more
private?'

The three siblings were chatting to each other, not paying
much attention to them at that moment.

It was curiosity that was making Chloe want to know.
Surely feeling each other's pulse wasn't going to cause any problems. It was simply to clarify it wasn't imagined.

'We've got something we'd like you to have,' Isabelle said,
interrupting them.

'You don't need to give us anything. Tea and cake is more
than enough,' Chloe was quick to say.

'We're not sure that it's a useful gift. But it's more likely to
get used by one of you. Come and have a look.'

'We were just going to feel each other's pulse quickly, if
that's all right? We may have been friends for a while and
known that our hearts shared a history, but we've never checked
that.'

'Of course. We'll go and open the shed,' Phil said, and all
three of them left the pair to it.

'This isn't going to be easy. We both need to locate our own
pulse first, then the hard bit – keeping hold of that while feeling
for each other's.'

'Are we going to be okay?' Chloe asked.

'Everything's going to be okay,' Zack said, in an echo of the
words she'd said repeatedly to him when he'd needed to hear
them.

'What if...?' Chloe said, but then she didn't know how to end the sentence, not when there were so many options. What if this didn't give them the answers they were hoping for? What if they were stuck in each other's company for life? What if they weren't?

'No what-ifs. People can lose a whole life to what-ifs, when the only thing we can deal with is the here and now. Let's just take each other's pulse and go from there.'

Chloe nodded. She knew she was worrying about things that she had no earthly way of knowing or understanding. They'd brought comfort to their donors' family. That had to be enough. She located her pulse with two fingers, Zack doing the same.

They then had to try and find each other's pulse at the same time, keeping two fingers connected to their own skin and using the free fingers from the other hand to connect to the other's pulse.

They looked like two referees about to toss a coin at the beginning of a match.

It took a moment to get completely coordinated with feeling her pulse as well as tracing Zack's, and getting her brain to register which was which, but when she had, it didn't take long to confirm what they'd been told was true. Each beat had a parallel response. They were completely in sync.

'What are the odds of that?' Zack said, neither of them letting go.

Chloe let out a puff of air. 'I don't think they've ever done any studies on humans with the exact same heart rate.'

'I wonder what would happen if we were doing different things. If we were, whether they'd beat differently.'

'I think it's happening like a sign. The family needed one and this is the hearts' one sure way of giving it.'

'So do you think our hearts will beat differently from now on?'

It was a strangely intimate moment. This man who'd come into her life unexpectedly, who she'd fallen a bit in love with, but then he'd left... Only the invisible string that linked them brought them back together. And here was a piece of proof. Not one that would stand up in a court of law, but one that everyone here believed in. 'I'm not sure.'

'Would you want them to?' Zack asked.

Pulse. Pulse. Pulse. She felt the rhythm in her wrist.

Pulse. Pulse. Pulse. She felt the same rhythm in Zack's wrist.

'I don't think it's safe to fall in love with you for a second time.' There, she'd said it. If he didn't know how much it had hurt her before, maybe he would now. And now she was having to live with the bittersweetness of her hurt sitting next to the need to be with him. Not necessarily because she wanted to be there, but because this seemed to be their destiny. Even their heartbeats sang the tune of how true it was.

Zack moved nearer, if that was possible given what they were doing. 'I'm so sorry. I was so preoccupied with the history of our hearts, I forgot about the present.'

'Who knew that history could ever make the present so strange?' Because here she was in Susan and Mike's garden, feeling both of their heartbeats, but knowing that Zack and Chloe had to continue on their own journeys.

'I'm glad it has, though. It's made me re-evaluate and appreciate things like I never did before. Can you feel it?'

'Feel what?'

'Our pulses are changing.'

Now Zack had said it, it was more obvious. The gap between beats was shorter, their heart rates speeding up, but once again at the same pace. And Chloe realised it was because he was close. It was because he was so close they'd be able to kiss if they wanted to.

'I'm going to do something that I should have done properly

before. With my heart and my head totally in it. But only if you're all in as well?'

Chloe didn't need to think twice to work out what he meant. It was the same thing that had crossed her mind. But thinking about what she wanted for herself and only herself, she knew she didn't want to kiss him. Not now. Not here. Not with Susan and Mike's family looking on at them expectantly (because they were now) and with her emotions all over the place.

'There's an audience,' Chloe whispered. 'I can't answer with an audience. You'll have to ask me again later.'

With that realisation, the spell was broken. They took their hands off each other, no longer able to tell if their heartbeats were the same. All Chloe knew was that her heart had been through too much, more than a heart should go through in a lifetime, and here she was knowing hers had experienced the heartache of two lifetimes. She didn't want to risk breaking it again in case it wasn't strong enough. Being here, meeting Susan and Mike's children, was enough. It was helping her heal and that was exactly what she needed right now.

Completing the circle was enough. Completing the circle had brought her here and, as Zack had said, being present was important. They were closing a circle. She didn't want to open up another.

CHAPTER FIFTY-TWO

ZACK

Pinpointing the exact moment it happened would always be something Zack would struggle with. Was it when he'd woken up in a room full of people knowing she'd been the one to save him? Would it be on their first walk after being reunited when he'd realised the flush in her cheeks was for him? Or was it in that moment of feeling each other's pulse in a suburban garden that wasn't theirs, but felt as if it had been?

Whenever it was, like his suggestion of kissing again, he knew that without doubt the timing was awful. Who was that slow to catch up with their own feelings? Only a man, he decided as their moment was interrupted.

'I'm not sure how you're going to get it out of here, but we'll arrange something,' Phil said, as he slowly wheeled the gift out of the shed.

'What is it?' Chloe asked.

'It's a Triumph Bonneville. My dad bought it as a do-it-up project with the idea of taking my mum on a fortieth anniversary tour around the UK. Only he never got it up and running. The house is going on the market soon, so we need to finish clearing. It seems fitting that if either of you want it you have it.'

The outer shell of the motorbike was gleaming. It had obviously been renovated with care but, as Phil demonstrated, when the key was turned, nothing came to life like it should.

'My friend's got a van. We can load it into the back of that in the next day or two, but only if you're sure? I don't want to take something that should be going to the family.'

'None of us have been able to get it to work. We've tried. If you manage to, it'll mean – like you were both meant to find each other – that you're also meant to be the ones riding it. Our mum and dad might never have made it to that point, but it doesn't mean that you two won't.'

After agreeing on when to pick up the bike, with Phil and Stuart set to help Larry (they were all adamant Zack wasn't to help with the heavy manual handling), the goodbyes were emotional. As the house was due to go on the market imminently, Zack sensed it was as much about saying goodbye to their childhood home as their parents for the three siblings. This was a final goodbye and even though they made promises to keep in touch, he guessed it would be as Facebook friends rather than for any further emotional meet-ups like this one. It would perhaps be enough to know that their parents' organ donations had gone on to give life once more as had been their wish.

The following day, Zack went as a passenger with Larry to collect the bike. It was only once it was stowed in the back of the van that he realised he'd not thought about where to store it.

'Where we heading with this then, Zee? Billy said he'd help me unload if I tell him where to meet us.'

'I don't suppose your mum has room in her shed?'

Larry shook his head. 'You know Mum won't let you take that across the lawn.'

Zack smiled because he'd already known the answer. Kathy loved gardening as much as Zack and Larry, and she wouldn't want a motorbike being dragged across her pristine grass.

'Hang on. Let me make a call and see if it's a possibility.' He should have done this already, but the past twenty-four hours had gone by in a bit of a blur.

His dad's care home answered quickly and responded with an enthusiastic yes. The shed they had there primarily housed gardening tools for Zack's use, and they were more than happy to have him visiting regularly while he got the bike up and running.

Once that decision was made, Billy was told where to head by Larry, and Zack let Chloe know where it would be housed. She replied saying she'd be able to walk there and meet them.

The journey wasn't a long one and Zack was smiling because he was certain his dad would approve, having had a love of motorbikes himself.

His wife was pillion, and the engine started without an issue. At long last they were on their way.

It was a fleeting glimpse of a flashback as they took the bike on its way to its new destination, and somehow Zack knew it would be the last one. Because he also recognised, with the bike still redundant in the back, that it wasn't a memory, it was a wish.

With the bike in situ at the care home's shed, it wasn't long before visiting with Chloe in tow was part of a new daily routine. They'd both described having a moment when they felt as if Mike and Susan had left them, that their actions were now their own and not the desires of their hearts' previous owners. It meant they had a period of rebuilding their friendship. In the time that Zack was tinkering with the motorbike, Chloe busied herself with her easel, having at last reached a point where she was able to paint for long periods of time. She was capturing different parts of the garden, as if she was taking a series of close-up photographs. Zack was keeping the garden in check as always, and intermittently trying different tricks that he'd learned about on the internet with the bike – none of which had been successful yet. On the days they weren't there, they were at their cardiac rehab class or visiting the art gallery, or checking on Larry and his nephew. Even though the disconnect had occurred as they'd hoped it would, they'd still become inseparable.

'Do you think we'll ever get it running?' Chloe asked, one morning at the garden. She delivered a takeaway coffee with the question while Zack was attempting yet another trick that wasn't working.

'If it takes until my dying day, I'm going to get this running.'

'Don't say that. I've seen you far too close to the other side for a joke like that to ever be funny.'

'I'm not joking. I'm not talking about anytime soon. I just mean that if I haven't sorted this in fifty years, I'll still be working on it.'

'No wonder Susan was fed up.'

'What do you mean? How could you know Susan was fed up? Did one of the children say something?'

Chloe crossed her arms and leaned against the shed's door frame, offering a wry smile at the same time. 'It was one of the things I felt. I wasn't having flashbacks in the same way you did, but sometimes I sensed these things. Like an echo from the past had found its way to me.'

Zack abandoned what he was doing, giving Chloe his full attention. 'Me too! At the time I thought I was beginning to go a bit mad.'

'Beginning?' Chloe pushed herself off the door frame and headed in his direction.

'You know what I mean. I shouldn't be able to sense someone else's thoughts, but sometimes they seemed to be there. I'm glad that's gone now. It was confusing, to say the least.'

'I know exactly what you mean. For a while, it kind of blurred my thoughts. Made it hard to understand what I was doing for me and what I was doing for someone else. I'm glad

that we seem to have broken whatever spell we were under.'
Chloe's hair, which reminded him of flowers, was newly
dipped pink and whenever she got close, Zack wanted to touch
it and take in its scent. He kept having to remind himself
not to.

'Do you think we've really disconnected from whatever had
a hold over us? Do you think we can go ahead and have lives of
our own now, without the worry we'll end up in cardiac arrest
again?' He'd often wondered if that was why she was still
hanging out with him.

'Do you want to be disconnected?' Chloe asked.

'Yes and no. I want us to hang out with each other because
we want to hang out together. Not because we're being made to.
What about you?'

'Yes.' Chloe's answer was instant. 'I want to be able to go on
holiday without feeling like I need to pack you in my luggage to
make sure you're okay. No one is meant to be with another
person all of the time.'

'We can stop hanging out. Experiment again. See if we fare
better being apart from one another. I mean, we've both said
we've stopped having those altered feelings. We just haven't put
any distance between us to check the theory. I think we've been
too scared to.'

'We should check our pulses again. See if they're doing
their own thing yet.'

'Okay.' Zack wiped his hands clean so they were free of oil.

Using the same formation they'd used a few weeks before,
they both placed their fingers in the quadrant position that
allowed them to take their own pulses while also taking each
other's.

It took some moments of concentration for them both to
find the beats they were looking for.

'They're out of sync,' Chloe said, somewhat triumphantly.

Zack didn't know whether to be pleased or disappointed. 'I

wish we'd known before. We could have checked more times to know whether this is a significant development or not.'

'I'd say it's significant.'

'How come?'

'Because now if we kiss, we're doing it because we want to, not because our hearts are telling us to.'

'Does that mean...? Can I?' Zack's usual smoothness abandoned him and he became a jabbering idiot instead. He'd wanted to ever since they'd been to Mike and Susan's house. He wanted to every day they'd spent in his dad's memorial garden. He wanted to, but knew he could never hurt Chloe again so he wasn't going to be the one to make the first move.

'Only if this won't cause you to run away in a week's time.'

'The only direction I'll be running in is towards you, and not because my heart wants to. Oh shit. That sounds so wrong. I mean *my* heart wants to as well as my head. Nobody else's desires are involved here. I'm the one that loves you. And the only person that's steered me to that realisation is me.'

Chloe placed a finger on Zack's lips. 'Has anyone ever told you that you talk too much when you're nervous?'

'I'm not without flaws,' he managed to muffle through the pressure of her finger. But knowing that she was right, he shut up and kissed her finger until she moved her hand and he was able to reach her lips.

Zack didn't have a clue what her heartbeat was doing or whether it matched his. The only rhythm he was concentrating on was that of their lips, because this time he wanted to make it count. He'd been given a second chance in more ways than one. He didn't intend to waste a moment from now on.

'I'd say that kiss was pretty flawless,' Chloe said, when they finally pulled apart.

'There's more where that came from.' Zack gave her a quick kiss on the cheek, then dispensed another on the other cheek for good measure.

'Before you get too carried away, let me try the key.'

Chloe hadn't tried to switch the engine on yet.

'Will you steal the glory if it goes?'

'We'll call it a joint effort.'

Zack passed her the key, and like the way their hearts had synchronised before, the engine roared into life as if it had been waiting for this moment. The same way Zack had had to wait for the right moment.

'I love you,' he shouted over the noise of the engine.

Zack lip-read Chloe's identical response.

And there it was. Mike and Susan's hearts may have stopped, but the love hadn't. And on their own terms, eventually, Zack and Chloe were going to love each other in this next lifetime.

EPILOGUE

It was another year before the final five rest home gardens were completed. Zack and Larry took on Billy as a permanent member of staff and Zack went down to three days of physical work, realising the limits of what he could manage were different now and he needed to respect what his body was telling him.

Still, every Saturday was spent completing the promise he'd made to himself as a tribute to his parents. Chloe had also got involved, creating an art piece of each garden and carrying out some art therapy groups with the care home residents. And when there were offers of help, Zack took them, turning the last part of the project into more of a community challenge. Even Chloe's sisters turned up most weeks to help, and they gradually seemed to warm to him.

During that year, Zack and Chloe had experimented with being together and being apart to check what effect it had on them. These days their desire to be together was more to do with feeling flesh on flesh rather than the need to keep each other alive. They spent far more time together than they did apart and their nights were either in Chloe's newly decorated bedroom, Zack's flat, or the occasional night of watching the stars in the back of the flatbed truck.

A year post-surgery, the doctors were happy to reduce them to six-monthly appointments. Chloe's family home was on the market as a clear sign that she was on the mend enough for her sisters to be happy for them all to get their independence. Zack's flat was also on the market so they'd be able to get a place together, but first there was the big adventure they'd been planning for some time. In fact, it hadn't been their adventure. It was Mike and Susan's. But instead of following the route their predecessors had planned, they were heading to the Wild Atlantic Way to finish the journey Zack should have completed, but barely started.

It sounded like the perfect romantic trip, and Chloe would almost have been inclined to agree, if it weren't for the van that would be following them for the entire journey in case the Triumph broke down on the way. The van containing Larry and his new girlfriend, Leona. They'd been hanging out during the garden project with notable frequency until finally declaring themselves a couple. And because neither of her sisters wanted to be left out of anything, Alice was also along for the ride.

It certainly wasn't the perfect recipe for romance, but Chloe and Zack hoped (and possibly Mike and Susan did too) that it was the recipe to heal a broken heart. They all needed plenty of that.

A LETTER FROM CATHERINE

Dear Reader,

Thank you so much for reading *The Crash*. If you did enjoy this book and want to keep up to date with all my latest releases, just sign up at the following link. Your email address will never be shared and you can unsubscribe at any time.

www.bookouture.com/catherine-miller

I want to share my own miracle with you. The one where I only have the medical notes for reference...

My first daughter was born and it quickly became evident that her twin sister was having problems. Because my epidural hadn't been fully effective, the medical team put me under anaesthetic to perform an emergency C-section. I woke at some point later in the recovery room, not knowing if she was alive.

She was. After seventeen long minutes of reviving her, the decision to put her on cooling jacket therapy in PICU was made to reduce the chance of any long-lasting brain injury. Today, she is a happy, healthy eight-year-old – as is her twin sister. I can only tell you about those seventeen minutes because it's written down. I have no recollection of them and am often very thankful for that fact.

So she and her twin sister are my miracles, and much like Zack and Chloe, sometimes we don't have to witness miracles to believe they can happen or know that they exist. Thank you for going on this reading journey and believing that the impossible is possible. I think we all have days when we need to hold on to the hope of a miracle in whatever form it takes.

I hope you loved *The Crash*, and if you did I would be very grateful if you could write a review. Every one of them is appreciated and I'd love to know what you think, and it makes such a difference helping new readers to discover one of my books for the first time. I love hearing from my readers – you can get in touch on my Facebook page, through Twitter, Goodreads or my website.

As with life, sometimes miracles only exist when they are side by side with tragedy. If you haven't already, perhaps this story will make you think about becoming a donor. Whether that be blood (blood donors saved me when I needed four units after the birth of my twins), bone marrow, organs, or even just your time. Sometimes for miracles to exist, people have to create them.

Wishing you your own small miracle, with love and light,

Catherine x

www.katylittlelady.com

facebook.com/katylittlelady.author
twitter.com/katylittlelady
instagram.com/katylittlelady

ACKNOWLEDGEMENTS

We moved house ahead of starting this book and as my office area isn't sorted yet, this novel has been written from my seat on the sofa. Throughout this, Tara, our dog, has been resting her butt upon me. Therefore, I've been told, I have to add her to the acknowledgements first. I've never known anyone able to sleep or emit gases as much as she has. I'm not sure it's been helpful, but I love her all the same.

Next I have to thank my family: Ben, Amber and Eden, and my mum. They support me through all the moments when I'm 'happily in the vortex' and I couldn't do this without their love and support. That applies to all the extended family as well.

I had the idea for this book, but when it came to writing it I realised that in reality, it would be unlikely Zack and Chloe would ever meet each other or the donors' family because of the guidelines surrounding organ donation in the UK. I therefore had to sculpt a story in a way to make these things possible. I hope I've done it justice. It is a work of fiction and I'm aware of the guidelines that are in place, but in this story I've bent reality slightly to make it as feasible as possible. If you'd like to know more about organ donation or to make your wish clear, you can do so in the UK at: www.organdonation.nhs.uk.

For some of the knowledge in this book, I've relied on my previous experience as a respiratory physiotherapist. I'd like to thank my old boss, Denise Mills-Goodlet, for clarifying some facts on whether certain things have changed.

Finally I'd like to thank the people who've worked on this

book: editors Christina Demosthenous and Caroline Hogg, and my agent, Hattie Grunewald. And for their support and encouragement: Karren and my fellow word wranglers. And as always, the readers and book reviewers who've supported me. A thousand thanks for all of you.

Printed in Great Britain
by Amazon

79098901R00162